FOOTSTE]

TWO WOMEN, TWO LIVES, ONE DESTINY....

A NOVEL

BY JULIET CAROLAN

To Eddie

With all my love

TABLE OF CONTENTS

Prologue

PART ONE
Chapter One
Chapter Two
Chapter Three
Chapter Four
Chapter Five
Chapter Six
Chapter Seven
Chapter Eight
Chapter Nine
Chapter Ten
 Chapter Eleven
Chapter Twelve
Chapter Thirteen
Chapter Fourteen
Chapter Fifteen
Chapter Sixteen
Chapter Seventeen
Chapter Eighteen
Chapter Nineteen
Chapter Twenty
Chapter Twenty-One
Chapter Twenty-Two
Chapter Twenty-Three
Chapter Twenty-Four

Chapter Twenty-Five
Chapter Twenty-Six
Chapter Twenty-Seven
Chapter Twenty-Eight

PART TWO
Chapter Twenty-Nine
Chapter Thirty
Chapter Thirty-One
Chapter Thirty-Two
Chapter Thirty-Three
Chapter Thirty-Four
Chapter Thirty-Five
Chapter Thirty-Six
Chapter Thirty-Seven
Chapter Thirty-Eight
Chapter Thirty-Nine
Chapter Forty
Chapter Forty-One
Chapter Forty-Two
Chapter Forty-Three
Chapter Forty-four
Chapter Forty-Five
Chapter Forty-Six
Chapter Forty-Seven
Chapter Forty-Eight
Chapter Forty-Nine
Epilogue

This is a work of fiction. Names, characters, businesses, places, events, and incidents are either the products of the author's imagination or used in a fictitious manner. Any resemblance to actual persons, living or dead, or actual events is purely coincidental.

Copyright © 2024 by Juliet Carolan. All rights reserved.

All rights reserved. No part of this publication can be reproduced or transmitted in any form or by any means, electronic or mechanical, without permission in writing from Juliet Carolan.

Previous Novels

The Book of Shadows

Synopsis

Footsteps of Fate is a haunting tale of love and loss, that weaves together the lives of two women separated by centuries but bound by a shared destiny.

In 1906 Isabella de Lacy finds herself torn between duty and desire when she falls in love with a mill owner of humble origins. As their forbidden romance blossoms amidst the disapproval of her father and the expectations of society, Isabella's world is shattered when tragedy strikes leaving her with a decision that will change her life forever.

In present-day Lancashire, Amelia's life is turned upside down, and her dreams of a happily ever after are shattered instantly. Seeking solace in her work she finds herself employed at the mysterious Milburn Manor in the village of Slaidburn, where the ghost of Isabella de Lacy walks the halls. As she delves deeper into the mysteries, she stumbles on an old journal written by a housemaid,

Florence Wilson. As she is drawn into Isabella's world, Amelia finds herself compelled to unravel the truth behind the whispers of betrayal and heartache that echo through the halls of the manor.

As past and present collide, Amelia and Isabella's lives become intertwined, their shared experiences forging a bond that transcends time. Together they must confront the ghosts of the past and embrace the promise of a future, all against the backdrop of the sun-drenched shores of Elounda on the island of Crete, where the ancient ruins and timeless beauty serve as a link to their intertwined destinies.

Footsteps of Fate

Prologue

Lancashire Milburn Manor

Milburn Manor stood shrouded in the mist of a restless night, its grand stone walls whispering secrets of a bygone era. Moonlight filtered through the skeletal trees, casting shadows that danced like mournful spectres across the overgrown gardens. The air was heavy, saturated with a chilling sense of loss, as if the manor itself were grieving.

    A figure moved silently along the corridors, her dark tattered gown trailing behind her like the remnants of forgotten dreams. Isabella de Lacy. She wandered the dim halls of her once beloved home, her presence barely more than a ripple in the darkness, yet unmistakable to those who dared to look closely. Her auburn hair, now a ghostly shade in the moon's pale light, framed a face etched with sorrow. Tears, glistening like frost, streaked her cheeks, caught between this world and the next.

She paused at the window overlooking the garden, the very place where her life had once brimmed with promise. Now it was nothing more than a twisted memory, tangled in the vines that choked the path below. A faint, mournful wail drifted through the night, carried on the wind. Was it the wind, or was it something else? Isabella clutched her chest as if still feeling the unbearable weight of heartbreak and betrayal.

A distant, haunting melody echoed faintly, a lullaby she could not forget. The sound stirred the shadows, and for a moment, she was not alone. Wisps of past laughter flickered in the corners of her vision, fading as quickly as they appeared. She reached out, her translucent fingers grasping at nothing, as if trying to hold on to something, someone, lost to her forever.

The manor's walls seemed to breathe with her sorrow, each creak and groan a reminder of lives unfulfilled, of love that ended in tragedy. Isabella's weeping grew softer, more desperate, as she vanished into the darkness, leaving only the faint scent of rosewater and despair.

Milburn Manor, steeped in centuries of secrets, held its breath, waiting for the next footstep of fate.

"We must be willing to let go of the life we have planned, so as to have the life that is waiting for us." –

From "A Room with a View"

By E.M. Forster

PART ONE
Chapter One
Amelia
Present day

Amelia stood at the entrance to St Ambrose Church, bathed in a golden light that seemed almost too perfect. The aisle stretched out before her, a path lined with bouquets of wildflowers and filled with the faces of friends and family. Their smiles were warm and welcoming, their eyes filled with joy. Her dress hugged her figure perfectly, flaring out at the hips into a cascade of delicate fabric that shimmered with each step. The bodice was adorned with delicate intricate lace, and the off-the-shoulder neckline accentuated her graceful collarbones. A long flowing train trailed behind her, adding an air of timeless elegance to her appearance. Her hair was swept up into an elegant chignon, with a few loose tendrils framing her face, and a delicate veil of the same lace completed her look.

Behind her, the bridesmaids stood in a line, each wearing a dress of soft blush pink that complemented Amelia's gown beautifully. Their dresses were simple yet elegant, with flowing skirts and fitted bodices. They each held a small bouquet of wildflowers, tied with satin ribbons that matched their dresses. The bridesmaids' smiles were radiant as they supported Amelia, their eyes filled with love and happiness for her.

She took a deep breath and began to walk. Her heart pounded with excitement and love as she took each step toward Jack, who stood at the altar waiting for her. But with every step she took, the aisle seemed to lengthen. The distance between her and Jack grew wider, the altar receding further and further away. Confusion clouded her mind. She quickened her pace, but it felt like she was moving in slow motion, her feet sinking into the floor as if it were quicksand. The whispering started softly at first, a low murmur that grew louder and more distinct with each passing second.

"She'll never make it," someone hissed.

"Look at her struggle," another voice sneered.

Amelia's steps became frantic as she tried to reach Jack, her breathing shallow and panicked. Laughter erupted around her, a cruel, mocking sound that echoed off the church walls. She looked around, seeing the faces of her guests twisted into grotesque masks of ridicule and scorn. Her beautiful gown began to tear and tangle around her legs, the lace and silk turning to rags. The flowers lining the aisle began to wilt, their sweet fragrance turning sour. The church itself seemed to transform, the walls darkening and closing in on her.

Amelia's vision blurred with tears as she called out for Jack, her voice barely heard amongst the sneers and laughter. He stood motionless at the altar, his face expressionless and distant. The vicar beside him had turned into a shadowy figure, eyes glowing with a sinister glare.

"Jack!" she screamed, but he didn't respond. He simply turned and walked away, disappearing into the darkness. The laughter grew louder, the faces around her becoming more grotesque and monstrous. Hands reached out from the pews, grabbing at her dress, and pulling her back. She struggled against them, desperate to break free, but their grip was too strong.

Suddenly, the floor beneath her feet gave way and she plummeted into darkness, the laughter echoing around her. She screamed, a sound of pure terror until there was nothing but silence.

***

Amelia jolted awake, her heart racing and her body drenched in sweat. She sat up abruptly, gasping for breath, her mind struggling to separate the nightmare from reality. It took her a few moments to realize she was not in the dark twisted church but in a sunlit room with white curtains gently billowing in the breeze. Amelia swung her legs over the side of the bed and stood up, walking over to the open window. The warm sun kissed her skin, and she took a deep breath, inhaling the salty air.

She gazed out at the shimmering crystal-clear waters of the Mirabello Bay coastline and mountains, her heart heavy with the weight of dashed dreams and broken promises, but no amount of beauty could ease the ache in her heart. Despite the pleas of her family and friends, she had decided to make this trip alone. She could feel the emptiness beside her in the bed on what should have been her honeymoon.

She could still feel the stares of family and friends in the church. She could still see the discarded wedding dress where she had left it on the bedroom floor. She had cut all contact with Jack; despite all the messages he kept leaving on her telephone. She couldn't face the reality of her situation at present. Just days ago, she had stood at the altar, trembling with anticipation as she waited to say her vows, but he had left her, stranded in a sea of uncertainty and heartache. Now, as she gazed out at the azure waters stretching before her, she couldn't help but feel adrift in a vast ocean of loneliness. The warmth of the Mediterranean sun offered little solace as she grappled with the sudden unravelling of her carefully laid plans. The ache in her chest was a mix of disbelief, betrayal, and the unbearable weight of unanswered questions. Her thoughts circled back to that day at the church, the whispers of guests, the pitiful glances as Jack had left her at the altar, simply saying "I'm sorry, Amelia, I can't do this."

      They had planned the wedding for months; they'd talked about their future in such detail that it felt solid, real. And then, without warning, he'd pulled the rug out from under her. Amelia tried to piece it together, had she missed the signs? Was there someone else? The humiliation of facing everyone back home lingered in her thoughts. She imagined the sympathetic looks, the probing questions, the embarrassment of returning to a life that now felt fractured. Here in Elounda, she was surrounded by the beauty of Crete, but all she could feel was the sting of betrayal and the uncertainty of what came next.

Chapter Two

Amelia
Present Day

Elounda was a charming fishing village on the eastern coast of Crete, Greece. It was the perfect place to enjoy the sun, the sea, and the Greek culture. There was a sandy beach, turquoise water, and nearby islands and historical sites. It had a traditional and authentic vibe, with whitewashed houses, colourful boats, and friendly locals.

The views from her balcony were breathtaking and she could see the island of Spinalonga, a former leper colony that she intended to visit while she was there. She was staying at Tasmania Village; a lovely complex of apartments where she had a studio apartment on the top floor at the front of the building. The owners Anna and George were lovely and welcoming and despite her heartache, she felt a certain sense of peace just being there. The apartment block was situated halfway between Elounda village and the even sleepier fishing village of Plaka. That evening she had decided on Anna's recommendation, to walk to Plaka. The views of Spinalonga were supposed to be incredible from there and she had even recommended a local taverna to eat at, The Carob Tree Taverna.

The walk to Plaka took around twenty minutes and followed a coastal path all the way. She followed the winding trail that hugged the shoreline, the rhythmic crashing of the waves against the rocks guiding her way. To her right the cerulean waters of the sea stretched out before her, the water shimmering and dancing in the sunlight. The scenery was beautiful with the surrounding mountains in the background and the island of Spinalonga coming into view in the distance, the nearer she got to Plaka. As she got closer, she could see fishing boats bobbing in the harbour and the tantalizing aroma of Greek seafood and spices wafted through the air, tempting her tastebuds, and invigorating her senses.

She walked around the old harbour, pausing to investigate some of the lovely gift shops, and gradually worked her way around the small village until on a little back street she found the taverna that Anna had recommended. It was set in a square surrounded by other shops and tavernas but stood slightly raised with all the tables and chairs set out around a lovely large Carob tree in the centre. The tables and chairs were a wonderful mix of old wooden furniture with brightly coloured cushions, each table and chair individually designed.

As the evening sun dipped low over Plaka, casting a golden glow across the quiet village, Amelia sat at her table, nursing her glass of white wine, and gazing at the early evening scenes around her. The small restaurant buzzed softly with the chatter of locals and tourists, the clinking of glasses, and the sizzle of food cooking in the kitchen. Above her the branches of the ancient carob tree rustled gently in the breeze, their shadows dancing across the sun-bleached tiles.
Amelia shifted in her seat, feeling the weight of her solitude more than ever. She hadn't planned to spend her honeymoon alone in Crete, but here she was, half a world away from the life she'd hoped to begin. She tried to distract herself with the stunning view of Spinalonga, the island looming across the bay, its ancient walls glowing amber in the fading light.

The evening air was heavy with the scents of oregano and grilled meat, and Amelia's stomach rumbled. She glanced around, trying to catch the attention of the waiter. That's when she first noticed him. A tall man in a simple white shirt, sleeves rolled up, moving between the tables with an easy grace. He wasn't like the other waiters; there was something different about him, a casual confidence that made him stand out.

As he approached, carrying a tray of steaming plates, Amelia saw him flash a quick smile at a nearby table, and for a moment, everything else seemed to fade. His eyes were dark, with a warmth that hinted at stories untold. He came to her table, setting down a small plate of olives and bread.

"Something to eat?" he asked in lightly accented English, his voice smooth and unexpectedly gentle. "The moussaka is the special today and it's very good." Amelia glanced up, surprised by the kindness in his tone.

"I'll have whatever you recommend," she said, managing a faint smile. He nodded, jotting down her order on a small pad.

"You're not from here," he observed, not unkindly, but with the curiosity of someone who had seen many strangers pass through.

"No," she replied, glancing away. "Just visiting." The man studied her for a moment, and Amelia felt a flush of embarrassment. She must have looked every bit the lost tourist, alone, with sadness written across her face. But if he noticed, he didn't show it. Instead, he extended his hand.

"I'm Nikos. I have a taverna in Vrouchas, but I'm helping out my friend tonight."

"Amelia," she replied, shaking his hand. His grip was firm but gentle, a contrast that caught her off guard. As Nikos moved back towards the kitchen, which was in a separate building on the other side of the road, Amelia found herself watching him, noticing the effortless way he navigated the space, the familiarity with which he greeted everyone. There was something reassuring about his presence, like he was exactly where he was meant to be.

A few minutes later, Nikos returned, setting down a dish of sizzling moussaka. "Best in the region," he said with a wink, leaning slightly closer. "And I'm not just saying that because I cooked it." Amelia laughed, the sound feeling foreign to her after days of silence. She took a bite, savouring the delicious rich flavour.

"It's amazing," she admitted. "You're not bad at this, you know."

Nikos shrugged playfully, "I'm a man of many talents." He leaned against the nearby tree, crossing his arms as if he had all the time in the world. "So, what brings you to our little corner of Crete?"

Amelia hesitated, unsure how much to share with a stranger. "I just needed to get away," she said finally. Nikos nodded, as though he understood far more than she was letting on.

"Sometimes, being far away is the best way to feel close to yourself again." His words struck a chord, and for a moment, Amelia felt seen in a way she hadn't in a long time. She looked down at her plate, suddenly aware of the quiet strength that Nikos exuded. It was as if he had been through his own trials and found his way back, and she couldn't help but wonder what those stories were. They continued to talk, the conversation flowing as easily as the wine. Nikos told her about his life in Vrouchas, about the taverna and the simple joys of a village life that revolved around food, family, and tradition. Amelia found herself captivated by his stories, the vivid pictures he painted of sunlit olive groves and moonlit festivals.

By the time the last light faded from the sky, Amelia realised that she didn't want the evening to end. There was a comfort in Nikos's presence, a quiet strength that felt like an anchor in her turbulent sea of emotions.

As Nikos gathered the empty plates, he looked at her and said, "You know, sometimes the most beautiful journeys start with the most unexpected detours." Amelia watched him walk away, a mix of gratitude and longing settling in her chest.

That evening as she went to bed, her skin tingled with the effects of the sun, and she felt happy and drowsy after the food and wine. Her phone showed several messages from Jack and one from her best friend Chloe. She made the decision that in the morning she would call Chloe and see what was happening back in England. She couldn't face calling her father yet but knew that she should as he would be worried. She glanced briefly at the messages from Jack most of which were begging her to call him. She absentmindedly twisted the engagement ring she still wore on her finger, a painful reminder of the wedding that never was.

A single tear slipped down her cheek as she remembered the joy and excitement she had felt when Jack proposed. She had been so certain that he was the one, that their love was meant to last. Now, all she felt was a deep sense of betrayal and a fear of the unknown future.

Slowly, she removed the ring and placed it on the little table beside the bed. She stared at it and allowed herself one last moment of sorrow. One last moment to mourn the life she had lost before she began the journey to find the life she was meant to live.

Chapter Three

Isabella
1906 Milburn Manor

Isabella de Lacy stood at the window of her room in Milburn Manor, gazing out at the rolling hills of the Lancashire countryside. The morning sun bathed the estate in a golden glow, casting long shadows across the manicured gardens. The manor, with its stone walls and ivy-covered turrets, had looked over the village of Slaidburn for many years. The interior of Milburn Manor was a blend of elegance and tradition. The grand foyer, with its sweeping staircase and marble floors, spoke of generations of wealth and status. Portraits of stern-faced ancestors lined the walls, their eyes following Isabella's every move as she made her way through the house. The air was filled with the faint scent of lavender, mingling with the aroma of freshly baked bread wafting from the kitchens.

Isabella was the daughter of Sir Rafe and Lady Eleanor de Lacy, a prominent family with deep roots in the region. At nineteen, she was poised and graceful, with long curly auburn hair that framed her delicate features, and her eyes held a depth of curiosity and intelligence.

On this particular morning, Isabella was preparing to visit the village, which was nestled in the heart of the countryside, and was a picturesque array of stone cottages, narrow lanes with dry stone walls, and a daily bustling local market. It was a place where time seemed to stand still, and the rhythm of life was dictated by the changing seasons.

Lady Eleanor had tasked Isabella with delivering a basket of provisions to the village church. The basket, filled with bread, cheese, and fresh fruits, was a token of the family's gratitude for the village's unwavering support over the years. On top of the basket, the cook Mrs Hargreaves, had placed two of her infamous cheese and onion pies, and the aroma was making Isabella's mouth water. Isabella was eager to make the journey, as it provided a welcome respite from the formalities of manor life.

Dressed in a simple yet elegant gown, Isabella made her way towards the front door, her footsteps echoing through the hall. She paused briefly to exchange pleasantries with Florence, her loyal lady's maid, who handed her a bonnet and gloves.

"Be sure to take the path through the gardens, my lady," Florence advised. "The flowers are in full bloom, and it's a sight to behold."

Isabella smiled warmly. "Thank you, Florence. I shall do just that."

As she stepped outside, the beauty of the manor gardens took her breath away. Beds of roses, lilies, and lavender created a wonderful scene of colours and scents. Birds sang from the branches of ancient oak trees, and a gentle breeze rustled the leaves. Isabella took a moment to savour the tranquillity before setting off towards the village. The path to Slaidburn wound through fields of wildflowers and pastures where sheep grazed lazily.

Upon arriving in the village, Isabella was greeted with warm smiles and friendly waves. She made her way to St Andrews Church, a modest stone building that stood in the heart of the village. Inside, Reverend Thomas, the village vicar, welcomed her with open arms.

"Miss Isabella, it's always a pleasure to see you," he said, his eyes twinkling with kindness.

"Good morning, Reverend Thomas," Isabella replied, handing him the basket. "My mother sends her regards and these provisions for the church and those in need."

"Thank you, my dear. Your family's generosity knows no bounds," Reverend Thomas said, placing a gentle hand on her shoulder. "How is Lady Eleanor?"

"She is well, thank you. She asked me to convey her gratitude for your prayers," Isabella said, her voice tinged with sincerity. After a brief chat, Isabella took her leave and wandered through the village. She visited the market stalls, exchanging pleasantries with the vendors and purchasing a few trinkets. The village children, their faces alight with curiosity, followed her, giggling and whispering amongst themselves. As she walked, Isabella's thoughts drifted to the nearby mills, the backbone of the local economy. She had often heard stories of the workers' long hours and harsh conditions. While her family enjoyed a life of privilege, she couldn't help but feel a pang of guilt for those less fortunate. She admired the resilience of the working people and wondered how she might one day make a difference to their lives.

As the morning wore on, Isabella made her way to the edge of the village, where the path led back to Milburn Manor. She paused at the top of a hill, taking in the sweeping view of the manor and the surrounding countryside. It was a place of beauty and history, a place where she felt a deep connection to her family and her heritage. But beneath the surface, Isabella knew there were secrets and struggles that came with being a de Lacy. The weight of her family's legacy often felt heavy on her shoulders, and she longed for the freedom to carve her own path.

As she made her way back to the manor, Isabella noticed an old gypsy caravan by the side of the road. Its once vibrant paint had faded over the years, now a patchwork of muted reds, greens, and blues, peeling and worn by time and travel. The wooden panels, carved with intricate floral patterns, bore the marks of countless journeys, each scratch and dent telling the stories of the caravan's past. A small wrought-iron chimney jutted from the roof, the faintest wisp of smoke curling into the morning air, hinting at a warm fire within. The roof itself was arched and covered in canvas, patched, and repaired in places where the elements had taken their toll. At the front of the caravan, a pair of wooden steps led up to a narrow door, its edges decorated with delicate carvings of swirling vines and blooming flowers.

Around the caravan, an assortment of colourful fabrics hung from a makeshift clothesline, fluttering gently in the breeze. Brightly patterned rugs and blankets faded but still vibrant, added a touch of warmth and homeliness to the otherwise rustic scene. A small table, set up outside, displayed an array of trinkets and charms. The wheels of the caravan were large and sturdy, their spokes thick with years of accumulated dirt and grime. At the rear, a small window, framed by lace curtains, offered a glimpse into the cosy interior, where a flickering candle cast a warm, inviting glow. The air around the caravan was filled with the scent of herbs and spices, mingling with the earthy aroma of the countryside.

Nearby, a small, shaggy pony grazed contentedly. Its coat was a mix of brown and white patches, thick and slightly matted in places and its mane and tail were long and unkempt. The pony's large dark eyes were gentle and intelligent. Its ears flicked occasionally, attentive to the sounds of the surrounding countryside, while its sturdy legs and broad hooves dug into the soft earth, steady and sure-footed. A simple leather bridle hung loosely around its neck, worn but well-cared for, with intricate patterns etched into the leather by skilled hands. Now and then, it would lift its head to look around, nostrils flaring slightly as it took in the scents of the area, before returning to its meal with a contented snort.

A gypsy woman, her colourful skirt swirling around her sat outside behind the table, selling various trinkets and charms. Drawn by curiosity Isabella approached the woman.

"Good afternoon," Isabella greeted, her voice gentle. The gypsy woman looked up and smiled, her eyes twinkling with a knowing light.

"Good afternoon, miss. Would you like to see my wares?" Isabella nodded, her gaze falling on a delicate silver pendant. She thought she could give it to Florence as it would suit her well and she wanted to thank her for all that she did for her.

"It is lovely, isn't it. It will bring the owner luck and wealth," the gypsy explained.

"I'll take it," Isabella decided, handing the woman a few coins. As the gypsy took her hand to exchange the money, her expression changed, her eyes widening with a sudden fear.

"Is something wrong?" Isabella asked, her heart skipping a beat. The gypsy woman hesitated, then tightened her grip on Isabella's hand. She traced the lines of Isabella's palm, her fingers trembling slightly.

"What is it?" Isabella asked, unnerved by the woman's sudden change in demeanour.

The gypsy's voice dropped, her words heavy with foreboding. "You carry the weight of fate upon your shoulders, my lady. Dark times lie ahead, and a great sorrow will haunt your steps. You will be betrayed by those you trust and lose everything you hold dear."

Isabella pulled her hand back, a shiver running through her. "What do you mean?" The gypsy woman looked at her, eyes filled with a strange mixture of pity and fear.

She leaned in closer, her breath warm against Isabella's ear. "Beware the footsteps of fate. You cannot escape what is already written." Isabella recoiled her heart racing. She turned to leave, but the gypsy called after her, her voice echoing with a chilling certainty: "You'll find yourself far from home, in a strange land where even the stars are unfamiliar."

Isabella hurried away, her mind swirling with the gypsy's ominous words. She clutched the necklace tightly, it's cool weight suddenly feeling like a burden. The path back to Milburn Manor felt longer, the shadows darker, as if something unseen was watching her every step. As she reached the gates, she glanced back, but the gypsy and her caravan were gone, vanished as it they had never been there. Isabella's breath caught in her throat, fear gripping her heart. What did the woman mean? What fate awaited her that even a stranger could sense?

Isabella stood alone in the twilight, the chilly wind biting at her skin, the gypsy's words echoing in her mind: *"Beware the footsteps of fate."*

Chapter Four

Amelia
Greece Present Day

As the days passed by in a blur of uncertainty and heartache, Amelia found herself confessing her situation to Anna, the lady who owned the apartments. She had also found herself chatting with another solo traveller, Angelina, who was a lovely lady and easy to talk to. They had shared their stories over a few evenings, enjoying the little copper carafes of wine that Anna served and the three of them had become good friends. They encouraged Amelia to reach out to her father, or her friend Chloe as they understood that Amelia didn't want to confront Jack yet.

"I will do, this evening," Amelia said, once again putting off the inevitable. "But today I just want to escape, maybe go to Agios Nikolaos or something, I'm not sure." She looked at Anna for help.

"Get the train up to the mountains," Anna said, "It is called the Happy Train. It looks a little touristy but Andreas the guide is lovely and highly informative, and you will see old villages that few people see, the real Greece." Anna encouraged her. "It leaves at noon and returns at 6 pm."

Amelia decided that she would make the trip and went up to her apartment to get her things and have a quick shower before setting off into Elounda. The walk to Elounda was beautiful the coastal road flat and the views breathtaking. She wandered around the harbour, looking into the various gift shops and soaking in the atmosphere of the village. She stumbled across a wonderful bookshop at the top of some stone stairs. Unfortunately, it was closed but she made a note to return and look inside.

From the main square, she followed the sea path and came to a causeway. In the shallows lay the sunken city of Olous and from there, past the windmills she continued until she got to a seafood restaurant called Kanali which looked out onto the sea of Elounda Bay. It looked so pretty with its white tables and chairs and from a quick look at the menu, she could see that it specialised in the most amazing seafood.

On the way back towards the main square she stopped off at a lovely taverna called Dimitri's which was on a corner of the harbour opposite an old church. Amelia sat at a small table by the edge of the taverna on a narrow-cobbled street. The scent of the sea mingled with the rich aroma of grilled fish and herbs. The owner an elderly man named Dimitri shuffled over to her table with a warm smile. His tanned skin was weathered, etched with lines that spoke of years spent under the Cretan sun. His son, Dimitri, followed closely behind, a younger brighter version of his father, with the same kind eyes and easy charm.

"Welcome, welcome," Dimitri said, setting down her plate of fava, a creamy split puree topped with a drizzle of olive oil and a scattering of red onions. "This has been on our menu for generation. My father made it, and his father before him."

Amelia smiled, grateful for the small comforts of this family-run place. "It's perfect. Thank you." As she took a bite, the earthy, slightly sweet flavour melted on her tongue, grounding her in the present moment, even as her mind wandered to the past. She couldn't help but think of how many stories were bound up in places like this. Families who had endured through wars, hardships, and joys, much like her own tangled history. The younger Dimitri leaned on the counter nearby, wiping his hands on a towel.

"You're English, right? We get many visitors from England. My grandfather used to tell us stories about the English soldiers who would eat here during the war."

Amelia nodded, savouring the fava. "I imagine this place has seen a lot."

Dimitri chuckled softly, his gaze faraway. "Oh yes. But it always stays the same. The sea, the sun, the food. We keep them as they were. It's our way of keeping the past alive." Amelia looked around, feeling the weight of those words. There was a comfort in the continuity, a quiet resilience that mirrored her own need to hold on to the pieces of her life that still made sense.

"It's beautiful," she said simply, glancing at her watch. Realising she had just enough time, she stood to leave, thanking Dimitri and his father for their kindness.

"I've got to catch the Happy Train," she explained. Dimitri grinned and pointed Amelia in the direction of the playground where she could catch the train. "It's a bit bumpy but you'll get amazing views. Enjoy and come back anytime." As Amelia walked away, she felt a sense of bittersweet calm. The fava had warmed her belly, but it was the stories and the spirit of Dimitris that lingered most.

She got to the meeting point for the train just before noon and was slightly sceptical when she saw the little vehicle. It was a small train engine with three carriages behind it and looked like a child's toy train. She smiled to herself and got on board.

Andreas was indeed delightful, and very enthusiastic, and kept her and the other people on board informed all the way along. They stopped at Plaka first and were given an hour to explore the village. Amelia had been there the day before, so she went back to the Carob Tree and had a coffee whilst she waited to re-board the train. There was a different waiter this time, and although he was lovely and friendly too, she had half hoped it would be Nikos again. As the small train wound its way out of Plaka, Andreas, the guide stood at the front, his voice filling the open carriages.

"Ladies and gentlemen, as we begin out journey into the mountains, take a look around. You'll see these trees around us-carob trees. These trees have been growing her for centuries. During challenging times, like the wars, they were a vital food source. They call it 'the black gold' of Crete." He pointed to the gnarled, ancient trunks scattered along the rocky terrain. They provided flour, animal feed, and even sweet treats. Life in the villages up there depended on them." Amelia looked out at the landscape, feeling the weight of the history beneath the bright sky. She had read about the resilience of the Cretan people, but seeing it up close, hearing about how even the trees helped them survive, touched something deep inside her.

As the train climbed higher into the hills, passing olive groves and rugged cliffs, she felt the wind whip through her hair, a welcome coolness against the warmth of the day. The scent of pine and wild herbs filled the air. The carob trees, with their thick twisted trunks, stood like silent witnesses to centuries of struggle and endurance. There was something comforting about their endurance, and yet, she couldn't help but feel a pang of loneliness as the train ascended into the old villages. The distance from her life back home, from Jack, felt even greater as she was carried further from the coast.

Andreas continued, his voice warm and full of pride. "We'll pass through villages that haven't changed in hundreds of years. The people who live here, they carry traditions, the same as their parents and grandparents." Amelia found herself drawn to the idea of life in these remote villages. Something about their timelessness, their detachment from the modern world, felt like a mirror of her own current detachment; from the life she thought she'd be living. The further they went, the more she could feel herself slipping away from her own world, as though the mountains were carrying her somewhere else entirely. Amelia's heart ached as the wind brushed her face, whispering secrets she wasn't quite ready to hear. She thought of the empty chair beside her, the seat Jack was supposed to fill and swallowed the lump in her throat.

Amelia found herself lost in a whirlwind of emotion; her thoughts drifting back to the shattered remnant of her wedding day. The memory of Jack's sudden departure from the altar hung heavy in the air; a painful reminder of the dreams that were shattered in an instant. But, amidst the wreckage of her broken heart, a flicker of determination began to take root, a resolve to confront the ghosts of her past and seek the closure she so desperately craved. With each passing mile, Amelia found herself drawing closer to the realisation that she could not move forward until she confronted the demons that haunted her. As the train slowed to a stop in the charming village of Vrouchas, Amelia resolved to speak to her father and Chloe. She knew her father had sent her an email which she would open on her return to her apartment.

The tour of Vrouchas took them to the Church of the Holy Trinity and then on to another village, Selles. It was like stepping back in time, old ladies in black sat on their doorsteps, the bleating of goats, and donkeys that were still ridden carrying hay. There was bougainvillea everywhere which as well as being visually stunning left a glorious scent in the air. On their return to Vrouchas, they stopped at a tiny taverna. It was called Nikos Taverna and Amelia wondered if it was the taverna that the waiter from the previous evening had mentioned that he owned. As it was busy at the front, Amelia decided to walk through to the back where there was a lovely small courtyard. She wasn't hungry and couldn't face sitting with others. She looked up as the owner approached. It was Nikos from the Carob Tree.

"So, you found me then?" he smiled enthusiastically. "What can I get you? The others on the train are all eating. You didn't want to join them?" he queried.

"No not now, sorry. Could I just get a small water, please? "Amelia smiled at him. He was very striking with his brown eyes, tanned skin, and lovely smile.

"Of course, "Nikos replied and returned with an ice-cold water for her. Sometime later Nikos reappeared.

"The train is ready to return if you've finished, "he said.

"Is there any other way back to Elounda, it's so peaceful here, I'd like to stay longer."

"I can run you back a little later if that's ok" Nikos replied "I need to go into Elounda for some supplies anyway. You are more than welcome to stay. Why don't you come and sit at the front and take in the atmosphere of the village?" Amelia followed him back through the taverna and sat at a little table in the front. An old lady was sitting on a chair opposite. She was dressed all in black and was sporting a rather surprising white beard. Amelia nodded to her and got a toothless grin back. There were no other tourists in the taverna now and Nikos came over to join her bringing with him two glasses of chilled white wine.

"I thought you might appreciate this," he said as he handed her one of the glasses. "Do you mind if I join you?" Amelia who hadn't wanted any company found herself accepting and they chatted easily for a while. Nikos told her more about the village and she told him about her life back in the UK, omitting the terrible events that had led to her being on holiday alone. Eventually, Nikos persuaded her to stay for some food. He had made a lamb kleftiko and he proceeded to tell her the history of the dish as it was cooking.

"It's a traditional Greek dish made with slow-roasted lamb cooked in parchment paper along with potatoes and vegetables. Kleftiko is named after the kelphts, a group of bandits who lived in the mountains of Greece around five hundred years ago." He explained as he topped up her glass of wine.
"The kelphts were rebels who waged a perpetual war against the Turkish rule. They considered anything belonging to the Turk as a lawful prize and that included food. The name lamb kleftiko translates to stolen lamb." Amelia was fascinated and could already smell the tantalising aromas of rosemary, garlic, and rich succulent lamb.

"Your English is very good, where did you learn to speak so fluently," Amelia said.

"I trained in Athens and took some classes too. With so many foreign visitors it made sense to learn English." Nikos replied. As they enjoyed the lamb which Nikos served with a large Greek salad, Amelia felt herself relaxing for the first time since that awful day. It was a wonderful couple of hours and as

Nikos took her back to Elounda they arranged for him to collect her in the afternoon of the following day as his taverna was closed. He had to go into Agios Nikolaos and had invited her to join him. He also suggested that if she wanted to go to Spinalonga, she should catch the first boat as it was not too hot on the island at that time and there were fewer tourists.

Amelia went back up to her apartment and sat on her balcony overlooking the ocean. She felt happy as she had spent such a lovely day, and she was looking forward to tomorrow. With a heavy sigh, she knew that she needed to make a phone call. She would call Chloe first and then open the email from her father.

With trembling hands, Amelia dialled Chloe's number, her heart heavy with anticipation and dread. As the phone rang, she braced herself for the conversation that lay ahead, knowing that whatever came next would change everything.

"Hello?" Chloe's voice came through the line, filled with concern and compassion.

"Chloe, it's me," Amelia said, her voice barely above a whisper.

"Thank goodness, I've been trying to get hold of you for days, are you ok?"

"Yes, no, I don't know." Amelia poured her heart out to Chloe re-living the events of her wedding day, how painful it felt, still felt, and how she didn't know what to do next. She was crying and eventually could hardly speak. Chloe listened with unwavering compassion. Amelia was her best friend and she wanted to be there for her. Eventually, Amelia calmed down and they talked a little bit about Greece, the weather, the food, both putting off the inevitable conversation.

"Jacks' been trying to call you, Amelia." Chloe suddenly said, knowing she had to be the one to start. "I know, I just can't face speaking to him yet," Amelia replied with a sob in her throat.

"Amelia, I'm sorry for how things turned out," Chloe began, her voice soft and empathetic. "I need to tell you something about Jack. You deserve to know the truth." Amelia held her breath,

"What is it, Chloe?" her voice was a mixture of sadness and curiosity. Chloe took a deep breath.

"The reason Jack left you at the altar… It wasn't just cold feet or second thoughts. There was another woman." Amelia's heart sank, and she felt a cold wave of betrayal wash over her.

"Another woman?" She echoed.

"Yes," Chloe said. "Jack had a fling with a woman at his office. He says it was a brief affair, but it had consequences. The morning of your wedding, she called him in a panic. She told him she was pregnant."

"I don't understand." Amelia was crying again. "How could I not know? Why did he leave it until we were about to get married."

"I know it's awful, and I can't imagine how hurt you must be. But Jack's actions were cowardly and selfish. He didn't handle things the way he should have." Chloe wished she could be there to hug Amelia.

Amelia's mind raced as she processed the revelation. The image of Jack, the man she had trusted and loved, was now tainted by betrayal. She had been left in the dark, humiliated in front of her friends and family, while he had fled from the consequences of his actions. Amelia sighed, the weight of the betrayal pressing heavily on her.

"I thought I knew him. I thought he loved me."

"You'll get through this, Amelia." Chloe was trying her best to be positive. you're strong, and you have so much ahead of you. Maybe your time in Greece will give you a chance to heal and find yourself again."

Amelia calmed down "Thank you, Chloe, for telling me the truth and for being here for me. I don't know what I would do without you."

They talked for a while longer and then Amelia said goodbye to Chloe promising that she would call her again in a couple of days. As the truth sank in, waves of despair washed over her, threatening to drown her in sorrow and regret. She reached for her phone again and immediately deleted all of Jack's messages and blocked his number. She thought back to the weeks before the wedding. He had been working later than usual but he had said that he wanted to clear his workload before the wedding and honeymoon. They had even abstained from sex, laughing, and saying they were waiting until they were married. Amelia had thought it strange but had just accepted it. Now she knew why. Because he had been sleeping with another woman.

She sat still and silent on the balcony but after a while amidst the wreckage of her shattered dreams, a spark of defiance was igniting within her, a determination to rise above the pain and reclaim the life that was stolen from her.

Chapter Five

Amelia
Greece

The following morning Amelia clicked on her father's email, steeling herself for whatever it might contain. She had been dreading this moment, unsure of how to respond to her father's well-meaning messages.

Dear Amelia

I hope this email finds you well and you are making the best of your time in Greece. I've been thinking about you a lot after everything that happened with Jack. I know how hard it must have been for you, and I want you to know that I am here for you, and your room at home is all ready for you.

I came across a job opportunity that I think might be perfect for you. It's a position at Milburn Manor, in Slaidburn working as a historian. They are looking for someone with your skills in history and archival research to organise their extensive library. I've attached the job description for you to review.

I believe a new project might do you good, and this could be a wonderful chance for you to focus on something you are passionate about. You've always been fascinated by history, and I think this could be a fantastic way for you to heal and find a new purpose after the events with Jack. You know you can stay here and it's not a long drive to Slaidburn.

Please let me know what you think, and give me a call soon, love.

With love.
Dad xx

Amelia sat back, the words blurring slightly as tears filled her eyes. Her father's kindness and understanding touched her deeply. He had always supported her, even when she felt lost and unsure of herself. She wiped away the tears and opened the attachment with the job description.

Clitheroe Advertiser

Wanted: Historian specializing in the Edwardian Era

Are you an enthusiastic historian with expertise in the Edwardian period? Do you have a keen eye for detail and a love for preserving historical collections? If so, we have an exciting opportunity for you.!

We are seeking a knowledgeable historian to sort and organize our extensive library housed within a charming Edwardian-era manor house. The ideal candidate will possess:

A deep understanding of the Edwardian era, including its cultural, social, and political aspects.

Experience in archival research and cataloguing, with a meticulous approach to organisation.

Excellent communication skills with the ability to collaborate with the owner.

A commitment to preserving and highlighting the historical significance of our collection.

This is a unique opportunity to immerse yourself in a rich historical environment and

make a meaningful contribution to the preservation of our heritage. If the above is relevant to you and you have a passion for the Edwardian era, we invite you to apply.
Please submit your resume and a cover letter to:
Rafe De Lacy
Millburn Manor
Slaidburn
BB7 3AE

Amelia had a degree in history and had completed her Masters in historical research and library sciences, specialising in the Edwardian Era. She had an in-depth knowledge of the period 1901 to 1914 and extensive knowledge of archives and digital research. She would apply for the job she decided and then see what happened. She had to do something when she went home and couldn't think beyond that at present. She replied to her father, thanking him, and promising to call and assuring him that she would apply for the position.

Curious to know more about Milburn Manor, she opened a new tab and typed the name into the search engine. A plethora of images and articles appeared, highlighting the manor's stunning architecture and lush gardens. It looked like a place straight out of a fairy tale. As she scrolled through the results, one headline caught her attention:

The Haunting of Milburn Manor: The Ghost of Lady Isabella

A chill ran down Amelia's spine. She hesitated for a moment before clicking on the link. The article opened with a hauntingly beautiful image of the manor bathed in moonlight, a ghostly figure barely visible in one of the windows. According to the story, Lady Isabella de Lacy had lived there in the late 19th century. She had fallen in love with a man beneath her station and the romance was doomed by her family's disapproval. A tragedy occurred and Isabella was sent away from the manor, to later die of a broken heart. Legend had it that Lady Isabella's spirit still roamed the halls of Milburn Manor, her soft mournful sobs echoing through the empty rooms. Fascinated, Amelia couldn't help but feel a mix of excitement and trepidation. The idea of working at a place with such a rich history and a resident ghost was both thrilling and daunting. She closed her laptop, her mind racing with possibilities.

***

Looking at the time, she began to make her way to the harbour to catch the first ferry to Spinalonga. As the boat cut through the azure waters of the sea, she felt a sense of apprehension mingled with the salty breeze. The sun hung high in the sky casting a golden glow upon the rippling waves that lapped at the sides of the vessel. Around her, the rugged coastline of Crete loomed, its craggy cliffs and verdant slopes an attestation to the timeless beauty of the island. As the boat drew nearer to its destination, a shadow seemed to fall over the horizon and a palpable sense of foreboding sent a shiver down Amelia's spine.

Spinalonga, the island of exile and despair lay before her like a ghost from a half-remembered nightmare. Once a bustling Venetian fortress, it had been transformed into a leper colony in 1904 a place of isolation and suffering for those afflicted with the dreaded disease and had only ceased being a leper colony in 1957. As the boat docked at the weathered stone quay, Amelia stepped onto the sun-baked earth with a mixture of trepidation and curiosity. The air was heavy with the scent of salt, mingling with the distant cries of seabirds that circled overhead like vultures. As she passed through the entrance tunnel known as Dante's Gate, she thought about the lepers and how seeing this meant that they probably wouldn't see the outside world again. Walking through the narrow pathways and streets Amelia could feel the weight of centuries pressing down upon her, a tangible presence that seemed to whisper of the countless souls who had walked these same paths before her. The ruins of stone buildings stood as silent witnesses to the suffering that had once taken place within their walls, their crumbling facades a poignant reminder of the fragility of life. Amelia glanced over at Elounda and Plaka. They were so close, yet the people sent to Spinalonga could never go back there. But surely, they must have seen the lights in Plaka where their families lived and heard the distant laughter of children. It was sad and as Amelia wandered the island's labyrinthine streets, she felt a sense of kinship with those who had come before her. She was adrift in a sea of uncertainty, her heart weighed down by the bitter sting of betrayal.

    She had been cast out from the sanctuary of her relationship and abandoned at the altar. She couldn't shake the feeling of being branded as damaged goods, a modern-day leper, shunned by society. As she navigated the haunting ruins of Spinalonga, her sense of isolation echoed across the sea, a silent cry for help in the face of overwhelming despair.

Amelia wandered along the deserted paths of Spinalonga, her footsteps echoing against the ancient stone walls. She had read about the island's history but nothing could have prepared her for the overwhelming sense of loss that lingered in the air. The sun was high, casting sharp shadows, yet the warmth did little to dispel the chill that settled deep in her bones. She passed crumbling houses with faded shutters and peered into windows where time seemed frozen. As she ventured deeper, an inexplicable heaviness took hold, a feeling as though she was intruding on something private, something not meant to be disturbed.

Drawn by a pull she couldn't explain, Amelia stepped into one of the old homes, its door hanging ajar on rusted hinges. The air inside was thick and stale and dust particles danced in the sunlight streaming through the cracks. She traced her fingers over the rough walls, imagining the lives once lived within. In the corner, a broken chair lay toppled, its seat worn from use, and a faded rug was draped haphazardly on the floor, as if hastily abandoned. The room seemed to close in on her, and as Amelia turned to leave, her foot slipped on the uneven stone floor. She fell hard, the impact jolting through her, and for a moment, everything went black.

When she opened her eyes, the room around her was changed. The air felt thicker, warmer, carrying the faint scent of wood smoke and something else she couldn't quite place. She struggled to her feet, her head spinning, and stumbled outside. But as she emerged, the island no longer looked the same. The light had dimmed, softened by a dusky glow, and the sounds of distant voices floated on the breeze, too faint to understand but unmistakenly human. Amelia blinked, disorientated. The streets seemed alive with an energy she hadn't felt before, as if the echoes of the past were reaching out, intertwining with the present. She could hear the faint creak of a door, the rustle of fabric, and the distant murmur of conversation as if people were just out of sight, living their everyday lives. The empty windows now seemed to watch her, no longer just hollow frames but portals to another time. Amelia's heart raced; the island felt alive in a way that was both beautiful and deeply unsettling.

She turned quickly, her breath catching as she tried to steady herself. Everything felt so real, yet impossibly out of reach. Amelia stumbled back towards the entrance, the feeling of being trapped between two worlds overwhelming her senses. Just as she reached the main gate, she slipped again, catching herself on the rough stone wall. The world flickered, and she blinked hard, the eerie glow of the past dissolving into the harsh brightness of the present day. Spinalonga was as it had been, empty, still and steeped in silence.

Amelia gasped, gripping the stone for support as the lingering sense of disorientation faded. She looked back, half expecting to see the island as she had moments ago, but there was nothing. Just ruins and the relentless sun overhead. Back on the boat, Amelia couldn't shake the experience. She sat quietly, her mind replaying those moments over and over. Had it been a trick of the light? A fleeting moment of dizziness? Or had she truly glimpsed into the past, felt the pulse of the lives that once filled those streets?

***

Amelia sat at a local bakery in Elounda, which was simply called Elounda's Bakery overlooking the main harbour whilst she waited for Nikos. She had a Greek coffee and a bougatsa. As she took her first bite her senses were greeted by an intoxicating aroma of freshly baked phyllo dough. It was a delicate pastry rolled out paper thin and layered to perfection. The golden-brown crust crackled with each bite giving way to a symphony of textures that danced upon her palate. Inside was a velvety smooth cheese filling and with each mouthful the creamy filling oozed out enveloping her taste buds in a blissful embrace, which left her craving for more.

The journey from Elounda to Agios Nikolaos was a picturesque one, marked by stunning coastal views and charming villages along the way. As Nikos and Amelia departed from Elounda, they wound along the coastal road, with the shimmering waters of the Aegean Sea on one side and rugged cliffs on the other. Passing through small traditional villages adorned with whitewashed houses and colourful flowers, Amelia felt that she was getting a glimpse of authentic Cretan life. Each bend in the road revealed a new vista, with olive groves, vineyards and citrus orchards dotting the landscape. As they approached Agios Nikolaos, the scenery became even more captivating. The road hugged the coastline, offering panoramic views of the turquoise sea and the distant mountains.

Later that afternoon they wandered around the bustling town of Agios Nikolaos. Surrounded by water on three sides, Agios Nikolaos combined the sleepy feel of a seaside resort with all the amenities of a cosmopolitan port. Villas and tavernas spilled over the town's three hills to meet a harbour dotted with mega yachts and fishing boats. They settled in a lovely taverna by the lake with a glass of wine and a wonderful Gyros each. Nikos explained that Gyros was chicken or pork cooked on a vertical rotisserie. The meat was then sliced and served in pitta bread with onion, tomato, tzatziki sauce, and thin chips. The word Gyro came from the Greek "turn." As they enjoyed their food, Amelia turned to Nikos.

"Something happened on Spinalonga today," she began, her voice thick with the weight of her confusion. "I felt...I was there, but it wasn't now. It was like I stepped back in time, just for a moment. I can't explain it."

Nikos listened, his expression serious. "The island has its secrets, Amelia. Sometimes the past and present aren't as separate as we think. Maybe you felt a connection, something that was meant just for you." Amelia nodded, still haunted by the feeling. It was as if Spinalonga had reached out to her, drawing her into its forgotten world for just a heartbeat.

They talked long into the evening. Nikos told Amelia all about his life in Vrouchas and how he had lost his beloved wife, Maria, to breast cancer a couple of years ago. Amelia could sympathise as she too had lost her mother to cancer. Amelia suddenly found herself telling Nikos about the wedding, Jack, and her despair. Nikos looked at Amelia

"What you have gone through is terrible, but I feel you will be ok. You are a beautiful, strong woman Amelia "

"I don't feel beautiful" Amelia replied looking into his eyes. "I go home tomorrow, and I am dreading it."

"You'll find the strength and if you get the job that you have applied for, it may help to take your mind off your troubles "Nikos took hold of her hand.

"Thank you. And you have been wonderful I'm so glad we met." Amelia knew she found Nikos incredibly attractive but was she ready for anything more? She toyed with the rim of her glass, her thoughts a whirlwind of conflicting emotions. She knew she should be packing, preparing for her journey home tomorrow, yet a part of her longed to linger in this moment, to bask in the warmth of Nikos's smile and the easy camaraderie they shared.

Nikos leaned in closer, his voice a whisper against the backdrop of the bustling taverna. "You know Amelia, there's something I've been meaning to tell you…." But before he could utter another word the chime of the taverna's closing bell shattered the spell jolting them back to reality. With a resigned sigh, Amelia rose from her seat.

"I should be going," she said, her voice tinged with regret. "Tomorrow's an early start, and I still have so much to do." They made their way back to Elounda. Amelia hugged Nikos and made her way slowly back up to her apartment. Nikos gazed at her retreating figure as she made her way to the door.

"Until we meet again, then," he said softly, his words a silent promise of things yet to come.

As Amelia stepped into her apartment, she felt a sense of longing stir within her. A longing for the warmth of Nikos's embrace, the laughter they had shared. But for now, she would have to content herself with the memories of this fleeting moment, a moment that had left an indelible mark upon her heart.

Chapter Six

Amelia
Lancashire

Amelia's return to Lancashire brought with it a sense of both familiarity and uncertainty as she navigated the winding roads that led her back to the place, she once called home. The rolling hills and countryside stretched out before her like an open embrace, offering solace amidst the tumult of her shattered dreams. She pulled up outside her childhood home, Highcliffe House. It was a large house situated on Lower Chapel Lane in the village of Grindleton with a converted barn attached and a large orchard full of damson trees to the other side. Her father was there to greet her with a tight-lipped smile, his eyes betraying a hint of concern beneath their stoic façade. Since losing her mother she had become close to her father.

"Welcome home Amelia, "he said, his voice gruff yet tinged with warmth. "I trust your journey was uneventful?"

Amelia nodded, the weight of recent events heavy upon her shoulders. "It's good to be back "she replied her voice soft with emotion.

In the days that followed, Amelia settled into a routine of quiet contemplation, finding some comfort in the familiar rhythms of home. She had not had any contact with Jack and Chloe had told her that he had gone to Thailand to see his parents where they had retired. Amelia was glad that she wouldn't bump into him and was still struggling to process what had happened. She had received a lovely text message from Nikos and hoped that they would stay in touch. She knew she would go back to Elounda, however she had no idea when that would be.

A letter arrived a week after Amelia had been home. She had been offered an interview for the job at Milburn Manor and for the first time in a while, she began to feel excited about the future. The letter also explained that there was accommodation with the job if she were successful and although her father wanted her to stay at home, Amelia knew it would be better to be away for the time being, to be somewhere completely new.

***

As Amelia approached Milburn Manor, in the lovely village of Slaidburn, a sense of awe washed over her like a gentle wave, leaving her breathless in its wake. The grand estate stood perched atop a gentle rise; its majestic silhouette outlined against the backdrop of the Lancashire countryside. Tall ivy-covered walls encircled the property hinting at the secrets that lay hidden within its hallowed halls. Slaidburn was a village and civil parish within the Ribble Valley district of Lancashire. It lay near the head of the River Hodder and Stocks Reservoir both within the forest of Bowland, an area of outstanding beauty.

The Manor itself was a masterpiece of architectural splendour, a vision of a bygone era of opulence and grandeur. Its towering turrets and soaring spires reached towards the heavens while intricate carvings adorned every surface, a masterpiece of craftsmanship of generations past. As she made her way up the winding driveway the imposing façade of the manor loomed ever larger casting a shadow over the landscape below. The scent of freshly cut grass mingled with the faint aroma of blooming flowers, creating a heady bouquet that tantalised the senses. At the entrance, twin oak doors stood sentinel, their polished surfaces gleaming in the dappled sunlight. Amelia's heart quickened as she crossed the threshold her footsteps echoing in the cavernous foyer beyond. As she was ushered into the heart of the manor, Amelia couldn't help but feel a sense of reverence for the history that permeated every corner of the estate.

As she settled into the plush armchair that awaited her in the drawing room, she felt in her heart that this was more than just a job interview, it was the beginning of a journey that would take her to the very heart of Milburn Manor. Amelia had researched the manor before coming and had read more about the ghost that allegedly roamed the corridors and gardens. They called her the "Weeping Widow" and Amelia resolved to ask Mr de Lacy all about her.

Mr Rafe de Lacy came into the drawing room. He greeted her warmly and took a seat in the chair opposite her. He was a well-built man, possibly around the age of fifty-five, Amelia guessed, with thick chestnut brown hair with hints of silver at the temples. He wore well-fitted trousers with a cashmere sweater and polished leather shoes. She noticed he had a vintage wristwatch on his wrist, a subtle nod to his heritage. His strong jawline and high cheekbones gave his face a chiselled look, softened by the warmth of his smile.

After the usual introductions, they chatted amicably for a while, discussing her background, her passion for history, and her previous work experiences. After some time, Mr de Lacy, or Rafe as he insisted, she called him, rose from his seat, and gestured for Amelia to follow him.

"Come, let me show you something, "he said with a twinkle in his eye. Leading her through a maze of corridors, Rafe finally stopped in front of a set of double doors. With a flourish, he swung them open to reveal the most magnificent library Amelia had ever seen. The room was vast, with lofty ceilings adorned with intricate mouldings that spoke of the manor's storied past. Tall, leaded windows allowed streams of soft, golden light to filter in, casting a warm glow over the chestnut oak panelling that lined the walls. A rolling ladder, polished to a gleaming finish, stood ready to assist in reaching the highest shelves, adding a touch of old-world charm to the space. In the centre of the room, a grand mahogany desk stood as the focal point. On its surface lay an assortment of neatly stacked books, a vintage brass reading lamp, and a leather-bound journal. Plush deep green armchairs were strategically placed around the room, inviting one to sit and lose themselves in the world of literature.

Above the fireplace, which was framed by an imposing marble mantelpiece, hung a portrait of a stern-faced ancestor, their eyes seemingly following Amelia as she moved through the room. The scent of aged paper and polished wood mingled in the air, creating an atmosphere that was both soothing and invigorating. Amelia took a deep breath, feeling a sense of awe and reverence. The library was not just a room; it was a sanctuary of knowledge and history, a place where the past and present converged in quiet harmony. She felt a twinge of excitement at the thought of exploring the countless stories contained within these walls, each book a gateway to another world.

Her eyes widened in awe as she took in the rows upon rows of books that stretched as far as she could see.

"Oh, it's beautiful," she breathed unable to tear her gaze away from the countless volumes that surrounded her. Rafe smiled at her reaction, a hint of pride in his eyes.

"I thought you might appreciate it," his voice tinged with satisfaction. "And I have a proposition for you Amelia."

Amelia turned to face him; her curiosity piqued. "Yes?" she prompted, eager to hear what he had to say.

"As you know we are looking for someone to sort through the manor's archives and historical records and put them all in some sort of order and to sort out the books for valuation. I think you would be perfect for the job but there is one condition." He explained.

"Ok what's the condition as I am very interested in taking the job" Amelia said eagerly.

"We need someone to live in for this position. There is a lovely suite of rooms available for free. I think that to truly get to know the manor and its history it would be better to live here, would that be something you could do?"

"Absolutely." Amelia was delighted "My family home is in Grindleton but living here would be amazing and I would love to."

"Well then, welcome aboard Amelia," Rafe said clapping his hands together. With that he led her out of the drawing room and down a long corridor, pointing out various landmarks and points of interest along the way. Finally, they arrived at a set of ornately carved doors, which Rafe opened to reveal a spacious suite overlooking the gardens.

"This will be your accommodation during your time here, I hope you find it to your satisfaction" Rafe looked expectantly at Amelia."

"It's fabulous, thank you, she said "turning to him with a grateful smile. The sitting room was the first thing she saw. It was a spacious area, adorned with tasteful antique furnishings. A large, soft sofa sat in front of an ornate fireplace. The mantelpiece adorned with delicate porcelain vases and a beautifully carved clock. Two wingback chairs flanked the sofa creating a cosy seating arrangement. A polished walnut coffee table held a vase of fresh flowers, their scent subtly perfuming the air. The walls were lined with dark wood panelling and tasteful paintings of serene landscapes added a touch of colour.

As she stepped further in, to the right of the sitting room was the bedroom. A four-poster bed, draped in soft, cream-coloured linens and adorned with plush pillows, dominated the room. The bed's headboard was carved with floral designs, and the heavy velvet curtains around it could be drawn for added privacy and warmth. An antique wardrobe, with mirrored doors and brass handles, stood against one wall, providing ample storage space. A delicate vanity table with a matching stool, complete with a large oval mirror, sat near the window, which overlooked the manor's sprawling gardens. The window was framed with heavy, brocade curtains that matched the bed's drapes.

Connected to the bedroom was a small but luxurious en-suite bathroom. It featured a clawfoot bathtub and the floor was tiled in a classic black and white pattern, whilst neatly stacked on a heated towel rail were an assortment of fluffy towels. A door from the sitting room led to a small study. It was furnished with a sturdy oak desk and leather chair and a built-in bookshelf filled with classic literature. The colour palette of the entire suite was a mix of deep burgundy, creams, and warm woods, adding to the cosy and inviting atmosphere.

"You do know that the manor has a resident ghost? I'll tell you what I know about the legend later, but it is said to be Lady Isabella. Some say she is cursed and others that she is searching for something." Rafe explained. "There are many stories, but none have been proven. All we know is that she's been here haunting these halls, for as long as anyone can remember."

Amelia still wasn't sure she believed in ghosts but was excited and curious, and as she looked around the room, she felt a sense of peace settle on her. This was just what she needed and once she was settled and had started the daily routine of the job, she resolved to contact Jack and try and get some sort of closure.

***

The following week, having packed her belongings from home and promising her father they would meet for lunch that Sunday at the Spread Eagle in Sawley, she moved into Milburn Manor. She settled comfortably in her rooms and decided to go for a look around the hall before she was due to have a drink and a welcome chat with Rafe and some of the other members of staff. The air hung heavy with the weight of centuries-old secrets as Amelia wandered the dimly lit corridors of Milburn Manor. The dim bulbs cast eerie shadows that danced along the walls, and a chill wind whispered through the ancient halls. As Amelia ventured deeper into the dimly lit corridors, an icy chill settled over her, causing her breath to mist in the frigid air. She wrapped her arms tightly around herself, seeking solace against the chilling cold that seemed to seep into her very bones.

Suddenly a bloodcurdling scream pierced the silence echoing through the empty halls with a haunting intensity. The sound sent a jolt of terror coursing through Amelia's veins, freezing her in place as she struggled to comprehend the source of the unearthly wail. Before she could react, a powerful force slammed into her, sending her sprawling to the ground with a cry of pain. The impact knocked the wind from her lungs, leaving her gasping for air as she struggled to regain her bearings. And then, as she lay there dazed and disoriented, she saw her. A figure shrouded in tattered rags crouched in the shadows with a look of utter anguish etched upon her twisted features. Was this Lady Isabella, the ghostly spectre whose presence had haunted Milburn Manor for centuries? Amelia's heart hammered in her chest as she watched in horror, unable to tear her gaze away from the tortured apparition before her. Lady Isabella's eyes bore into her with an intensity that sent a chill down her spine, her mouth contorted in a silent scream of torment.

Unable to bear the sight any longer, Amelia scrambled to her feet, her pulse racing with fear as she stumbled backward, desperate to escape the chilling presence of the ghostly figure. She fled from the corridor, her mind reeling from the terrifying encounter she had just witnessed. And yet, even as she fled, Amelia couldn't forget the anguished wail that still echoed in her ears, a haunting reminder of the darkness that lurked within the walls of the ancient manor.

Chapter Seven

Amelia
Milburn Manor

Amelia's encounter with the ghost had left her shaken but she had to go to the drawing room that evening to meet Rafe and the other employees. Rafe could see that she was visibly shaken and passed her a glass of red wine. He explained about the legend of the Weeping Widow.

"The de Lacys had lived at the Milburn Manor for over three hundred years and Lady Isabella was the daughter of Lord Rafe de Lacy and Lady Eleanor de Lacy. Unfortunately, she had fallen in love with a wealthy mill owner, but her parents were horrified and forbade her to see him due to a difference in status. It was said that she continued to see him, but some tragedy occurred, and Lady Isabella left the manor and later died of a broken heart, but as I say, no one really knows the true story. I do hope this hasn't put you off the job and staying here Amelia," Rafe looked concerned. "She doesn't mean any harm, and although I have never seen her, I know that some have. I've never heard anyone recounting her screaming although many say they hear her sobbing. She is often spotted in the gardens near the chapel, where it is believed she used to meet her lover."

"Not at all, although it was a bit of a shock, "Amelia lied. Inside she was terrified but resolved to put this to one side and not mention that the ghost she had seen was not only dressed in rags but was disfigured and obviously in pain. In a way it had made her even more determined to stay and see if she could find out more about the poor Isabella whilst organising and sorting through the archives in the library. As she went to bed that night it took her a while to settle as she kept staring around her bedroom expecting to see the ghostly figure. She also had ghosts of her own to deal with as she had arranged to meet Jack finally and talk things through. He had returned from a brief visit to Thailand, and she was meeting him after work the following day and they had arranged to meet at the local pub in Slaidburn, The Hark to Bounty. The old Inn was a fabulous pub with lots of character and a lovely large open fire. The inn was reputed to date back to the 1300s and was known as The Dog until 1875. Amelia loved the story behind the name, which came from the squire of the village who had a pack of hounds. One day whilst out hunting, the party had called at the inn for refreshments. Their drinking was disturbed by a loud and prolonged barking from the dogs outside. The squire's dog, named Bounty was the loudest one and this prompted the squire to call out "Hark to Bounty"! Upstairs was the courtroom which was used as the local court from the early 19th century and the old pub had still retained much of its original features and charm.

***

The air inside the pub was thick with the mingling scents of beer and smoke from the fire. Amelia's heart hammered in her chest as she scanned the crowded room searching for Jack among the throng of people. And then, there he was, sitting alone at a corner table, a half-empty glass of beer clutched in his hand. As she approached Jack looked up and they simply stared at each other, the weight of unspoken words hanging heavy in the air. Finally, it was Jack who broke the silence, his voice rough with emotion. "Amelia, I'm sorry," he said, his tone a mix of sadness and regret.

Amelia met his gaze, her own eyes brimming with a mix of sadness and determination.

"We need to talk, Jack," she said, her voice steady despite the tumult of emotions swirling within her. As they settled into their chairs, the sound of raucous laughter and clinking glasses faded into the background, leaving them cocooned in a bubble of awkward tension.

Jack began, "It started as a stupid fling. I was feeling the pressure from work, and I made a terrible mistake. There was this girl, Sophie, and…it just happened. I never meant for it to go anywhere."

Amelia's eyes narrowed, her anger simmering just below the surface. "And the morning of our wedding? The phone call?"

Jack sighed deeply, running a hand through his hair. "She called me that morning and said she was pregnant. I panicked. I didn't know what to do, so I ran."

Amelia clenched her fists under the table. "And now? What happened to her?"

"She admitted she lied about the pregnancy. She just wanted to get back at me for ending things with her. It was all a manipulation," Jack said, his voice tinged with bitterness. "I know I hurt you, and I regret it every day."

Amelia felt a mix of relief and anger. "You've ruined everything, Jack. Our house, our plans, our future. I had to face everyone alone. Do you have any idea how humiliating that was?"

Jack's eyes filled with tears. "I'm so sorry Amelia. I wish I could take it all back."

There was a long pause as Amelia let his words sink in. Everything he said seemed to belong in the past and it all felt so distant. She thought about Elounda, about Nikos and her new job at Milburn Manor. She looked at Jack.

"I can't do this, Jack" she said finally, her voice trembling. "I can't go back to what we had. It's too broken."

Jack looked devastated. "But I still love you Amelia. I want to make things right."

Amelia shook her head. "It's too late. You made your choice, and I need to move on with my life." He reached out to take her hand, but she pulled away.

"Thanks for talking Jack, but I think we will leave it to our solicitors from now on." She said bravely as she got up. With a strength that she didn't know she had, she walked out of the pub, without looking back.

That night she emailed Nikos and told him all about her meeting with Jack. She wanted Nikos to know that her relationship with Jack was definitely over and she was looking forward to moving on. She went to bed with a heavy heart but also a determination to move on with her life, whatever that might be.

Chapter Eight

Amelia
Milburn Manor

Amelia's fingers trailed along the weathered spines of the books that lined the shelves of Milburn Manor's library. Sunlight filtered through the tall windows casting golden rays that danced across the polished wooden floor. As she worked, the silence of the room was broken only by the soft rustle of pages and the occasional creak of floorboards beneath her feet. Lost in her task, Amelia hardly noticed the passage of time until a glint of light caught her eye. She turned to see an ornate brass key nestled among the books, its intricate design standing out against the faded covers. Curiosity piqued, Amelia reached out and carefully plucked the key from its resting place. It felt cool and heavy in her palm, its weight a tangible reminder of the secrets hidden within the old manor.

With a sense of anticipation, Amelia set off in search of the lock that matched the key. She wandered deeper into the labyrinth of shelves, her footsteps echoing softly in the quiet of the library. Finally, she came upon an ancient oak cabinet built in a shadowy corner of the room. The cabinet bore a small brass plaque engraved with the words "Archives," and Amelia knew that she had found her destination. Taking a deep breath, she inserted the key into the lock and turned it with a soft click. The cabinet swung open on silent hinges, revealing row upon row of neatly organised files and folders.

Amelia's heart quickened as she reached for a weathered leather-bound volume tucked away on the bottom shelf. Dust motes danced in the shafts of sunlight that filtered through the dusty air as she lifted the diary from its resting place. As she flipped through the yellowed pages, her excitement grew. The handwriting was elegant and precise, the ink faded with age, but the words jumped off the page with a clarity that sent a shiver down her spine.

***

.

Florence Wilson, the diary's author, chronicled her days as a servant at Milburn Manor with a keen eye and sharp wit. Her entries were filled with details of the lives of the manor's inhabitants and from her brief first look, Amelia could see that Florence was Lady Isabella's personal lady's maid.

June 3rd, 1906

This was my first day of service at Milburn Manor and it has been one of both excitement and apprehension. As I pen these words in the dim light of my room, I cannot help but reflect on the events of the day.

Milburn Manor is a grand estate, its towering spires and ivy-clad walls casting shadows that seem to stretch to the very horizon. From the moment I arrived, I was swept up in a whirlwind of activity. The scullery maids are the first servants up in the morning and they must get the kitchen range hot enough to make tea whilst the hall boy cleans boots and empties chamber pots. The housemaids make tea for the lady's maids and the housekeeper before getting all the fires going around the house. There is such a lot of work to do. The kitchen maids make breakfast for all the servants before the cook makes the breakfast for the family. There are many servants, and many names to learn. I am sharing my small room with Daisy who is Lady Eleanor's lady's maid, which makes her senior to me, but she seems very friendly and has made me very welcome.

Today marked my first day as Lady Isabella de Lacy's lady's maid and I felt both excited and anxious about my new position. The grandeur of Milburn Manor is unlike anything I have ever seen before. The walls are adorned with exquisite paintings, and the halls echo with the footsteps of distinguished guests and household staff alike. This morning, I was introduced to Lady Isabella. She was a vision of grace and beauty, with delicate features and kind eyes. She welcomed me with a warm smile, instantly putting me at ease. Despite her noble standing, she seems gentle and approachable, qualities I did not expect from someone of her standing.

My duties began with assisting Lady Isabella in dressing for the day. Her wardrobe is vast, filled with the finest fabrics and intricate designs. As I helped her into a stunning emerald green gown, I couldn't help but admire the craftsmanship of each piece. Lady Isabella takes pride in her appearance, and I must ensure she always looks her best. Throughout the day, I attended to various tasks: brushing her hair, arranging her jewellery, and ensuring her chambers were in perfect order. Lady Isabella has a serene presence, and I found myself enjoying the rhythm of my work. In the afternoon, Lady Isabella took a walk in the gardens, and I accompanied her. The gardens are breathtaking, with vibrant flowers and meticulously maintained hedges. She picked a few blooms and handed them to me, saying that every flower has its own story and beauty. I felt a connection to her in that moment, understanding that beneath her noble exterior lies a soul that appreciated the simple pleasures in life. Tonight, as I sit in my modest quarters and reflect on the day, I feel a sense of fulfilment. Serving Lady Isabella is an honour and I am determined to perform my duties with the utmost care and dedication. I hope to earn her trust, and perhaps in time, her friendship.

Now I must rest because tomorrow there is to be a grand party. Guests from near and far have been invited to enjoy an evening of festivities amidst the picturesque surroundings of the estate's beautifully manicured gardens. There will be live music, dancing, and a sumptuous feast prepared by the cook. Daisy told me that cook is doing her special roast saddle of lamb and I'm hoping that we get to taste some of it. Oh, Daisy has come to bed now, so I will sign off and write again tomorrow. So excited, I hope I shall sleep.

June 4th, 1906

All was set for the grand party and the meal took place in the dining room which is a grand hall with its walls adorned with ancestral portraits. A long-polished dining table stretched across the room and was set meticulously for the evening meal. China delicate as a whisper graced each place setting and shining silverware rested beside crystal goblets. Candles flickered casting a warm glow on the scene. Downstairs the kitchen staff bustled around, the cook overseeing the preparations. She is a bit scary but exceptionally good at what she does. The guests gathered in the drawing room sipping cocktails and engaging in conversation. I could hear the piano's notes weave through the air. The meal that I had seen the cook preparing looked amazing. There was to be a delicate consommé to begin and then the roast saddle of lamb accompanied by Yorkshire pudding with buttered asparagus and potatoes dauphinoise. I had seen the kitchen staff prepare the dessert which was a magnificent trifle with layers of sponge cake, custard, fruit, and whipped cream, crowned with a single candied violet.

Isabella was dressed in a beautiful long gown in blue with silk and lace and her earrings and necklace were sapphires. She was a vision of beauty and elegance.

I watched as she swept down the long staircase and into the drawing room to meet the guests ....

Amelia closed the diary; she would continue reading it later when she had gone to bed. She wondered whether to inform Rafe about the discovery, but she was reluctant to do so at that time and wanted desperately to read the diary for herself and discover more about Isabella. A sudden chill swept through the room, raising goosebumps on her arms. She looked up and reflected in the mirror opposite her she could see the ghostly figure of Lady Isabella standing behind her. Amelia's breath caught in her throat as she met Isabella's gaze, her eyes wide with wonder and fear. For a moment, the two women stood locked in a silent exchange, the weight of centuries hanging heavy between them.

Then as quickly as she had appeared, Isabella faded from view, leaving Amelia alone in the quiet of the library once more. Later that evening in the quiet of her bedroom, unable to resist the temptation she opened the diary once more and began to read…

Chapter Nine

**Isabella 1906
Lancashire**

Isabella de Lacy descended the grand staircase of Milburn Manor, the soft rustle of her gown echoing through the opulent halls. Tonight, the manor buzzed with anticipation, as distinguished guests were set to arrive for an evening of elegance and refinement. Her gown, a vision of silk and lace in hues of midnight blue with a plunging off-the-shoulder decollete draped gracefully around her slender frame, accentuating her delicate features and fiery auburn curls. Adorned with pearls and satin ribbons, she exuded an air of timeless sophistication, befitting her status as the jewel of Lancashire society. She had a fair complexion, with a natural healthy glow, which spoke of her privileged upbringing. She had high cheekbones and a delicate jawline that added to her aristocratic appearance, while her full lips often carried a gentle smile that could light up a room. Despite her outwardly serene appearance, there was a quiet strength in Isabella. Her intelligence and wit made her a captivating conversationalist and she had a knack for putting people at ease. Beneath her composed exterior, lay a heart burdened by unfulfilled dreams and unspoken desires. Her longing for true love and freedom from societal expectations often brought a wistful look into her eyes, especially when she thought no one was watching. In her private moments, Isabella found solace in music and literature. She was an accomplished pianist with a beautiful singing voice and books were another escape, providing her with a sense of adventure and a window into worlds far beyond the confines of her aristocratic life.

As Isabella reached the foot of the staircase, she paused to survey the scene before her. The drawing room, aglow with the warm flicker of candlelight, beckoned invitingly, its plush furnishings arranged in anticipation of the evening's festivities. With a graceful sweep of her hand, Isabella pushed open the doors to the drawing room, stepping into the opulent space beyond. The air was alive with the murmur of voices and the tinkling of crystal glasses, as guests mingled in clusters, exchanging pleasantries, and gossiping in hushed tones.

Isabella's eyes swept across the room, taking in the familiar faces of Lancashire's elite. She saw her mother Lady Eleanor resplendent in a gown of emerald green, her laughter ringing out like music amidst the chatter of the assembled guests. And there standing by the grand piano was their neighbour Sir Geoffrey, his silver hair catching the light as he regaled his companions with tales of his latest travels abroad. As Isabella made her way through the room, she greeted each guest with a gracious smile and a polite exchange of pleasantries. Her presence radiant and commanding drew the attention of all who beheld her, casting a spell of enchantment over the gathering. Isabella played her role with effortless grace, her every movement a testament to her impeccable breeding and refined sensibilities. But beneath the façade of social grace and refinement, lay a heart that longed for something more, a heart that yearned for love, passion, and the promise of a future outside of the confines of Milburn Manor.

***

As she accepted a glass of champagne from a passing waiter she noticed James Wycliffe, the enigmatic mill owner whose reputation preceded him. James stood near the fireplace, his tall frame dressed in a tailored suit of deep charcoal grey, his dark hair swept back from his forehead with effortless elegance. Despite his presence being unconventional at such gatherings, James possessed an undeniable charisma that commanded attention.

As Isabella observed him from across the room, she could not help but feel intrigued by the mill owner. Rumours swirled about James's wealth and influence, his rise from humble beginnings to become one of Lancashire's most successful industrialists. His presence at the party was a testament to his ambition and determination to be accepted among Lancashire's elite.

For a moment, time seemed to stand still as Isabella and James locked eyes across the crowded room, the world around them fading into insignificance. In that fleeting moment, Isabella felt a spark of something indescribable, a connection that went beyond the boundaries of social convention and expectation. As the evening wore on, Isabella found herself drawn inexorably to James's side, their conversation flowing effortlessly as they exchanged small talk and witty banter.

Their conversation moved on to other matters and she found herself fascinated by his stories of the mill and the way times were changing, especially for women. With each passing moment, Isabella felt herself falling deeper under his spell.

Isabella's father Lord Rafe de Lacy, stood with stoic formality near the entrance of the drawing-room, his gaze sweeping across the assembled guest with a watchful eye. He was dressed in a tailored suit of dark velvet, adorned with a gold pocket watch. He was a formidable man and a stern father to his daughter and his son, also christened Rafe as was tradition but he was known by his second name of William. As Lord Rafe's eyes settled on Isabella, he noted with displeasure her animated conversation with James Wycliffe, the mill owner. A frown creased his brow as he observed the interaction between his daughter and James, a sense of unease settling in the pit of his stomach. He had heard whispers of James's reputation, rumours of his humble origins, and questionable business dealings. With a stern expression, Sir Rafe approached Isabella and James, his footsteps measured and deliberate as he sought to intercede in their conversation. His voice was tinged with thinly veiled disapproval as he addressed Isabella, his tone clipped and authoritative.

"Isabella, my dear, there you are," Lord Rafe began, his gaze flickering briefly to James before returning to his daughter. "I trust you have met Mr Wycliffe?"

Isabella tensed imperceptibly at the sound of her father's disapproving tone, her smile faltering slightly as she nodded in acknowledgment. Beside her James maintained a polite façade, his demeanour respectful but guarded as he addressed Lord Rafe in turn.

"Indeed, my lord," James replied, his voice measured and polite. "It has been a pleasure to make her acquaintance." Lord Rafe's gaze lingered on James for a moment longer, his expression inscrutable as he assessed the mill owner with a critical eye. Though he offered a perfunctory nod, there was an unmistakable tension in the air, a silent exchange of scrutiny between the two men of vastly different worlds.

As the evening wore on, Lord Rafe kept a watchful eye on Isabella and James, his disapproval simmering beneath the surface as he contemplated the implications of their burgeoning acquaintance. For Lord Rafe, the prospect of his daughter becoming entangled with a man of James's ilk was anathema, a threat to the social order and familial reputation that he held dear.

***

Meanwhile, downstairs in the bustling servants' quarters, a hive of activity unfolded as the household staff prepared for the evening's festivities. The air was alive with the clatter of dishes, the hiss of steam from the kitchen, and the hum of whispered conversations as maids and footmen hurried to and fro, attending to their respective duties.

Among them was Florence Wilson, the headstrong and spirited lady's maid to Isabella de Lacy. With her chestnut curls pulled back in a neat bun and her apron tied securely around her waist, Florence moved with purpose and determination, her hazel eyes sparkling with a mischievous glint. As she bustled about the servants' quarters, Florence could not help but overhear the whispers and gossip swirling among her fellow servants. The topic of conversation, of course, was the evening party upstairs and the notable presence of James Wycliffe, the mill owner whose arrival had sparked no small amount of speculation amongst the household staff.

"Did you see the way Master James was eyeing up Miss Isabella?" one of the kitchen maids whispered conspiratorially to her companion, her eyes wide with excitement. Florence rolled her eyes at the gossip, dismissing it with a shake of her head as she focused on her tasks. She had little interest in the romantic entanglements of the upstairs world preferring to devote herself to her duties as Isabella's lady's maid.

Yet even as she worked, Florence could not shake the feeling of unease that lingered in the air, a sense of foreboding that whispered of impending change. The arrival of James Wycliffe had disrupted the delicate balance of life at Milburn Manor, casting a shadow of uncertainty over the household and its inhabitants.

Chapter Ten

Amelia
Lancashire

As she put the diary down, Amelia heard the ping of her email. Eagerly she opened the computer, hoping it was a reply from Nikos.

Hey Amelia

It was so good to hear from you, you made my day. The diary you have found sounds interesting. Keep me updated as you read more. I can't believe your old manor house actually has a ghost. I don't know much about the supernatural but make sure you take care, please.

The taverna has been busy which is good, and I seem to have acquired a dog!! She just turned up. I have been feeding her and it looks like she has decided to stay. I've called her Nina. It suits her as she is slender and sophisticated, she's tan with a white stripe on her face. I'll attach some photos. She is a Cretan hound. Anyway, no more news from here. Please keep in touch and let me know more about your mystery. You never know maybe we can solve it together someday, back here at my taverna, with some of my lovely lamb kleftiko that you enjoyed. Wish you were here.

Take Care

Nikos xx

With her spirits lifted considerably from the email, she went down to the library to continue some work. She was seeing her father later for lunch, so she pressed on with some more archiving. She was itching to read more of the diary but that would have to wait until later.

***

As Amelia drove through Grindleton on her way to Sawley to meet her father she reminisced about her childhood. She had lived in a large house on Chapel Lane next to the Methodist church. There was a barn attached to the house which her parents had converted into a lounge and bedrooms with a stable underneath where her beloved horse Nesta had slept. They had spent many wonderful days riding around the countryside, but she had let her go when she went to university and often thought about the horse with affection. Maybe she would start riding again one day. There were two village pubs in Grindleton, The Duke of York, and The Buck Inn. She had spent many evenings in The Buck when she was still living at home and chuckled to herself at some of the memories. The Duke of York had passed through many hands but now sadly stood empty and abandoned and The Buck had recently been converted into a restaurant and bar called The Rum Fox. She passed the little village school that she had attended which was attached to the church where she had nearly got married and where her adored mother was buried. Opposite the school were the local playing fields where she had spent many happy hours as a child, with other local children from the village.

***

Sawley was a lovely village and the pub, an old coaching inn called the Spread Eagle was located on the banks of the river Ribble with a view of the ruins of the old abbey which used to be a Cistercian monastery founded in 1146. The cosy ambiance of the local pub enveloped Amelia as she stepped inside, the familiar scent of beer and hearty meals instantly washing over her senses. She scanned the room until her eyes settled on her father, seated at a secluded table near the back, a welcoming smile lighting up his weathered face.

"Dad," Amelia greeted, her voice tinged with warmth as she approached the table. "Thanks for meeting me here." Her father rose from his seat, a twinkle of pride gleaming in his eyes as he enveloped her in a fond embrace.

"Now, let's get you seated and fed. I'm sure you've got plenty to tell me." As they settled into their seats, the waitress approached to take their orders, and soon they were savouring steaming plates of pub fare, the clatter of cutlery, and the lively chatter of fellow patrons providing a comforting backdrop to their conversation. As always when they went out to eat, they ended up ordering the same dishes. They both started with a crisp Yorkshire pudding filled with creamy liver pate and then the beer-battered haddock with mushy peas and tartare sauce. Their table had wonderful views over the river, and it was a delightful setting.

"So, tell me about this new job of yours," her father prompted, his gaze warm with genuine interest. "How's it going at Milburn Manor?" Amelia smiled, a sense of excitement bubbling up within her as she recounted her experiences at the manor, from the eerie encounters with the ghostly apparition to the fascinating discoveries within the dusty old library. She mentioned the diary but didn't go into too many details about what it contained.

"Just be sure to take care of yourself, all right?" her dad remarked, "I don't want you getting too wrapped up in this ghost business and forgetting to enjoy life." Amelia chuckled, a warmth spreading through her chest at her father's words.

"Don't worry I'll make sure to keep one foot firmly planted in the real world, even as I delve deeper into the mysteries of Milburn Manor." Their conversation drifted to other topics, but before long the subject turned to Jack.

"Dad," Amelia began, her voice faltering slightly as she broached the delicate topic. "I saw Jack the other day. It was…... awkward, to say the least. Her father's expression softened with sympathy as he reached across the table to gently squeeze her hand.

"I'm sorry Amelia," he murmured, his tone filled with compassion. "I know how much he hurt you."

"It's been tough Dad," she admitted, her voice soft. "But I'm trying to move forward, to focus on things that matter, the job, my friends, finding closure." Her father nodded in understanding, his eyes reflecting a depth of emotion that spoke volumes.

"You're stronger than you know, Amelia," he assured her, his voice tinged with pride. "And you have an entire world of possibilities waiting for you. Just don't forget to lean on those who love you, especially when times get tough."

As they continued to chat and laugh over their meal, Amelia felt a profound sense of gratitude for the bond she shared with her father, a connection that had only grown stronger in the face of life's many twists and turns. As they lingered over their empty plates, lost in the warmth of each other's company, she knew that no matter what challenges lay ahead, they would always face them together, united in love and unwavering support.

Chapter Eleven

Isabella 1906
Lancashire

James Wycliffe stood amidst the bustling activity of his cotton mill, the rhythmic hum of machinery filling the air as workers bustled about their tasks. As the owner of one of Lancashire's most prominent mills, he took pride in the efficiency and productivity of his operation, yet his thoughts often strayed from the business at hand to a certain lady who occupied his mind more often than he cared to admit.

Isabella de Lacy, her name alone conjured a flurry of emotions within him, from admiration to longing, and a hint of apprehension at the obstacles that lay between them. She was unlike any woman he had ever met, her grace and intelligence captivating him from the moment they first crossed paths. As he watched the workers deftly operating the machinery, James couldn't help but wonder what Isabella would think of it all. Would she find beauty in the intricate dance of gears and spindles as he did, or would she only see the toil and sweat of those whose livelihoods depended on the relentless churn of the mills? Lost in thought, James recalled the first time he laid eyes on Isabella, the grandeur of the evening party, the sparkle of candlelight against her porcelain skin, the grace with which she moved through the room as if she were born to command attention. But beneath her regal exterior, James sensed a depth of spirit and resilience that intrigued him. A woman unafraid to challenge convention, to defy expectations, even at great personal cost. And although he knew the path ahead would not be easy, he couldn't shake the feeling that Isabella was worth every sacrifice, every risk.

      James had been born into modest circumstances in rural Ireland. From an early age, he displayed a keen intellect and unwavering work ethic, traits that would serve him well in the years to come. Despite the hardships of his upbringing, James harboured dreams of a better life, one filled with opportunity and prosperity. Determined to carve out his path in the world, James left his small village behind and set out for the bustling industrial centres of Lancashire. It was there, amid the clatter of machinery and the roar of steam engines, that he found his calling in the textile industry. Starting as a lowly apprentice in a local mill, James quickly proved himself to be a diligent and resourceful worker, earning the respect of his peers and mentors alike. With each passing year, James rose through the ranks, his natural talent and tireless dedication propelling him ever closer to his goal. When the opportunity arose to purchase his own mill, James seized it with both hands, determined to turn his vision of success into a reality.

Through shrewd business acumen and a knack for innovation, James transformed his humble mill into a thriving enterprise, renowned throughout Lancashire for its quality textiles and efficient production methods. But amidst his professional triumphs James never forgot his roots, remaining humble and grounded despite his newfound wealth and status.

As the day wore on, James found himself immersed in the intricacies of mill operations, his thoughts drifting back to Isabella time and time again. Yet amidst the whirlwind of activity and the constant hum of machinery, one thing remained clear; no matter what the obstacles that lay ahead, he was determined to find a way to win

Isabella's heart and prove himself worthy of her love.

***

The kitchen of Milburn Manor buzzed with activity as the newest addition to the staff made his grand entrance. Tall, with a shock of unruly dark hair and a twinkle in his piercing blue eyes, Pierre LaFontaine brought an air of sophistication and charm that instantly captivated the attention of the kitchen staff.

Mrs Mary Hargreaves, the seasoned head cook of Milburn Manor, watched with a mixture of curiosity and apprehension as Pierre sauntered into the bustling kitchen, his confidence palpable as he surveyed his new domain. She had heard whispers about the talented French chef who had been hired to elevate the manor's culinary offerings, but she couldn't help but wonder how his arrival would affect the balance of the kitchen.

As Pierre began to assert his authority, issuing commands in his melodious French accent and effortlessly commandeering the culinary chaos around him Mary found herself both impressed and slightly unnerved by his presence. There was no denying his culinary skill, his deft hands moving with precision as he whipped up elaborate dishes with effortless grace.

Florence was making some tea and a light snack for Isabella in the kitchen and couldn't help but notice the handsome French man. Beneath his suave exterior, she felt there lurked an enigmatic aura, a sense of mystery that piqued Florence's interest and set her heart aflutter in a way she hadn't felt in years. She tried to ignore the flutter of excitement in her chest as she focused on her duties but try as she might, she couldn't shake the feeling that Pierre LaFontaine would prove to be more than just a skilled chef.

***

In the grand drawing room of Milburn Manor, Rafe de Lacy sat regally in his favourite armchair, his brow furrowed in deep concentration. Across from him, Eleanor de Lacy, his elegant wife, reclined gracefully on the plush sofa, a look of concern etched upon her features.

"Rafe, we must discuss Isabella's future," Eleanor began, her voice soft but resolute. "She's of age now, and it is time we found her a suitable match."

Rafe nodded solemnly; his gaze fixed on the crackling fire before him. "Indeed, my dear. Our daughter is a woman grown, and we must ensure her future happiness and security."

Eleanor sighed, her thoughts turning to the delicate matter at hand. "I have received word from Sir Edmund Ashcroft. He has expressed a keen interest in Isabella as a potential match for his nephew, Sir Percival Ashcroft." Rafe's brow furrowed at the mention of Sir Edmund Ashcroft, his expression unreadable.

"Sir Edmund, you say? A man of considerable wealth and influence to be sure. But is Sir Percival truly the right match for Isabella? She's very headstrong with opinions of her own.

Eleanor nodded, her gaze steady.

"I believe so, Rafe. Sir Percival may be slightly older than Isabella, but he is a respected gentleman with a distinguished reputation. His connections and resources would provide Isabella with security and stability, and his maturity may prove to be an asset in their union."

Rafe considered his wife's words carefully, his thoughts drifting to the future of his beloved daughter.

"Very well, Eleanor. If you believe this match to be in Isabella's best interests, then we shall proceed, but we must tread carefully. Isabella's happiness is my foremost concern, however, as I said she can be headstrong and may not welcome this match."

Eleanor smiled, "Of course Rafe. I shall speak with Isabella and arrange for her to meet with Sir Edmund and Percival. With any luck this union will bring prosperity and happiness to our family. I think I will arrange a theatre evening; Isabella loves the theatre."

As the fire crackled merrily, they continued to chat and discuss the future of their daughter.

Chapter Twelve

Amelia
Lancashire

As days turned into weeks, Amelia found herself increasingly immersed in the diary of Florence Wilson whose words offered a tantalizing glimpse into the past. She still hadn't mentioned the diary to Rafe, and she was reading it mostly in the evenings so that she could concentrate on her job of archiving records and sorting out the vast library in Milburn Manor. Despite the unsettling encounter with the ghostly apparition in the corridor, Amelia found solace in her work at the manor. The quiet serenity of the library provided a welcome refuge from her thoughts about Jack, and she threw herself into her tasks with renewed determination.

One afternoon, as she sifted through a stack of dusty manuscripts, Amelia's thoughts turned to her friend Chloe, whose comforting presence had been a source of strength in the wake of her shattered wedding. With a pang of guilt, she realised that she had neglected her friend in recent weeks, consumed as she was by her job and the diary. Determined to make amends, Amelia called Chloe and arranged to meet her in Clitheroe later that afternoon.

They decided to meet at The Emporium. This was a restored and rejuvenated former Methodist chapel at the bottom of Moor Lane in Clitheroe. It was a fabulous brasserie, coffee shop, wine bar, and pizzeria across three floors and under one roof. The ambiance was elegant and timeless but warm and welcoming. They hugged as they met and settled into a comfortable sofa in the corner on the ground floor. They decided on the Greek mezze platter to share which consisted of halloumi, sunblushed tomatoes, balsamic onions, falafel, hummus, and pitta, and then the Spanish Chorizo pizza which came with crushed olives and Manchego.

Over a lovely glass of chilled white wine, they discussed the events that had transpired since their last meeting, their conversation ranging from light-hearted anecdotes to the weightier matters that weighed on Amelia's mind. When the topic turned to Jack, Chloe's expression softened with sympathy, her unwavering support a balm to Amelia's wounded heart. Their conversation turned to the tangled web of emotions that had ensnared Amelia's heart as she struggled to make sense of the conflicting feelings that had plagued her since Jack's abrupt departure. With each word, Chloe listened intently, her empathy a soothing presence amid turmoil. Chloe squeezed Amelia's hand; her gaze filled with compassion.

"Whatever you decide, I'll be right here beside you." She vowed, her voice unwavering. "And if you ever need someone to talk to, to lean on, I'll always be here, no matter what."

"I don't know what to do, Chloe," Amelia admitted, her voice trembling with uncertainty. "Part of me wants to see Jack again, to demand more answers, but another part just wants to move on, to put it all behind me and start fresh."

"And what about Nikos?" Chloe inquired, her gaze searching. "Have you spoken to him again?"

Amelia hesitated, her thoughts drifting to the handsome Greek waiter who had captured her attention with his easy charm and warm smile.

"I have," she admitted, a blush creeping into her cheeks. "We've been emailing each other quite regularly, and I feel that there's a connection there, do you think I'm being stupid?"

Chloe grinned, knowingly, her eyes twinkling with mischief "Not at all, he sounds lovely and who knows where it might lead." Amelia nodded, still blushing and the conversation turned to the diary that she had found.

"Chloe, you won't believe what's been happening," she began, her voice tinged with a mix of exhilaration and trepidation. "First, there's this diary I found at Milburn Manor. It belonged to a lady's maid who worked there in the early 1900's and it is simply captivating." Chloe's excitement mirrored Amelia's own as they delved deeper into the details of the diary's contents. But as the conversation flowed, Amelia couldn't shake the memory of her recent encounters with the ghostly figure of Lady Isabella at the manor. She explained the legend to Chloe.

"I've seen her, Chloe. In the corridors of Milburn Manor. She was dressed in rags, her face tormented and twisted." Amelia shuddered as she remembered the vision she had seen. Chloe's eyes widened in astonishment.

"You've seen a ghost? Wow, why didn't you tell me sooner?"

"I don't know, I suppose I didn't want you to worry," Amelia smiled at her friend. They continued chatting for a while, enjoying their food and wine and each other's company. As they left, Amelia promised to keep Chloe informed of any more ghostly sightings and more of the secrets of the diary as they were revealed.

As night fell over Milburn Manor, casting long shadows across the grounds, Amelia made her way through the corridors to her bedroom. She turned on the bedside lamp and got into bed with the diary, looking forward to the next pages. But as she settled down into the soft bed with the warm glow of the lamp, she couldn't shake the feeling that she was being watched. She kept looking around the room because, despite the warmth of the radiators, there was a chill in the air.

As she continued to read, in the darkest corner of the room, obscured by shadows and half-forgotten whispers, the ghostly figure of Lady Isabella watched silently, her ethereal form a haunting reminder of the mysteries that lay hidden within the walls of Milburn Manor.

Chapter Thirteen
Isabella
Lancashire 1906

They arrived at the Theatre Royal in Manchester dressed in elegant attire befitting the grandeur of the occasion. Liveried footmen opened the doors and assisted the ladies with their wraps. The theatre entrance was magnificent with a central portico adorned with Corinthian columns and pilasters. Lord Rafe de Lacy had driven them himself in his brand-new Rolls Royce Silver Ghost which was his pride and joy.

As they made their way through the opulent foyer, Sir Edmund and his nephew Percival were coming towards them. Isabella had talked with her mother about this introduction and although she hated the idea of him being selected as a prospective husband, she knew for her parents' sake that she must be polite and charming.

Sir Percival Ashcroft was a man of unremarkable appearance, a stark contrast to the beauty and grace of Isabella. In his early forties, he had a slightly stooped posture that gave the impression of someone burdened by the weight of his own existence. His hair was a dull shade of brown, thinning at the crown and streaked with premature grey. It was meticulously combed back, revealing a high forehead and deep frown lines etched into his skin. His face was long and gaunt, his eyes a cold steel grey that peered out from beneath heavy brows. His eyes though sharp and calculating, lacked warmth and depth. Sir Percival's nose was long and slightly hooked, casting a shadow over thin colourless lips that rarely curved into a genuine smile. His jawline was weak and receding, hidden beneath a neatly trimmed but sparse beard that did little to enhance his appearance. He was dressed in a tailored suit, perfectly pressed but despite his outward appearance of wealth and status, there was an air of discontent and dissatisfaction about him, as if he were constantly striving for something just out of reach.

Instantly Isabella's heart sank, her initial impression of Percival confirming her worst fears. Despite his impeccable manners and polished exterior, she sensed something dark and foreboding lurking beneath the surface. Suppressing a shudder, Isabella forced herself to smile politely as Percival took her arm to lead her into the theatre, her mother behind beaming with pride at the prospect of this prestigious introduction. The ushers showed them to their seats, smart in their uniforms.

They were watching a production of Romeo and Juliet by the playwright William Shakespeare and Isabella was enthralled. During the interlude, when the odious Percival had gone to get some refreshments Isabell's gaze landed on a familiar figure seated in the audience. It was James Wycliffe the mill owner she had been talking to at the party. Despite their brief interaction that other evening Isabella found herself inexplicably drawn to him, a flutter of excitement stirring in her chest at the sight of his handsome features. As their eyes met across the crowded theatre Isabella felt a spark ignite within her. He smiled at her and raised his hand, a silent acknowledgment of the undeniable attraction that simmered beneath the surface. In that fleeting moment, Isabella glimpsed a glimmer of hope amidst the stifling constraints of her society, a tantalising promise of forbidden desire that she hoped would consume them both.

***

As the soft rays of the evening sun filtered through the lace curtains, Florence bustled about Isabella's bedroom tidying and straightening the luxurious furnishings in anticipation of her mistress's return. With practiced efficiency, she smoothed the crisp linens, plumped the pillows, and arranged fresh flowers in a delicate porcelain vase on the dressing table. As she worked, Florence couldn't help but reflect on the dynamics among the household staff, particularly since the arrival of the new servants. Thomas, the young footman, had seemed friendly enough, always quick with a smile and a helping hand. Mrs Thornber, the stern housekeeper, took a more cautious approach, her watchful gaze leaving no detail unnoticed and the butler, Mr Edmund Rogers was positively scary. But it was Lily Bates, the timid maid of all work from the workhouse, who had stirred the most curiosity amongst the staff. Whispers and murmurs followed her wherever she went, some expressing sympathy for her difficult circumstances, others casting suspicious glances her way. Then there was the new chef Pierre who despite Florence trying to engage in conversation seemed to resent her for some reason. Despite her initial attraction to the chef, she was now a little wary of him.

She knew all too well the challenges that came with being in service, the unspoken hierarchy that dictated one's place in the household pecking order, but despite the underlying tensions, Florence remained determined to perform her duties with diligence and grace, ever mindful of her responsibilities to her mistress. As she put the finishing touches on Isabella's room, she made her way down to the servants' hall for supper.

As the evening descended upon Milburn Manor, the servants gathered in the bustling kitchen for their nightly supper. The warm glow of the hearth cast dancing shadows across the room as they settled around the sturdy wooden table, eager for a moment of respite after a long day's work. At the head of the table, Mrs Thornber, the formidable housekeeper, presided with a stern yet watchful eye, ensuring that order was maintained amidst the lively chatter and clatter of cutlery. Opposite her, Mr Rogers, the dignified butler sat with an air of quiet authority, his gaze sweeping over the assembled staff with a sense of paternal concern.

On one side of the table, the French chef Pierre Lafontaine regaled the company with animated gestures and exaggerated expressions, his thick accent lending an air of exoticism to his culinary tales. The cook, Mrs

Hargreaves, eyed him warily, her lips pursed in thinly veiled disapproval as she stirred a bubbling pot on the stove.

"Ah, but you see, Madame Hargreaves," Pierre exclaimed, a mischievous twinkle in his eye, "in France, we do not just cook. We create masterpieces and culinary works of art that delight the senses and elevate the soul! Here try my escargot please, you will enjoy it, voila!." Pierre exclaimed as he put the dish in front of her. As Mrs Hargreaves took a mouthful of the food presented to her, the other servants all held their breath.

"Well, the plating is somewhat messy! what is it anyway, escar...what?"

"Why it is our famous recipe made with snails of course "Pierre retorted with a flourish. Mrs Hargreaves snorted derisively; her cheeks flushed with indignation as she spat her mouthful of food into the sink.

"Masterpieces, you say. Snails? you are a heathen Mr LaFontaine. I'll take good Lancashire fare over your fancy French concoctions any day." She spluttered and went back to her cooker in a huff.

The other servants chuckled appreciatively, caught up in the playful banter between the two culinary rivals. Amidst the laughter and camaraderie, Lily the young maid of all work, sat quietly at the end of the table, her eyes wide with wonder at the lively scene unfolding before her.

Lily had grown up in the cold unyielding confines of the workhouse in Clitheroe, a place where hope was as scarce as warmth. Born to a destitute mother who died soon after childbirth, Lily was thrust into the unforgiving world of institutional care, where the walls seemed to echo with the cries of abandoned children and the heavy footsteps of strict masters. From her earliest memories, Lily was acquainted with hardship. The days were long and gruelling, filled with monotonous chores and harsh discipline. She learned quickly to keep her head down and her emotions in check, for any sign of rebellion or sadness was met with swift punishment. The meals were meagre, often just enough to stave off starvation, and the children fought over scraps like famished animals. The workhouse was a place devoid of tenderness. The matrons were stern, their faces etched with the hardness of years spent enforcing rigid rules. Instead, she was met with the stinging crack of a cane or the cold dismissive glares of those in charge. The other children were both allies and rivals, forming fleeting friendships that could be broken by a single misstep or misinterpreted glance.

Lily's nights were filled with nightmares. She would wake up shivering, the thin blankets offering little protection against the chill of the dormitory. In those quiet moments, she would curl up and try to remember the feel of a mother's embrace or the sound of a lullaby, but those memories were non-existent, just imagined.

Education was a luxury in the workhouse and Lily's schooling was sporadic and rudimentary. She learned to read and write in fits and starts, her lessons frequently interrupted by the demands of labour. Yet she possessed a sharp mind and an unyielding determination to rise above her circumstances. As she grew older, the nature of Lily's work changed. She was put to more strenuous tasks, her young body strained by the demands of manual labour. She scrubbed floors until her fingers bled, laundered clothes in icy water and tended to the sick.

The harsh realities of the workhouse left their mark and Lily learned to be wary of trust, to guard her heart against the disappointment that so often followed moments of vulnerability. She developed a keen sense of survival, an instinctual understanding of when to speak and when to remain silent, when to fight and when to flee.

When she secured her lowly position at Milburn Manor, it offered her a glimmer of hope, a chance to redefine herself, but even there, the memories of her workhouse years loomed large. She was wary of the other staff and in awe of the butler and the housekeeper. She had never met anyone like the new chef Pierre who she thought was the most handsome man she had ever seen, and she was completely under his spell.

Chapter Fourteen

Amelia
Lancashire

The quaint streets of Slaidburn embraced Amelia as she wandered through the village, her mind heavy with the weight of a secret she could no longer bear alone. She had made a discovery, one that would alter the course of her life, and she needed confirmation.

She wandered around the village taking in the sights. She passed the local pub The Hark to Bounty with the post office and local store opposite. She stopped at the unknown soldier bronze statue that stood on a pedestal situated at the meeting of three roads. Slaidburn was situated on a bridge over the river Hodder and was a peaceful village full of rural charm. Amelia loved the old stone cottages, the ancient church, and the picturesque picnic area down by the river. Amelia made her way down towards the local health centre where she had an appointment that morning. She laughed to herself as she entered the doors, it had been like trying to get an audience with the Pope, getting an appointment with the doctor, but she had managed to circumnavigate the frosty receptionist eventually and she gave her a big smile as she took her seat.

***

As Amelia sat in the waiting room, her heart was racing. The pastel-coloured walls and the faint smell of antiseptic did little to calm her nerves. She had been feeling off for a few weeks, chalking it up to stress and the emotional upheaval of recent events. But when her period was late, she decided it was time to see a doctor.

"Amelia?" the nurse called, breaking Amelia's thoughts.

She stood up and followed the nurse to an examination room. Moments later, Dr Carter walked in giving her a warm smile.

"Good morning Amelia. What brings you in today?" Dr Carter asked, taking a seat across from her.

"I've been feeling really tired and nauseous lately, and I've missed my period," Amelia said, trying to keep her voice steady.

Dr Carter nodded, making notes. "All right, let's run some tests to find out what's going on."

After a series of questions and a quick examination, the nurse came in to take a blood sample. Amelia's anxiety grew as she waited for the results, her mind racing with possibilities. A short while later, Dr Carter returned, a serious expression on his face.

"Amelia, the test results are back. You're pregnant."

Amelia's eyes widened in shock. "Pregnant?" she repeated, as if saying the word would make it more real.

Dr Carter nodded. "Yes. Judging by your symptoms and the test results, I'd say you're about six weeks along."

Amelia's mind whirled. She thought about Nikos and the evening in Greece.

"I didn't expect this," she said softly, tears welling in her eyes.

Dr Carter reached out, placing a reassuring hand on Amelia's.

"I know it's a lot to take in. Do you have a support system? The father? Family or friends to whom you can talk?"

Amelia nodded slowly. "Yes, I can talk to the father. But this is…it's just so unexpected."

Dr Carter smiled kindly. "Take you time to process this. There are resources available to help you, and I'm here if you have any questions or need support."

Amelia thanked the doctor and left the surgery, feeling a mix of emotions. As she walked down the street, she placed a hand on her stomach, trying to comprehend the new life growing inside her. The future felt uncertain, but she knew she had to be strong for herself and her baby.

She returned to Milburn Manor and decided to have an early night and read some more of Florence's diary but as the quiet Lancashire evening enveloped Amelia, she found herself lost in a whirlwind of memories. It was a night etched in the depths of her soul, one she had guarded fiercely, yet now, in the solitude of her room, it flooded back with startling clarity.

The memory carried her back to the warmth of a Greek evening, the air heavy with the scent of jasmine and the gentle hum of cicadas. Nikos had returned that fateful evening unexpectedly knocking on her apartment door. His presence ignited a spark of anticipation that she couldn't ignore. They took some wine onto the balcony and the conversation had flowed effortlessly, punctuated by shared laughter and stolen glances that spoke volumes of unspoken longing. As the moon rose high in the sky, casting a soft silvery glow over the room behind them, their inhibitions melted away, leaving only the raw, unbridled passion that pulsed between them.

In the tender embrace of the night, they shared whispered confessions and lingering touches, each moment a testament to the undeniable connection that bound them together. And as the first light of dawn painted the sky with hues of gold and pink, they had surrendered to the irresistible pull of desire, losing themselves in each other. Now, as Amelia traced the contours of that memory with trembling fingers, she felt a surge of longing wash over her, a bittersweet reminder of a love she had dared to dream of but never fully embraced.

Closing her eyes, she allowed herself to be swept away by the echo of that night, savouring every fleeting moment as if it were a precious treasure to be cherished for eternity. With a sigh, Amelia nestled deeper into the embrace of her memories, her heart awash with the warmth of their night together.

Unbeknownst to her, Isabella's spectral form loomed in the shadows, a silent sentinel bearing witness to the tumultuous emotions that stirred within Amelia's soul. And in that moment of vulnerability, Isabella's ghostly presence resonated with her own, a silent understanding passing between them like a whisper in the night. Though they were separated by centuries, Isabella's spirit reached out to Amelia in a silent communication of shared experience. For in the depths of her sorrow, Isabella once grappled with the same fears and uncertainties that now plagued Amelia's troubled mind. As she stood in the shadows, a silent witness to Amelia's anguish, Isabella offered her solace in the knowledge that she was not alone.

In the darkness of the room, Amelia felt a strange sense of comfort wash over her, a fleeting connection to a presence unseen yet keenly felt. And, as she struggled to come to terms with the daunting reality of her situation, she found strength in the silent companionship of the ghostly figure that lingered in the shadows, a silent guardian watching over her in her hour of need.

Chapter Fifteen
Isabella
Lancashire 1906

Milburn Manor was hosting a lavish garden party, held on a sunny afternoon at their grand estate. The air was filled with the scent of blooming flowers, and the sound of laughter and light music drifted through the manicured gardens.

Earlier that day Florence had dressed Isabella in a tea dress of the palest lilac. It had a high neckline, elbow-length sleeves, and intricate lace and embroidery with a wide-brimmed hat adorned with matching lace. She had put her lovely auburn hair up in an elegant chignon that went perfectly with or without the hat. She thought she looked perfect, and Isabella seemed pleased with the result.

The sprawling gardens of the manor were adorned with fountains, topiaries, and colourful flower beds. The cream of Lancashire society gathered there to see and be seen. Isabella knew that Percival was attending but was secretly hoping to see James Wycliffe and even have a dance with him.

The champagne was flowing freely and was served in crystal flutes. Florence had been in the kitchen earlier and had watched as Mrs Hargreaves and Pierre, for once working in harmony had prepared the food. Pierre was doing something special for the evening supper which was a guarded secret much to the annoyance of Mrs Hargreaves. But for the afternoon there were cucumber sandwiches, thinly sliced cucumber on buttered bread. Smoked salmon canapes, a large chicken salad, and devilled eggs. Pierre had made macarons and eclairs, all spread out on large tables within the garden. There was a string quartet playing quietly in the corner and William, Isabella's brother was setting up a friendly game of croquet on the manicured lawns.

The garden party was in full swing, with guests laughing and chatting, their colourful attire creating a vibrant tapestry against the lush greenery. Isabella took a deep breath, trying to calm her nerves. She hadn't seen James Wycliffe since the theatre, and her heart raced at the thought of encountering him again. The scent of blooming roses filled the air, mingling with the light floral notes of ladies' perfumes and the earthy aroma of freshly cut grass. The string quartet played softly under a white canopy, the music adding an air of elegance to the event. Isabella's gaze wandered across the crowd, searching for James. Her eyes landed on a group of men standing near the fountain, and there he was, engaged in animated conversation.

James Wycliffe stood out among the guests, his presence commanding attention despite his humble origins. His dark hair, slightly tousled by the breeze, framed a face that was both rugged and handsome. He wore a well-fitted suit that accentuated his broad shoulders and lean frame, a stark contrast to the more flamboyant attire of the other gentlemen. As he laughed at something one of the men said, Isabella felt a pang of longing. His laughter, so genuine and unrestrained, was a rare and beautiful sound. Gathering her courage, Isabella began to make her way toward the fountain, her steps deliberate yet graceful. She wove through the throngs of guests, exchanging polite nods and smiles, her mind focused solely on reaching James. As she approached, he glanced up and their eyes met. For a moment, the world around them seemed to blur, leaving only the two of them in it.

"Lady Isabella," James greeted her with a warm smile, bowing slightly as she drew near. His voice, rich and deep, sent a shiver down her spine.

"Mr Wycliffe," she replied, her smile brightening her features. "It's a pleasure to see you again."

"The pleasure is mine," he said, his eyes holding hers a moment longer than was proper. "How have you been?"

"Well thank you. And you?"

"Busy, as always. But this is a welcome respite." He said gesturing to the festivities around them. Their conversation flowed easily, the chemistry between them undeniable. As they spoke Isabella felt a warmth spread through her chest, a stark contrast to the cool formality she often experienced with Percival. James had a way of making her feel seen and heard, his attention unwavering and genuine. After a few minutes, the other men excused themselves, leaving Isabella and James in a semblance of privacy despite the bustling party around them. They stood in companionable silence for a moment, the sounds of the party fading into the background. The tension between them was palpable, a magnetic pull that neither could deny. Isabella's heart raced as she contemplated her next words, but before she could speak, James leaned in, his voice barely above a whisper. "Dance with me "his breath warm against her ear.

As the soft strains of music drifted through the air, Isabella found herself swept into a dance with James, their movements graceful and fluid as they twirled amidst the sea of guests. With each step, their eyes met in silent communion, a shared understanding passing between them that transcended the constraints of society.

"You dance divinely, Miss de Lacy" James murmured, his voice low and husky as he guided her across the dance floor that was inside a marquee on the lawn.

"As do you, Mr Wycliffe," Isabella replied, a blush staining her cheeks as she felt the warmth of his hand upon her waist. But amidst the heady throng of the garden party, their dance did not go unnoticed. As Isabella's father, Lord de Lacy, looked on with growing disapproval, Percival's jealousy simmered beneath the surface, his eyes smouldering with barely contained rage. Their conversation was cut short as Percival approached, his expression darkening with animosity.

"May I have this dance, Isabella?" he asked, his tone tinged with a hint of possessiveness. Isabella forced a smile, her heart sinking at the thought of being in Percival's company.

"Of course, Percival" she replied, her voice tinged with resignation as she allowed him to lead her away. As they danced, Percival's grip tightened around her waist, his words laced with bitterness as he spoke of James with thinly veiled disdain.

"You would do well to stay away from that man, Isabella," he hissed, his eyes flashing with anger. "He is not of our ilk, and I imagine that his intentions towards you are far from honourable."

Isabella's heart pounded in her chest as she struggled to maintain her composure, the weight of Percival's words pressing down upon her like a leaden shroud. As she stole a glance across the gathered guests, she saw James watching her from afar, his eyes filled with a silent plea that spoke volumes of the burgeoning love that bound them together.

***

Downstairs in the kitchen Florence was watching as the French chef Pierre presented Mrs Hargreaves with the menu for that evening's supper.

The appetiser was Escargot en Croute, snails delicately cooked in garlic and herb butter, served in flaky pastry shells. The soup was Vichyssoise Glacee, chilled potato, and leek soup, garnished with a dollop of cream and fresh chives. The main course was Canard a L'Orange, roast duck drizzled with a tangy orange glaze, accompanied by a medley of roasted root vegetables and pommes Anna. His dessert was Crepes Suzette, thin pancakes flambeed with Grand Marnier and orange liqueur.

As Pierre passed the menu over to Mrs Hargreaves, her reaction was a mixture of astonishment and apprehension. She peered down at the list of dishes, her brow furrowing in confusion as she scanned the unfamiliar French names and exotic ingredients.

"Snails, again! Cold soup, who ever heard of such a thing?" she muttered incredulously, her eyes widening in disbelief. "What on earth is all this?"

Pierre, ever the embodiment of culinary enthusiasm, beamed at her with an air of self-assurance. "Ah Madame, it is the epitome of haute cuisine, a symphony of flavours and textures that will tantalise the palate and elevate the dining experience to new heights!" he exclaimed, his French accent lending an air of elegance to his words. Mrs Hargreaves remained sceptical, her hands clutching the menu tightly as if searching for some semblance of familiarity amidst the culinary chaos.

"I don't know about all that, snails? what's next frogs? And cold soup. Never heard the like and whose Anna and Suzette" she muttered under her breath, as the other servants looked on and tried not to laugh.

As the evening unfolded and Isabella was commandeered by Percival, Lord de Lacy sought out James with a stern expression etched upon his features. He beckoned James aside, his voice low and commanding as he delivered his message.

"Mr Wycliffe," Lord de Lacy began, his tone tinged with disapproval. "I must ask you to leave this gathering and refrain from any further association with my daughter. Is it clear that your presence here is causing her undue distress." James's brow furrowed in confusion, but he held his tongue, sensing the gravity of the situation.

"I assure you, my Lord, my intentions towards Isabella are nothing but honourable" he replied evenly, though his heart ached at the thought of being separated from her. Lord de Lacy's gaze hardened, his resolve unyielding.

"Your intentions matter little, Mr Wycliffe," he retorted his voice carrying a note of finality. "You are a man of a lower station, and it would be best for all involved if you were to remove yourself from this situation." James swallowed hard; his jaw clenched with suppressed emotion. He knew the futility of arguing with Lord de Lacy but the thought of leaving Isabella behind, especially with Percival, tore at his heartstrings like a dagger through flesh. With a curt nod, he acquiesced to Lord de Lacy's demand, his gaze lingering on Isabella inside at the supper table one final time before he turned to depart, his footsteps heavy with the weight of unspoken longing.

***

A few days after the ball Isabella and her mother were scheduled to visit the mill in Grindleton. At the party, although Isabella had danced and mingled, her thoughts had been consumed by one person: James Wycliffe. She didn't understand why he had left so abruptly but their stolen moments amidst the crowd and his sudden vanishing had only deepened her longing to see him again, and now, with an unexpected opportunity, she felt a flutter of excitement mixed with apprehension. Visiting the mills was an important part of the duties of the manor, something she and her mother did together. However, Eleanor had taken ill but insisted that Isabella make the visit and take Florence with her instead. Florence, ever observant, had noticed Isabella's distracted demeanour since the night of the party and suspected that her mistress's heart lay not just with the mill, but with its owner.

As the carriage approached the mill, Isabella felt her heart pound. The imposing structure loomed ahead, its tall chimneys spewing clouds of smoke. James was waiting at the entrance, his expression both warm and wary. He greeted Isabella and Florence with the expected courtesy, but his eyes betrayed his true feelings. He led them through the noisy bustling environment, explaining the various processes with practiced ease. Florence, sensing the need for discretion soon found an excuse to linger behind, giving Isabella and James the opportunity for a private conversation. They moved to a quieter area, a secluded corner of the mill where the sounds of the machinery were more distant.

"I was worried your father wouldn't allow this visit" James confessed, his voice low.

"He doesn't know Mother hasn't come with me, and you left the party so suddenly I had to see you," Isabella replied.

"Your father asked me to leave, Isabella. I don't think he approved of us dancing and talking." James was looking at her tenderly but worried. "That's because of Percival Ashcroft, whom my parents have decided is the perfect match for me."

Isabella's eyes were shining with unshed tears. "I felt such a connection with you James, I can't explain it."

James took her hands in his. "I feel the same. We need to be careful, Isabella. Your family would never allow this."

"I know," she whispered, "but I can't help how I feel."

Their faces were close now, breaths mingling. At that moment, the world outside ceased to exist. James leaned in, and their lips met in a tender, urgent kiss. It was a promise, a declaration, and a lament all at once. They pulled apart, breathless, aware of the risk they were taking but unwilling to step back.

"We must find a way," Isabella said, her voice trembling.

"We will," James assured her. "Somehow we will."

Their moment was interrupted by Florence's discreet cough. She had kept watch, ensuring they were not discovered, and now it was time to return. Isabella squeezed James's hand one last time before stepping away, the weight of their situation selling heavily on her shoulders. The journey back to Milburn Manor was a quiet one. Florence did not press Isabella with questions, merely offering her silent support, understanding the turmoil her mistress was enduring. She vowed to help her in any way she could, understanding the precariousness of their situation.

Back at the manor, Isabella retired to her room, her mind whirling with thoughts of James. Their future seemed impossibly fraught with obstacles, yet her heart clung to the hope that love would find a way. That evening as she lay in bed, Isabella thought of their kiss, the warmth of James's touch, and the promise in his eyes. She knew the path ahead would be perilous, but for the sake of their love, she was willing to face whatever fate had in store.

After Isabella left, James remained in the secluded corner, the memory of their kiss lingering. He knew the risks they faced but felt a renewed sense of purpose. He would work tirelessly to find a way for them to be together, no matter what the cost.

Chapter Sixteen

Amelia
Lancashire

Amelia closed the diary with a sigh. Although it had distracted her for a while, and she loved every word she read she knew that she had to speak to Nikos. They had been emailing regularly but, in her heart, she realised that she would need to speak to him in person. Amelia hesitated for a moment and then with a deep breath she finally pressed the call button, her heart pounding in her chest as she waited for Nikos to answer. After a few rings, a voice came through the line, warm and familiar, yet tinged with a hint of apprehension.

"Hello?" Nikos's voice carried across the distance, filled with curiosity and concern.

"Hi Nikos, it's me Amelia" she began, her voice wavering slightly with nerves.

"Is everything all right?" Nikos's tone shifted instantly, a note of worry creeping into his voice. "You sound worried, what's happened?" Amelia took another breath, steeling herself for what she was about to say.

"There's something I need to tell you, "She started, her words tumbling out in a rush. "I…I'm pregnant." There was a moment of stunned silence on the other end of the line, broken only by the sound of their breathing mingling together across the miles. Then Nikos spoke, his voice soft yet tinged with disbelief.

"Pregnant?" he repeated as if trying to process the news.

"Yes," Amelia affirmed, her voice barely above a whisper. "I just found out." Nikos took a moment to respond, his words carefully chosen.

"Amelia, this changes things." He admitted, his tone heavy with the weight of their situation.

"I know," Amelia replied softly, her heart aching with the realisation of the implications. "I just…. I needed you to know." There was another pause, filled with unspoken thoughts and emotions swirling between them. Then, Nikos spoke again, his voice filled with a mixture of tenderness and resolve.

"Thank you for telling me, Amelia," he said gently. "We'll figure this out together, all right, but give me some time to process this will you?" Amelia nodded, even though he couldn't see her.

"All right," she echoed, a flicker of hope blossoming in her chest at his words. "Together."

***

"Pregnant!" shouted her father, "by a Greek waiter!" Amelia cringed and looked around the restaurant, but no one seemed to have heard. "Pregnant?" he repeated, his voice laced with disbelief. "Amelia, how could you let this happen?" Amelia winced at the accusation in his tone, her fingers tightening around the fork in her hand.

"It wasn't planned, Dad," she replied quietly, her gaze dropping to her lap. "But it is happening, and I thought you should know." Her father ran a hand through his hair, his frustration evident in the lines of his face.

"This is … unexpected." He admitted, his voice strained. "What does the waiter have to say about this."

"He's not a waiter dad, he owns a taverna and he's a lovely man. We've talked and he wanted some time to process the news, I'm sure we'll work something out between us, we just need to talk some more, I'm sure he will call or email later."

"I don't know what to say, Amelia, we need to discuss this more, I am so disappointed in you, really after all you have been through. You said you had met someone in Greece, not that you had slept with him "his voice was beginning to rise again. Amelia felt a surge of panic at her father's reaction, the weight of disappointment crushing down on her.

"Dad, please," she pleaded, her voice trembling. "I need your support more than ever right now until I decide what to do or hear what Nikos says." Her father sighed heavily, his features softening slightly at the desperation in his daughter's voice.

"Amelia, I also need time to process all of this," he replied, his tone weary. "But you know I love you, and we will navigate this together, as a family. Amelia nodded her eyes brimming with tears as she reached across the table to squeeze her father's hand.

"Thanks, Dad," she whispered, "That means everything to me."

***

"Pregnant?" exclaimed Chloe her eyes widening in disbelief. It was a couple of days later and Amelia had arranged to meet her friend at a local pub in the village of Bolton by Bowland. They were meeting at The

Coach and Horses, a lovingly restored former coaching inn, in the heart of the old village.

Chloe's eyes stayed wide, and her hand flew to her mouth in disbelief.
"Oh, my goodness, Amelia, are you serious?" she exclaimed, her voice filled with astonishment. Amelia nodded; her cheeks flushed with embarrassment.

"Yes, Chloe it's true, and Nikos is the father," she admitted. Chloe's eyes widened even further, her shock evident on her face.

"Nikos? As in your Greek fling Nikos?" she asked her voice tinged with disbelief. Amelia nodded miserably, her heart heavy with uncertainty.

"I don't know what to do" she confessed. "Since I told Nikos I haven't heard a word from him. Surely this can't happen again to me, I can't be abandoned again Chloe, I can't take it." Amelia had started to cry. Chloe reached across the table to take Amelia's hand in hers, her expression filled with sympathy.

"Oh Amelia, I'm so sorry. But you're not alone, you know that I'll be here for you every step of the way, whatever you decide to do." As they tucked into their Welsh Rarebit and apple slaw, they talked for a couple of hours and even though Amelia's mind was in a whirl she knew she had her father and Chloe by her side to support her in whatever might come next.

***

As Amelia trudged up the driveway to Milburn Manor, her thoughts weighed heavy with the recent revelations she had shared with Chloe. The cool evening air whispered through the trees, and an eerie stillness hung over the estate, casting long shadows across the path. Just as she reached the imposing front doors, Rafe's voice cut through the silence.

"Amelia," he called out, his figure emerging from the shadows of the entrance hall. "Someone is waiting for you in the library." Amelia's heart skipped a beat at the unexpected news, immediately thinking it must be Jack.

"Who is it?" she said to Rafe, her brow furrowed in confusion. Rafe glanced at her with raised eyebrows.

"Go and see for yourself, Amelia, and let me know if you need anything." He replied, gesturing towards the grand oak doors leading to the library.

With a sense of trepidation, Amelia pushed open the doors and stepped into the dimly lit room. The flickering glow of the fire cast dancing shadows on the walls, lending an otherworldly ambiance to the space. A tall figure was sitting in one of the high wing-backed chairs and Amelia's heart sank as she didn't want to face Jack again.

"Hello," she said tentatively. The figure rose and turned towards her.

And there standing in front of her was Nikos.

Amelia's breath caught in her throat at the sight of him, her heart fluttering with a mixture of relief and apprehension.

"Nikos? What are you doing here?" she stammered. Nikos turned to face her, his expression a mix of emotions she couldn't quite decipher.

"I had to see you Amelia, he replied "There's something important I need to tell you." Before Amelia could respond, a sudden chill swept through the room, causing her to shiver involuntarily. Out of the corner of her eye, she thought she caught a glimpse of movement, a shadowy figure lurking in the darkness its features twisted in anguish. Isabella…the realisation sent a shiver down Amelia's spine, her skin prickling with unease. She blinked and the apparition was gone, leaving her to grapple once again with the unsettling sensation of being watched.

Unaware of the ghostly presence, Nikos stepped closer, his gaze locking with hers.

"Amelia, I need you to listen to me," he began, his voice low and urgent. "There's something I should have told you before, something important that could affect us."

Isabella crouching in the corner, began to move forward….

Under the weight of the evening's silence, Milburn Manor held its breath as if the very walls were bracing for the secrets about to unfold. Amelia stood in the grand yet somber library, the air around her thick with anticipation. The tall windows framed the night, the moon casting a silver glow that danced upon the ancient tomes and whispered across the polished floor.

Nikos's arrival had stirred a storm within Amelia's heart, a mix of joy, fear, and uncertainty. She watched him warily as he looked at her and took hold of her hand.

"I came as soon as I could, as soon as I knew you were carrying our child" Nikos began, his voice a gentle rumble in the quiet room. "But there's something I need to tell you. I already have a child, a son." He paused, bracing for Amelia's reaction.

But as he spoke, a chill crept into the room. In the shadowed corner, where light dared not linger, Isabella listened. Her form a mere whisper of her earthly self, was drawn to the unfolding drama. Clad in the remnants of her past, her hands deformed by the cruelty of her fate, Isabella's gaze was fixed upon Nikos, her heart twisted by a misdirected sense of protection towards Amelia. Amelia taken aback, struggled with a tumult of emotions. Betrayal, understanding, love, and fear danced within her, each vying for dominance. Before she could respond, the air shifted, and the temperature dropped as if the manor itself reacted to the confession and the silent witness to their plight.

Isabella moved by a surge of protective fury and her tragic memories, saw in Nikos not the loving partner Amelia hoped for but a symbol of betrayal, a man threatening the happiness of another woman under the manor's roof. Her ghost, fuelled by centuries of anger and sorrow, began to manifest with greater intensity, her presence a growing storm of supernatural wrath.

As Nikos's confession lingered in the air, mingled with promises of a shared future, the library itself seemed to recoil at the weight of his words. Books flew from their shelves as if hurled by invisible hands, their pages fluttering wildly in a tempest of disapproval.

The heavy oppressive air crackled with energy, a physical manifestation of Isabella's indignation. A vase, once perched safely on a mantle shattered against the wall with a violence that mirrored the ghost's turbulent emotions.

Amelia and Nikos, caught in the eye of the unfolding storm, exchanged a glance, a silent agreement that there was no reasoning with the unseen forces at play. As a heavy book narrowly missed Nikos, grazing his shoulder before thudding to the ground, the danger of their situation became perilously clear.

With a decisive grip, Amelia seized Nikos's hand, her action born both of fear and a sudden fierce determination to protect her future.

"We need to leave, now" she urged. Together they made their dash for the exit the air around them alive with movement and a rising wind that howled through the room with the force of a winter gale. They burst through the doors, spilling into the corridor beyond, where the tumult of the library seemed like a distant nightmare. Behind them, the library door swung shut with a definitive thud as if Isabella herself had signalled the end of the encounter. Amelia leaned against the wall, her mind racing to process the night's harrowing events.

Still shaken by their encounter with Isabella's vengeful spirit, they sought out Rafe. He was in his office, surrounded by ledgers and estate documents. At the sight of their distressed faces, Rafe's expression shifted from concentration to concern.

"What on earth's happened?" Rafe asked, standing to meet them, his voice laced with alarm. Between them Amelia and Nikos recounted the surreal events in the library, their words tumbling over each other in their haste to explain. Rafe listened in stunned silence, his brow furrowing as the tale unfolded. The notion of a ghost haunting the manor was one thing, but Isabella's active malevolence was entirely another.

"I don't know what to say," Rafe admitted, the scepticism in his voice belied by the genuine worry in his eyes. "But you're safe now and that's what matters. We'll discuss it further tomorrow but, in the meantime, I think you should stay here tonight, Nikos." Gratitude mingled with exhaustion in Nikos's nod of acceptance. The offer was a welcome one and he didn't want to leave Amelia alone. He had been going to stay a few miles down the road at a small cottage he had rented in Harrop Fold, but he telephoned and cancelled the booking, the owner David, being exceedingly kind and understanding.

Later together in her room Amelia and Nikos found themselves in a reflective mood.

"It's been a bewildering day," Amelia began, her gaze meeting Nikos's. "But there's more we need to discuss. About what you told me in the library, about your son." Nikos took a deep breath, the weight of his past visibly settling on his shoulders.

"Yes, my son, Alexandros. He's three and lives in Athens with my parents. They have been his main caregivers since my wife's death. It was a dark time for me, Amelia. I was drowning in grief and unable to be the father he needed." Amelia reached for him and as they hugged each other, she touched his face.

"I can't begin to imagine how hard that must have been for you. But Nikos know this, you're not alone anymore. There's two of us here that need you and Alexandros" She gently pointed to her stomach as she said it. Nikos smiled and pulled her closer.

As they succumbed to the embrace of sleep, wrapped in the comfort of each other's arms, the night whispered secrets through the corridors of Milburn Manor.

Unseen by the couple, Isabella lingered in the shadowed corner of the room, a presence as still as the air before a storm.

Chapter Seventeen
Isabella
Lancashire 1906

The morning sun had barely kissed the sky with its golden hues when Isabella was summoned to the drawing room of Milburn Manor. The urgency in Florence's voice hinted at an announcement of significant importance, one that could not wait for the leisurely pace of the day to unfold. With a sense of foreboding Isabella dressed in haste with Florence's help, her thoughts a whirlwind of speculation.

The drawing room, with its opulent furnishings and portraits of ancestors gazing down in silent judgment, felt more imposing than ever. Her parents, Lord, and Lady de Lacy sat awaiting her arrival, their expressions solemn. The air was thick with expectation.

"Isabella, sit," her father commanded, gesturing to a chair opposite them. His tone brooked no argument, and she complied, her heart hammering in her chest.

"We have news that concerns your future," her mother began, her voice laced with a cheerfulness that did little to ease Isabella's growing apprehension.

"Your father and I have given this matter considerable thought and have decided upon a course of action that will ensure the prosperity and continuation of our family's legacy." Lord de Lacy's gaze was fixed on Isabella with an intensity that made her shrink back in her seat. Isabella's mind raced as she braced herself for the inevitable proclamation. She had always known that her marriage would be a matter of familial duty rather than personal choice, but the reality of facing such a moment was far more daunting than she had anticipated.

"You are to be betrothed to Percival Ashcroft," her father announced, the finality in his voice echoing ominously in the room. Percival Ashcroft, a name that sent a chill down Isabella's spine. A man of cold demeanour and calculating eyes, whose presence suffocated the air with his arrogance. Isabella had tried to keep her distance from him since the garden party, she found his manner and appearance quite repulsive. She knew he just viewed her as a pawn in his quest for power and influence.

The room spun as she absorbed the weight of her parents' decree.

"No," she whispered, "I cannot marry him."

"You will do as you are told, Isabella. "Her father stood up and banged his fist on the table in front of him. "This union is not merely about you; it is about the future of this family. Percival Ashcroft is a man of wealth and standing, your marriage will secure our position for generations to come."

"But I do not love him," Isabella protested, her voice gaining strength. "How can you ask me to bind my life to someone I could never love, respect, or even like?"

"Love?" her father scoffed, his voice rising in anger. "You speak of love as if it is a luxury you can afford. You are a de Lacy. Your duty is to this family and its name. Your desires are quite irrelevant Isabella." Isabella stood, fuelled by a courage she didn't know she possessed.

"Then I reject that duty" she declared, her defiance ringing clear. "I will not sacrifice my happiness for titles or wealth. I will not marry Percival Ashcroft." Her mother was looking at her in horror. The slap came swiftly, her father's hand striking her cheek with a force that left her stunned. The sting of betrayal hurt far more than the physical pain. Tears welled in her eyes, not from the blow, but from the chasm that had opened between her and her family.

"Leave us," her father bellowed, pointing towards the door. "You are confined to your quarters until you come to your senses. Consider the consequences of your defiance, Isabella. You risk everything with your selfishness."

Isabella fled the room, the weight of her parents' expectations and the loss of their affection crushing her. In the sanctity of her quarters, with the door firmly shut behind her, the tears came freely. She was trapped in a gilded cage, her future sold to the highest bidder.

Yet within her heart, a resolve took root. She would find a way to escape the fate her parents had chosen for her. Times were changing and Isabella de Lacy was her own person, and she would fight for her right to choose her path, come what may.

***

The drawing room of Milburn Manor was filled with the fading light of late afternoon, casting long shadows across the polished floor. Lord Rafe de Lacy stood by the window, his expression stern as he watched the last of the sun disappear behind the rolling hills. He turned away, frustration etched into every line of his face.

"She outright refused," he said, his voice tight with barely contained anger. "She behaved like some petulant child." Lady Eleanor de Lacy, seated gracefully on a high-backed chair, looked up from her embroidery. She had been expecting this, but it did not make hearing it any easier.

"She's spirited, Rafe. And she's still so young." Rafe clenched his fists, his temper simmering.

"Spirited is one thing, Eleanor, but this is sheer defiance and I will not tolerate it. You said yourself that Percival Ashcroft is a perfectly respectable match, and she knows it too." Eleanor set her embroidery aside, her expression troubled.

"Perhaps we've pushed her too quickly. She's barely had time to know him, let alone come to terms with the idea of marriage."

Rafe's eyes blazed. "She's had plenty of time, and she knows her duty. I won't have her ruin this. Percival is the future of our estates, without this match, we stand to lose everything we've worked for." Eleanor sighed, her gaze drifting to the ornate fireplace, where the flames flickered softly. She understood the stakes, her husband's relentless ambition, the family's reputation, and the financial strains they hid from the world.

"What do you suggest?" Eleanor asked quietly, though she already knew the answer. Rafe paced the room, his footsteps echoing in the grand space.

"We need to act quickly, before she has any more time to let these foolish ideas fester. We'll bring the engagement dinner forward."

Eleanor's eyes widened. "So soon? Rafe, she's not ready, and neither are we."

Rafe stopped, his gaze piercing. "She won't have a choice. Once it's announced in front of our friends and the entire county, she'll be forced to comply. There'll be no running back to her room, no more tantrums. She will have to play her part." Eleanor hesitated, torn between loyalty to her husband and her love for her daughter.

"Very well. I'll have the staff make the arrangements. The dinner will go ahead and the engagement will be announced."

Rafe nodded, a satisfied glint in his eye. "Good. And make sure Isabella knows exactly what is expected of her. This family has no room for rebellion." As Eleanor rose to leave, she glanced toward the corridor leading to Isabella's room. She felt a pang of guilt, knowing her daughter's dreams were being crushed beneath the weight of their expectations. But there was no time for sentiment now. Rafe and Eleanor had chosen her path, and the wheels were already in motion. The engagement dinner would be the turning point, whether Isabella was ready for it or not.

***

The following morning there was a soft knock on her door and Florence came in with a tray of food for Isabella. There was a delicious omelette and a small plate of cheese and fruit. Florence placed the tray down and looked at Isabella, her expression one of unwavering loyalty.

"Is there anything else I can get you, my Lady?"

Isabella looked up. "Florence, "she began, her voice barely above a whisper. "I need your help."

Understanding flashed in Florence's eyes, a silent nod affirming her willingness to stand by Isabella, no matter the request.

"What do you need me to do Miss Isabella?" she asked, her tone steady. Isabella handed her a letter, sealed with wax.

"Please, take this to James Wycliffe at the mill in Grindleton. Arrange for us to meet.

I must see him Florence, it's imperative." Florence took the letter, her fingers brushing against Isabella's in a moment of silent solidarity. Isabella explained about her meeting with her parents and their intention for her to marry Sir Percival. Florence had only come across Sir Percival a couple of times but had not liked him and knew in her heart that he was wrong for Isabella.

"I'll see it done, Miss. Trust me." She replied tucking the letter into her apron with a discreetness born of necessity. The risks were clear to both, a maid and her mistress caught in the act of defiance, but their shared resolve made them fearless.

***

In the quiet hours of the morning, with the manor still shrouded in the soft light of dawn, Florence slipped from the servants' quarters, the letter from Isabella clutched in her apron. The morning mist hung low over the gardens, casting a gossamer veil over the world as if protecting Florence on her secret mission. Her heart, though heavy with the responsibility entrusted to her, was determined. The path to the mill, where James worked, was familiar, yet today it felt charged with a new purpose. As she embarked on her journey from Slaidburn she wound her way through the rugged beauty of the fells. With each step, she felt the weight of the morning mist clinging to her cloak enveloping her in a delicate shroud. Navigating the undulating terrain of the fells required careful attention, but Florence welcomed the challenge. The rolling hills unfolded before her like a patchwork quilt, each rise and fall offering a new perspective on the landscape she called home.

The tranquillity of the fells was interrupted only by the occasional bleat of a distant sheep, or the rustle of leaves stirred by the gentle breeze. As she pressed onward, the village of Grindleton gradually came into view, its quaint cottages nestled among the foothills like a cluster of precious gems. Finally, she reached the imposing structure of the mill, its towering silhouette casting a shadow over the landscape. With a sense of purpose, Florence ascended the steps and entered the bustling hub of activity, ready to deliver her message and fulfil her duties with unwavering dedication.

Once inside the mill, Florence found James overseeing the day's work, his presence commanding yet kind. Handing him the letter with discreet urgency, she relayed Isabella's message, her voice low.

"Miss Isabella wishes to meet you by the chapel in the gardens of the manor. Lord and Lady de Lacy are currently away. Please, sir, be discreet for her sake." James's eyes scanned the letter, and upon reading Isabella's words, his resolve hardened. He nodded to Florence, a silent promise of discretion and honour, and offered Florence the use of his carriage to take her back to the Manor.

***

Later that day Isabella made her way to the chapel in the grounds of Milburn Manor. Her heart raced with anticipation and fear, the stakes of this meeting weighing heavily upon her. The chapel, a silent witness to countless whispered prayers and secret meetings, stood as a beacon of hope amid the carefully manicured lawns.

James was already there, waiting in the shadow of the ancient stone building, his figure a contrast to the vibrant blossoms that lined the path. Their eyes met, and in that gaze, a myriad of emotions passed between them, hope, fear, and an unspoken promise.

"Isabella," James began, his voice breaking the silence, "I have longed for this moment, though I wish it were under happier circumstances." Isabella stepped closer, her resolve at seeing James, strengthening.

"James, I cannot, I will not marry Percival. My heart belongs to you, and though the path before us is fraught with peril, I cannot deny it any longer." James took her hands in his, the touch a balm to her frayed nerves.

"Isabella, my love for you transcends any obstacle, any duty imposed upon us by others, we will find a way, together, I swear it. I know a little of Sir Percival and have heard a lot of gossip, things that no lady should know, trust me you will not be marrying that man." He said angrily.

"There's to be an engagement dinner tomorrow night, I don't think I can bear it James," Isabella sobbed, clinging to him.

"Don't worry my love, we will find a way, I promise." James took her in his arms.

In the garden, near the chapel that had stood for centuries, they pledged their love to each other, a vow as enduring as the stones beneath their feet. Their words though whispered in the shadow of the chapel, rang with a truth and passion that could not be contained.

***

Lily with her duties carrying her through the vast grounds of the manor found herself near the chapel on an errand that afternoon. As she moved closer to the chapel, intent on collecting the fresh herbs that Pierre the French chef had ordered her to find, the sight of Isabella and a man, clearly not Sir Percival, caught her eye. Curiosity, mingled with a sense of duty, urged her to retreat, yet her feet carried her closer, hidden by the thick foliage that bordered the garden path. From her vantage point, Lily could see the earnest expressions on their faces, the way they held each other's hands with a desperation that spoke of a love forbidden and fierce. Lily recognised the man as James, the mill owner from Grindleton, a figure of much speculation among the staff after Lord de Lacy had asked him to leave the garden party. Seeing them together, Lily's heart ached with a pang of sympathy. She had always admired Lady Isabella's beauty, kindness, and grace.

As they pledged their vows of love and promises of a future together, Lily stepped back, her heart heavy with the secret she now carried. The young maid knew the weight of what she had seen, the danger it posed not just to Isabella and James but to herself as well. In the hierarchical world of the manor, knowledge was as much a burden as it was a power. Torn between loyalty to her mistress and the implicit command of silence in the face of the manor's rigid social codes, Lily made her way back to the main house, the herbs forgotten in her hands. The questions that now plagued her were of a nature no training had prepared her for. Should she keep this secret, protecting Lady Isabella, at the risk of her position? Or was there someone she could trust, someone who could help navigate the treacherous waters ahead?

***

The greenhouse was a sanctuary, hidden at the edge of the estate where overgrown hedges and twisted ivy formed a natural barrier from the rest of the world. Isabella had often come here alone, seeking solace among the neglected plants, the once grand space now a tangle of broken glass, creeping vines, and wilting flowers. It was a place of solitude and silence-a forgotten corner that seemed to echo her own sense of isolation.

Tonight, however, the greenhouse was alive with new meaning. The moonlight filtered through the cracked panes of glass, casting fractured patterns on the dusty floor. James turned to look at Isabella with an expression of an unspoken longing that mirrored her own. They didn't speak at first. Words felt unnecessary, almost intrusive in the quiet of the night. Isabella moved toward him, her breath catching as his eyes met hers. The air between them was charged, filled with a tension that had been building since their first meeting in the gardens. It was as though every stolen glance, every lingering touch had been leading them to this moment. James reached out, his fingers brushing against her cheek, tracing the line of her jaw as if he were committing every inch of her to memory. Isabella closed her eyes, leaning into his touch, feeling the warmth of his skin against hers. The scent of the earth and faint remnants of flowers hung in the air, mingling with the soft rustle of leaves. It was intoxicating, a heady mix of fear and desire. They moved together as if drawn by an invisible force, an unspoken understanding that this was their only chance, their only refuge from the world that sought to keep them apart. His hands, roughened from work, were gentle as they pulled her closer, and she clung to him, the fabric of her dress tangling with the ivy that crept along the ground.

In the dim light, they found something new and undeniable. It was not just a physical connection but a meeting of souls, bound together in defiance of everything that stood against them. There was no lavish bed, no soft sheets, only the hard cold earth beneath them and the warmth of each other. But it was enough. As they lay entwined, Isabella knew that this moment would change everything. The weight of her family's expectations, the looming shadow of Percival, and the life she was being forced into seemed to fade away, if only for a breath. But the reality was there, lingering just beyond the broken panes of glass. The outside world would intrude soon enough, with its rules and judgements, but here in the greenhouse, they were free, if only for a night.

She looked up at James, her heart aching with a mix of love and fear. His eyes were dark, filled with the same desperate hope that burned within her. But in this fragile place, amidst the ruins of a forgotten garden, they had found each other. And for now, that was enough.

Chapter Eighteen
Isabella
Lancashire 1906

In the bustling heart of Milburn Manor, the kitchen was alive with the sounds and smells of preparation. Cooks and kitchen hands moved with practiced urgency, orchestrating a culinary symphony under the watchful eye of Pierre, who prided himself on perfection. The occasion was significant, an engagement dinner to formally announce the betrothal of Isabella to Percival, a union of great interest not just to the families involved but to the entire staff of the manor.

Lily, the young housemaid, slipped through the kitchen door, her entrance barely noticed amid the chaos. Her hands meant to be clutching the fresh herbs from the garden, were empty, a fact she hoped to conceal but which was quickly noticed by Pierre. With a sharp reprimand, he summoned her to his private quarters, a space rarely entered by the staff.

Once secluded from the prying eyes and ears of the kitchen, Pierre's demeanour shifted from anger to keen interest.

"Now Lily, tell me why you've returned empty-handed. This isn't like you," he prodded, sensing there was more to her forgetfulness than met the eye. Trembling, Lily confessed what she had witnessed in the gardens near the chapel. The secret meeting between Isabella and James, their expressions of love. She spoke of Isabella's refusal to marry Percival, her voice a whisper, fearful of the consequences of her words. Pierre listened, his mind racing with the implications of Lily's discovery. Here was a piece of information potent with potential, a secret that could indeed advance his standing with the de Lacy's if used with cunning. Yet, the revelation also placed him in a position of power over Lily and indeed possibly Mrs Hargreaves the long-standing cook, a leverage he was quick to recognise and exploit.

"Lily, you understand the gravity of what you've stumbled upon." Pierre began, his voice a low coercive hiss. "This knowledge could upset the plans of the manor's most influential guests. It could also serve my, and therefore your, future here should we play our cards right." He paced the room, considering his options before turning back to her.

"You will continue to observe and report back to me. Anything you see or hear regarding Lady Isabella and that mill owner, you tell me first. Do you understand? Your job and your future here depend on it. If not, I will ensure you are sent back to the workhouse." Lily nodded a mix of fear and resignation in her eyes. She was trapped in a web of intrigue, her simple life as a maid forever altered by the secrets she now carried. Pierre satisfied with her acquiescence, sent her back to her duties with a stern reminder of her obligation to him. As Lily returned to the kitchen, her mind was a tumult of thoughts and emotions. She regretted her accidental role in the unfolding drama, yet she also felt a burgeoning sense of responsibility.

Pierre, meanwhile, contemplated his next moves. The information Lily had provided was a valuable currency in the social economy of Milburn Manor. How he chose to spend it would determine his fate and that of those entangled in this scandal. For now, he decided to bide his time, letting the knowledge simmer like a well-crafted sauce ready to be served at the perfect moment for maximum impact.

***

Isabella's chamber, a study in muted elegance, was bathed in the soft glow of the late afternoon sun that filtered through the tall, draped windows. The room, spacious and adorned with the refined décor befitting the room of a lady, held a quiet air of anticipation. A large four-poster bed, its canopy, and bedspread crafted from the finest silk stood as the room's centrepiece, flanked by ornate bedside tables. Across the room, a mahogany dressing table bore an array of silver brushes and mirrors, reflecting the opulence of the era.

As the final preparations for the dinner were underway, Isabella stood before a towering armoire, its doors swung open to reveal a collection of gowns, each a masterpiece of fabric and design. Her choice for the evening was a dress that managed to capture both the essence of her beauty and the depth of her inner turmoil. A gown of deep emerald silk that complemented her eyes, with intricate lace detailing at the bodice and sleeves, tapering to a fitted waist before flowing out into a full skirt. The dress, while stunning, felt like a costume to Isabella, a mask to hide the uncertainties that churned within her. Isabella turned to Florence, a look of resolve upon her face.

"Florence, I cannot bear the thought of spending my life with Percival. He is everything I despise, cold, calculating, and utterly devoid of compassion. My heart belongs to James, and it always will." Florence, who had been laying out Isabella's jewellery on the dressing table, paused her hand still. She met Isabella's gaze in the mirror, her expression one of understanding and quiet determination.

"Miss Isabella, I know the depth of your feelings for Mr James, and I know the risk you take in defying your parents' wishes. But I stand with you, and I will do all in my power to help you and James find happiness." Isabella's eyes welled with tears, not of despair but of gratitude. Florence's loyalty, and her willingness to brave the dangers of their secret, offered a glimmer of hope in the encroaching darkness of her situation.

"Thank you, Florence. Your courage gives me strength. But I fear what the future may hold for us all." Isabella whispered, her voice barely audible over the rustle of her gown as she moved to sit at the dressing table.

As Florence helped Isabella with her final preparations, adjusting the fit of her dress and arranging her hair in an elegant updo adorned with pearls, the bond between them deepened. In the reflection of the mirror, amidst the soft light and shadows of the room, they shared a moment of silent solidarity, a pact forged in defiance of a future neither of them wished to embrace.

Downstairs, the manor buzzed with the anticipation of the evening's announcement, oblivious to the storm brewing in the heart of its heiress. Isabella, adorned in her emerald gown, the very picture of grace and nobility, descended the staircase with Florence's whispered assurances echoing in her heart. Tonight, she would play the part expected of her, but her soul, like the dress she wore, belonged to another, a secret defiance against the fate others had chosen for her.

Chapter Nineteen
Amelia
Lancashire

In the ambient warmth of the local eatery, a favourite spot nestled in the heart of the countryside near Milburn Manor, Amelia, Nikos, and her father shared a table laden with local specials. They had met at The Inn at Whitewell. This was a former 16th-century coaching inn set above the river Hodder overlooking open countryside with the fells in the distance. Amelia thought Nikos might like to experience this traditional Lancashire hotel with its mullioned windows, old stone-flagged floors, and the history of the Inn, which the late Queen Elizabeth had visited in 2006. They had all ordered the famous Whitewell fish pie.

The clink of glasses and the hum of conversation provided a backdrop to their exchanges, a blend of personal revelations and shared plans. Amelia's father, initially wary, had warmed to Nikos, impressed by his sincerity and the obvious depth of his feelings for Amelia.

As they delved into discussions about cultural differences, the challenges of long-distance relationships, the pregnancy, and the anticipation of Amelia's move to Greece the atmosphere around the table was one of tentative acceptance and growing understanding. Nikos with his engaging stories of life in Greece, painted a vivid picture of the world that awaited Amelia, a testament to their commitment to forge a shared life despite the hurdles. The day had unfolded smoothly, the initial apprehension giving way to laughter and shared anecdotes when an unexpected figure appeared at the entrance of the large dining area. Jack stood framed against the doorway, his sudden presence casting a shadow over the gathered group. The ambient noise seemed to dim, drawing the attention of Amelia to the man whose history she had relegated as a closed chapter that she had no intention of revisiting.

Approaching their table with a confidence that bordered on defiance, Jack's arrival was a cold intrusion.

"Amelia, I've heard the news, Slaidburn is a small place as you should know." He looked towards Nikos with a look that mingled disbelief with a hint of scorn. "I must say, you moved on quickly. I'm guessing you picked him up on our honeymoon?" The accusation hung heavy in the air, charged with tension and the spectre of past grievances. Amelia felt Nikos stiffen beside her, his protective instincts flaring at the implied challenge. Amelia met Jack's gaze squarely.

"Jack, you left me and what I do with my life and who I see is up to me now. My decisions are not yours to judge or comment on." But Jack wasn't done. His gaze swept over them again, landing on Nikos with a cold challenge.

"You may think you've won, taking my place so easily. But remember, happiness built on someone else's ruins doesn't last. I'll make sure of that."

Her father who had been observing the exchange with growing disapproval, finally spoke up.

"That's enough Jack. You're out of line and quite frankly after what you did, I can't believe you even have the nerve to come over and speak to Amelia. You need to leave Jack. Now. And if you ever threaten my daughter again, you'll answer to me." His voice firm and commanding left no room for argument. Jack, momentarily taken aback by the united front before him, clenched his jaw, the muscles working in silent frustration. He gave a cold dismissive laugh.

"Well, I wish you all the best, but take care of yourself Amelia as you never know what's around the corner." With a final, lingering look that seemed to encompass both malice and defiance, Jack turned on his heel and exited the eatery. Nikos got up ready to go after him the anger obvious in his face. Amelia's father stopped him.

"He's not worth it Nikos, just leave it." He said. They all sat quite stunned by what had just occurred and talked long into the afternoon. Amelia couldn't understand his attitude as the last time they had spoken Jack had seemed genuinely remorseful. Amelia felt a tumult of feelings as she processed the shift. Surprise initially at the stark change in Jack's attitude, confusion as she wondered what had sparked his anger, and then, a growing unease, considering the implications of his threats. The safety and happiness of her new family suddenly seemed fragile, vulnerable to the whims of a man she no longer recognised. Yet amidst the whirlwind of emotions, Amelia's resolve hardened. The encounter whilst unsettling, underscored the importance of the future she and Nikos were building together. It highlighted the strength of their bond, a contrast to the instability of her past relationship with Jack. She felt a protective surge, not just for her unborn child, but for the life and love she had chosen with Nikos.

***

The journey back to Milburn Manor was cloaked in an uneasy silence, the day's events casting long shadows over Amelia and Nikos. Upon their arrival, Nikos, with a reassuring squeeze to Amelia's hand, excused himself to make a long-distance call to his family in Greece, leaving Amelia to her thoughts and the weight of the confrontation with Jack. It wasn't long before Rafe sought Amelia out. His expression bore a mixture of concern and confusion as he gently informed her of an unexpected visit he'd had earlier in the day.

"Jack was here, Amelia, your former fiancé I believe. He mentioned your plans to relocate to Greece and raised questions about your ongoing commitment to the archiving project." Rafe revealed, his tone carefully neutral yet probing for the truth. The revelation struck Amelia with a mix of surprise and indignation. That Jack would go as far as to involve Rafe and potentially jeopardize her professional standing proved the depth of his resentment. Taking a deep breath, Amelia gathered her resolve, realising this was a moment for not just clarification but for honesty and openness.

"Rafe, there's much you don't know," she began. "Firstly, yes, I am planning to move to Greece with Nikos. But not immediately. There's something else, something deeply personal that has influenced this decision-I'm pregnant." The admission hung in the air, a declaration of her new reality and the future she was carefully weaving. Rafe's initial surprise softened into understanding, his features relaxing into a supportive smile.

"Congratulations, Amelia. That's wonderful news, albeit unexpected." Encouraged by Rafe's reaction, Amelia delved deeper, sharing not just her joy and apprehensions but also the profound connection she's discovered through the archiving project and more importantly the diary of Florence the Maid.

"This diary, Rafe, is more than just a piece of history. It's a story that needs to be told, a wrong that needs to be righted. Isabella's ghost, and her appearances to me, are not just hauntings. She is always dressed in rags, her hands disfigured, her face twisted in pain. I feel that it's a plea for help, for closure."

As she spoke, Amelia laid bare the journey she had undertaken since discovering the diary. She spoke of the love and tragedy encapsulated within its pages. She explained her belief that completing the archiving project and bringing Isabella's story to light was not just a professional obligation but a personal crusade to offer peace to a restless soul. Rafe listened intently, his initial scepticism giving way to intrigue and empathy. By the time Amelia concluded her tale, Rafe was fully invested, not just in the continuation of the project but in supporting Amelia through the challenges ahead.

"Amelia, your dedication to Isabella's story, in the face of your life changes, is admirable. Milburn Manor is fortunate to have someone of your passion and integrity involved in preserving this history." Rafe said, offering not just his understanding but his assurance of support. "We'll navigate these waters together. And as for Jack, consider it handled. Your focus should remain on the future, both Isabella's and your own."

As Amelia left Rafe's office, a weight lifted from her shoulders. As she walked down the corridor toward her room there was a sudden drop in temperature, heralding a presence she had come to recognize with a mix of apprehension and a deep compelling urge to understand. The flickering lights cast erratic shadows, elongated, and twisting as if beckoning her gaze forward.

There, materializing from the dimness at the far end of the corridor stood Isabella. Dressed in the tattered remnants of what once might have been a dress, she presented a poignant image of despair and enduring sorrow. Her hands and feet, visible beneath the frayed edges of her garment, bore the marks of her affliction, disfigured, a stark reminder of the isolation and pain she had endured in life. Amelia's breath caught at the sight, a wave of empathy flooding her for the tormented soul before her. Why was she dressed that way, and why was she so hideously disfigured? There was nothing in the diary so far that could explain any of this. Isabella's eyes, brimming with an ageless sorrow, met hers, conveying volumes of unspoken misery.

"Isabella," Amelia whispered, her voice suddenly loud in the chilling silence. "I'm reading Florence's diary; I will bring your truth to light."

For a fleeting moment, Isabella's form seemed to waver, a shudder passing through her as if Amelia's words had reached across the boundaries of time and death. As quickly as she appeared, she dissolved into the ether,

her presence receding into the fabric of the manor, leaving behind muffled sobs and a cold that slowly receded returning the corridor to its mundane reality.

Chapter Twenty

**Isabella
Lancashire 1906**

The grand dining hall of Milburn Manor was alight with the glow of candles, casting soft shadows over the opulent room adorned for the evening's dinner. It was an event marked by the expected grace and formality of the manor's traditions, yet beneath the surface, undercurrents of tension ebbed and flowed with the quiet clink of silverware and the murmur of polite conversation. The dinner commenced with a delicate amuse-bouche of smoked salmon and caviar, a hint of the extravagance to follow. This was succeeded by a rich creamy lobster bisque, its depth of flavour showing Pierre's skill and attention to detail. The main course, one of Mrs Hargreaves's specialties, was a roasted pheasant. Each course was paired meticulously with wines selected from the manor's extensive cellar, a hidden gem, nestled deep within the bowels of the grand estate. The cellar was accessible via a narrow spiral stone staircase descending from the main floor giving it an air of mystery and timelessness. The cool damp atmosphere spoke of centuries past, and the walls were constructed from ancient, rough-hewn stone indicative of the cellar's age and the consistency of its temperature and humidity. The air carried a faint, earthy scent mixed with the rich heady aroma of aged wine.

The room was vast, with a high vaulted ceiling supported by thick wooden beams that had darkened over time. The dim lighting was provided by wrought iron sconces holding flickering candles and old-fashioned lanterns, casting shadows across the stone floor and walls. Row upon row of wooden racks lined the walls and filled the central space, each carefully crafted to hold a vast collection of wine bottles. The racks were made from sturdy oak, their surfaces polished smooth by years of careful handling. Some sections were dedicated to specific vintages, meticulously labelled with handwritten tags that detailed the year, origin, and type of wine. The collection ranged from robust reds and crisp whites to vintage champagnes and delicate dessert wines.

In one corner of the cellar, a large intricately carved oak table served as a tasting area, and nearby a small antique wooden cabinet held an assortment of crystal decanters, wine glasses, and other tasting accessories. Hidden behind a sliding panel in the farthest corner of the cellar was a smaller, more secure room. This secret vault held the most valuable and rarest bottles in the collection. Throughout the cellar, the flickering candlelight revealed glimpses of history: cobwebs in the corner, old wine stains on the stone floor, and the occasional scurrying of a mouse. It was a part of the Manor's legacy, a sanctuary of appreciation of fine wine.

At the table, Isabella sat beside Percival, her betrothed, a man who wore his social standing like armour, impenetrable and polished. To the outside world, Percival presented as the epitome of gentility, a man of wealth, influence, and impeccable manners. However, this façade belied the truth of his character, a reality that Isabella knew all too well. His demeanour was as cold and distant as the frosty depths of winter. With sharp calculating eyes that missed nothing and a voice like ice, he commanded attention wherever he went. Yet behind his polished exterior lay a darkness, a secret that whispered through the halls of Milburn Manor like a chilling breeze. Isabella had heard the whispers, the subtle murmurs that danced on the edges of polite conversation. Gossip, they called it, but Isabella knew better. She had seen the way Percival's gaze lingered a little too long on the handsome footmen, the way his smile never quite reached his eyes when he was in her company. For Isabella, it was more than just idle speculation, it was a glimpse into the depth of Percival's soul. A man driven by duty and obligation yet shackled by the weight of expectation and societal norms, just as she was. Unfortunately, this was the man to whom she was to be married, unless she could find a way to be with James, but Isabella couldn't shake the feeling that behind his icy exterior, Percival hid a darkness that threatened to consume them all.

Throughout the dinner, Percival engaged with guests and family alike, his laughter resonant and his comments insightful, drawing admiration from those around him. Isabella played her part, her responses measured, her smiles carefully curated. Yet, her eyes betrayed a distant troubled light, glimpses of a spirit stifled by the impending reality of a life bound to a man she could neither love nor respect.

As the evening wore on, the opportunity arose for Isabella to escape the oppressive atmosphere of the dining hall under the pretence of needing fresh air. Much to Isabella's annoyance, Percival, ever the attentive fiancé in the eyes of their company, offered to accompany her, a gesture that elicited approving nods from the gathered guests.

The cool night air was a welcome relief as they stepped out into the gardens, the manicured beauty of the landscape a stark contrast to the turmoil brewing within Isabella. However, the solitude also peeled away Percival's mask of affability, revealing the cold, calculating demeanour he reserved for private.

"You should smile more, Isabella. It wouldn't do for rumours of your discontent to reach the ears of our esteemed guests," Percival remarked, his voice laced with a thinly veiled warning. His words, meant to chastise, hung heavy between them, a stark reminder of the power he wielded. Isabella, taken aback by his sudden shift in tone, found herself at a loss.

"Percival, I ..." she began, her voice faltering under the weight of his gaze.

"Isabella, you must understand, that our union is one of convenience and alliance. It's not affection I require from you, but obedience and the preservation of appearances," he interrupted, his words cutting through the chill of the night. The harshness of his statement, devoid of any pretence of kindness, crystallized Isabella's resolve. She understood then, with a clarity that pierced the fog of her uncertainty, that her future with Percival would be one of silent endurance, her every action scrutinized, her every feeling disregarded. The rest of their walk was marked by silence. Upon their return to the dining room, Percival resumed his role, the perfect gentleman, while Isabella was left to mask her growing despair. Finally, the guests left, and Isabella could escape to her room, to await her longed-for meeting with James that night.

***

Meanwhile, in the bustling environment of the kitchen, the atmosphere was a stark contrast to the refined air of the dining hall. Pierre overseeing the finishing touches to the evening's culinary delights, moved with a commander's authority, his eyes missing nothing. It was during these moments of orchestrated chaos that Florence caught a peculiar exchange between Pierre and Lily the young maid of all work. Florence who had come to fetch a tray of petits fours for the drawing room, noticed Pierre drawing Lily aside, speaking to her in hushed tones that seemed at odds with the celebratory nature of the evening. Lily's face, usually open and cheerful, was etched with concern as she nodded in response to Pierre's words, casting furtive glances toward the rest of the kitchen as if afraid of being overheard. The sight troubled Florence, her intuition whispering that the conversation was out of place, its secrecy incongruent with the simple duties of a maid. Her respect for Pierre earned through his culinary prowess, was tinged with a new caution. What business could he possibly have with Lily that warranted such privacy and apparent urgency?

Tucking away her observations, Florence returned to her duties. Yet the interaction between Pierre and Lily lingered in her mind. As the evening wore on, the seeds of doubt and curiosity sown in Florence's mind took root, her loyalty to Isabella compelling her to stay alert, to watch and listen more closely.

***

Under the veil of night, within the gardens of the chapel, Isabella and James found sanctuary in each other's presence. Concealed by the shadow of ancient oaks, their meeting was a fragment of stolen time, each moment precious and fraught with the danger of discovery. Isabella, her heart a tumult of love and defiance, clung to James with a desperation that belied her usual composure.

"Percival is not my choice," she whispered. "My father may have pledged my hand, but my soul remains my own, and it belongs to you, James." James with a quiet intensity, vowed,

"Then we shall write our destiny. I will not let their decision dictate our lives. I may not be in your father's eyes of the correct social standing, but I have money Isabella, and I can and will take care of you." His words, spoken with the conviction of a man who had known struggle, offered Isabella a sliver of hope in the encroaching darkness of her situation.

Unbeknownst to the lovers, their secret tryst was once again observed. Lily watched from the shadows, her heart heavy with guilt. Fear of losing her place at Milburn Manor, Lily had reluctantly become Pierre's eyes and ears. Each whispered word, each tender embrace observed by Lily, was a dagger to her conscience. Yet the threat of Pierre's wrath kept her silent. The lovers, oblivious to the watchful eyes, continued to lay their plans, their words a fragile tapestry of hopes and dreams. They spoke of a future free from the constraints of duty and expectation, a vision of a life together that shimmered with the possibility of happiness. As the night waned and the time came for parting Isabella and James shared a final lingering embrace. They separated, each step away from their secluded haven a step back into the roles imposed upon them by birth and circumstance.

Lily, her task complete, retreated from her hidden vantage point, the weight of her betrayal settling coldly around her. As she made her way back to the manor's kitchen, the information she carried felt like a chain binding her to a fate she neither desired nor could escape. Inside the manor, Pierre awaited her report, his ambition a dark flame that consumed all in its path. Lily's account of the lovers' meeting was received with a satisfaction that chilled her to the bone. Pierre, now armed with knowledge powerful enough to shatter lives, contemplated his next move, a predator poised to strike.

.

Chapter Twenty-One
Amelia
Lancashire

Under the early morning sky, a palette of soft blues and pinks, Amelia and Nikos shared a quiet breakfast, their last together before his departure to Greece. The air was thick with unspoken emotions, a blend of anticipation for the future and the immediate pain of separation.

Before Nikos's departure, Amelia had arranged to meet Chloe so that she could get to know Nikos. They had arranged to meet at Tom's Table in Clitheroe. This was a lovely French-inspired bistro located in Lee Carter House, in a secluded courtyard. The head chef, hailed from a local farming family and the atmosphere was tranquil and inviting. As they hugged and sat down, Chloe couldn't help smiling. Nikos was lovely and she was so pleased for her friend. Amelia and Chloe ordered the Twice Baked Souffle Suisse and Nikos opted for the Steak Frites. They all chatted amiably, their conversation meandering from plans about moving to Greece, and their shared dreams for their baby to reminiscences of past adventures, and Chloe was fascinated by Nikos's accounts of the taverna and life in a Greek village. When their food arrived, they all agreed it was delicious. Chloe couldn't get over the souffle, it was the lightest most delicious souffle she had ever tasted, and Nikos said the steak was outstanding.

After the meal at the restaurant, Chloe suggested a walk to let the food settle. Amelia had an appointment with her solicitors, Lewis Mitchell, whose offices were in an old converted dairy near the railway station in Clitheroe, leaving Chloe and Nikos with some time to explore Clitheroe. They strolled through the quaint streets taking in the historic charm of the town. They meandered through the local market and Nikos was delighted by the array of fresh fruit and vegetables and the local fare of cakes, pies, and pastries.

"So, how are you feeling about all this?" Chloe asked, glancing at Nikos as they walked. Nikos looked thoughtful for a moment before answering.

"It's a lot to take in. Finding out Amelia is pregnant, and now being here with her, seeing where she comes from, meeting you and her father…it's overwhelming."

Chloe nodded, understanding. "I can imagine. But you care about her a lot, don't you?"

"Yes," Nikos said firmly. "I care about her deeply. I want to be there for her and the baby. It wasn't planned but I'm ready for it. I can't wait for her to come to Greece, I think she'll love it." They continued walking, passing by charming shops and cafes. The streets of Clitheroe were bustling with activity, but there was a calmness to the town that Nikos found soothing.

"Amelia has been through a lot," Chloe said softly. "With Jack and everything. She deserves happiness." Nikos looked at Chloe, appreciating her insight.

"I know. I want to give her that happiness. I want to be the person she can rely on. I will be there for her, I promise."

Chloe smiled warmly. "I think you're already doing that Nikos. Just be patient and supportive, she needs that right now."

As they approached Clitheroe Castle, Nikos took in the sight of the ruined early medieval castle which stood proudly on a limestone mount. Chloe informed him that the keep was the second smallest surviving stone-built keep in England and that the views from the top were spectacular. They began the ascent, the path winding through lush greenery.

"Tell me more about Amelia," Nikos said, eager to learn more about the woman he had come to care for so deeply.

Chloe thought for a moment before speaking. "Amelia is one of the strongest people I know. She's been through so much, but she never gives up. She has this incredible resilience. And she's kind, too. She always puts others before herself." Nikos listened intently, feeling a deep sense of admiration for Amelia.

"I see that in her. She has this quiet strength." Nikos smiled and his eyes reflected the depth of emotion that he felt for Amelia. They reached the top of the hill, standing before the ancient walls of Clitheroe Castle. The view from the top was breathtaking, with the town spread out below them and the rolling hills of Lancashire in the distance.

"She loves this place," Chloe said, gazing out at the view. "It's like a part of her."

Nikos nodded, understanding. "I can see why. It's beautiful. Peaceful."

Chloe turned to face him. "Nikos, I think you're going to be a wonderful father.

Just keep being there for her, and everything will fall into place."

Nikos smiled, feeling a sense of hope and determination. "Thank you Chloe. That means a lot." They stood in silence for a moment, taking in the beauty of the landscape. As they began their descent, Nikos could see why Amelia loved Chloe so much and they chatted and laughed as they made their way through the streets of Clitheroe to meet Amelia.

***

As the day ended and Nikos's car disappeared down the long driveway of Milburn Manor, a profound solitude enveloped Amelia. The manor with its sprawling lawns and ancient stones felt more like a sentinel to the past than ever before. As night enveloped Milburn Manor, Amelia found herself adrift in a dream more vivid and sensory than ever she had experienced before. The soft rustling of the ancient trees outside her window seemed to merge with her dreams, pulling her deeper into a world that felt both familiar and strange. She found herself walking through a narrow, cobblestone street in a village she didn't recognise. The buildings were old, their whitewashed walls gleaming under the sun. Vines of bougainvillea spilled over the edges of rooftops, their vibrant pink flowers adding a splash of colour to the scene. The air was warm and fragrant, filled with the scent of the blooming flowers and the distant sound of the sea. Amelia's steps were light, almost as if she were floating. She felt an inexplicable pull, guiding her through the winding streets. She turned a corner and found herself in a small sun-drenched courtyard. There, sitting on a stone bench, was a woman dressed in a simple, flowing dress. Her long auburn hair cascaded over her shoulders, and her eyes held a depth of emotion that made Amelia's heart ache.

"Isabella?" Amelia whispered, recognizing her instantly. The woman looked up, her eyes meeting Amelia's. There was a moment of silent understanding between them, a connection that transcended time and space. Isabella stood and walked towards her, her movements graceful. As she approached, Amelia noticed a look of deep sadness in her eyes, mixed with a flicker of hope. Isabella reached out and took Amelia's hand, her touch cool and comforting. She opened her mouth as if to speak, but no words came out.

Instead, Amelia heard a faint whisper in the breeze, a name carried on the wind.

"Dimitri."

Amelia's heart skipped a beat. The name echoed in her mind, filling her with a sense of urgency and longing. She wanted to ask who Dimitri was, but the words caught in her throat. Isabella gave her a gentle smile, her eyes full of unspoken words. She squeezed Amelia's hand, then slowly began to fade, like mist in the morning sun.

"No wait!" Amelia called out, but it was too late. Isabella was gone, leaving Amelia standing alone in the courtyard. The warmth of the sun and the beauty of the flowers suddenly felt distant and surreal. Amelia woke with a start, her heart racing and her mind buzzing with questions. The dream had felt so real, so vivid. She could still feel the cool touch of Isabella's hand and hear the whisper of the name, Dimitri. She sat up in bed, the moonlight casting a soft glow through the window, illuminating her thoughts.

Who was Dimitri? And why had Isabella called out his name? Amelia knew she had to find answers, but she also felt a deep sense of sadness for Isabella, a woman whose story seemed to be intertwined with her own in ways she couldn't yet understand. As she lay back down, trying to piece together the fragments of her dream, Amelia felt the now familiar cooling of the room and as she looked up, there, at the end of her bed stood Isabella.

The ghost's appearance was less ethereal than before, her presence so palpable that Amelia could almost believe she was not alone. Isabella's eyes, filled with an ancient sorrow, locked onto Amelia's, and she whispered, "Dimitri. Dimitri." before fading away, leaving nothing but the echo of her voice and a chilling sense of urgency in her wake.

Amelia sat up, clutching the sheets to steady her trembling hands. The dream, Isabella's visitation, and that name, Dimitri, wove together into a tapestry of mystery that Amelia knew she could not ignore. The night air felt colder now, the shadows in her room deeper. Amelia knew she was standing on the precipice of discovery, one that could lead her further into the heart of Isabella's tragedy and closer to unravelling the secrets that bound her spirit to Milburn Manor. With the name Dimitri as her only clue, Amelia steeled herself for the journey ahead, into the unknown and the whispers of the past that refused to be silenced. Knowing she wouldn't go back to sleep, she reached for Florence's diary……

Chapter Twenty-Two
Isabella
Lancashire 1906

James stood at the threshold of his mill. The building, a sturdy structure of stone and timber, bore the marks of hard labour and the passage of time. Its wheels churned steadily, powered by the relentless flow of the river that coursed beside it, a testament to the enduring spirit of industry. As he stepped inside, the clamour of the mill greeted him, a cacophony of gears grinding, looms clacking, and the murmured conversations of the workers. The air was thick with dust and the heat intense. James's gaze swept over the workers, each absorbed in their task. Their faces, etched with the lines of fatigue and pallor of too many hours spent indoors, told stories of hardship and resilience. Men and women, some no older than mere children, toiled side by side, their hands moving with the practiced efficiency born of necessity. Despite the adversity they faced, there was a sense of camaraderie among them, a shared understanding that in the struggle for survival, they were united.

Yet, as he watched them, James's heart was heavy. He knew all too well the toll the mill took on its workers, the long hours, the dangerous conditions, and the meagre pay that barely kept poverty at bay. James had always striven to be a fair and compassionate master, but the limitations of his circumstances often hampered his efforts to improve theirs. Amidst the din and dust of the mill, James's thoughts invariably drifted to Isabella. Her image, radiant and gentle, was a stark contrast to the grim reality of his surroundings. He thought of their stolen moments together, of her laughter echoing in the quiet of the garden, of her hand in his. His thoughts drifted to the evenings when they had been carried away and consummated their love for each other in the grounds of the chapel. James knew that he now had to make a definite plan to elope with Isabella. The plan to flee to Ireland, to escape the constraints of their current lives and build a new one, was a beacon of hope in the dreariness of his days. Ireland, where his family lived, represented more than just a refuge; it was the promise of freedom, of a life lived on their own terms, away from scrutiny and expectations of society.

Yet, the thought of leaving the mill, uprooting himself from the life he had built, filled him with a sense of trepidation. It wasn't the loss of the mill that concerned him but the fate of the workers who depended on it. His departure would leave them vulnerable, at the mercy of whoever took his place. Could he, in good conscience, pursue his own happiness at the cost of theirs?

But then, he thought of Isabella, the love they shared, the life they could have together, and he knew he would brave any uncertainty, any sacrifice for the chance to be with her. In her eyes, he saw not just the promise of love but the possibility of a future where they could make a difference, not just for themselves but for others as well. He hoped the letter he had passed on to Florence would ease Isabella's mind and he couldn't wait to see her again. As the day wore on, and the mill continued its relentless churn, James made a silent vow. He would find a way to ensure the wellbeing of his workers, to leave the mill in hands as caring as his own. And then, he and Isabella would embark on their journey to Ireland, to a new beginning.

***

Florence moved with quiet urgency through the ornate corridors of Milburn Manor, the letter from James concealed within the folds of her apron. Her mission was one of secrecy and significance; the contents of the letter held the potential to alter the course of Isabella's life, to offer a glimmer of hope amidst the oppressive expectations that surrounded her.

Isabella, secluded in her room under the pretence of rest, awaited Florence's arrival with a mixture of anticipation and anxiety. The weight of her betrothal to Percival, a union devoid of affection and warmth, lay heavily upon her, a constant reminder of the future that had been chosen for her, not by her.

When Florence knocked and entered, Isabella's heart quickened. The trust between the maid and her mistress was a rare bond, forged in the shared understanding of Isabella's plight and her clandestine love for James.

"Miss Isabella," Florence whispered, her eyes scanning the room for any sign of intrusion. Assured of their privacy, she presented the letter. "From Mr Wycliffe," she said looking intently at Isabella. Isabella's hand trembled as she took the letter, her fingers brushing against Florence's in a silent expression of gratitude. With a nod, Florence discreetly exited, leaving Isabella to the solitude and anticipation of James's words.

James spoke of his undying love, of his unacceptance of the life that was being forced upon her, and of his daring plan for them to be together. He asked her to meet him by the old oak tree that night. Isabella's heart soared as she read and re-read the letter.

As the day waned and the appointed hour drew near, Isabella prepared herself with care. This decision to meet James was not made lightly. It was a choice born of love, a love that refused to be constrained by the dictates of society and family. Isabella made her way to the old oak tree with a mixture of fear and hope.

Under the canopy of whispering leaves and starlit skies, James revealed to Isabella his audacious plan. James took her hands in his, the connection a tangible affirmation of their bond.

"I've thought long and hard about this, about us, and there's a way, a way for us to be together, free from the constraints that seek to bind you here." He spoke of Ireland, his homeland, a place of rugged beauty and wild hearts, where the green of the earth seemed to touch the sky.

"It's there in Ireland, where I propose we start anew. My family has land, not grand like Milburn Manor, but rich in peace and freedom. There, we can live openly, as a married couple, away from the prying eyes and harsh judgments that ensnare us here." Isabella caught between the life she had always known, and the promise of a future filled with love and autonomy, felt a surge of daring alight within her. James's words painted a picture of a life vastly different from the one laid out for her, a life not of opulence, but of genuine contentment and togetherness.

"Ireland, she whispered, the name itself a beacon of hope. "But James, the journey, the scandal it would cause, are we truly ready to face all that?"

James's resolve shone in his eyes, unwavering and fierce. "Isabella, for us, for the love we share, I am ready to face anything. And I know deep in your heart, you are too. Together we are strong enough to forge this new path." The notion of fleeing to Ireland, of leaving behind everything was a daunting prospect. Yet in the face of a future that threatened to tear them apart, the choice became clear. Their plan, whispered between heartbeats and sealed with a kiss under the moon's watchful gaze was a declaration of war against the societal chains that sought to bind them.

As they parted that night, with the echo of their vows lingering in the air, Isabella and James were unaware of the shadow of Lily, hidden in the trees, who had heard everything of their plans.

Chapter Twenty-Three
Nikos
Greece

Nikos's return to Greece carried the weight of countless emotions and responsibilities, the foremost being the reunion with his young son, Alexandros. He was going to Athens to meet with his parents and son before returning to Vrouchas.

His parents' home in Athens was a familiar haven and the reunion with Selena and Stavros, his parents was warm, though shadowed by the apprehension of the news he carried. As he shared the story of Amelia and their unborn child, he watched his parents grapple with the news, their traditional views clashing with the undeniable love and commitment in Nikos's narrative. Their eventual acceptance spoke volumes of their love for him, a reluctant blessing that Nikos deeply cherished.

The moment Nikos had anticipated with a mixture of joy and anxiety finally arrived when he was reunited with Alexandros. The little boy, with his curious eyes and cautious demeanour was initially hesitant in the presence of his father, who was more like a stranger to him. This distance was a challenge Nikos was determined to overcome, his love a bridge he vowed to rebuild, no matter the effort it required. His parents, although they understood that the time had come for Alexandros to return with his father, were visibly upset and Alexandros clung to them, frightened and not really understanding what was happening. They promised Nikos they would visit very soon but would leave it a while so that Alexandros could settle in with Nikos. They were flying back to Heraklion where Nikos had left his car and driving the rest of the way to the village.

The journey to Vrouchas was slow and winding, the road climbing steadily upwards through olive groves and vineyards. Alexandros, sat in the back of the car wide-eyed and curious, his fingers gripping the seat tightly as he took in the new sights and sounds. Nikos smiled at his son in the car mirror, feeling a swell of pride and love that melted his heart. He pointed out landmarks along the way, telling Alexandros stories of his childhood adventures.

"Look, Alexandros," he said, gesturing towards an ancient, gnarled olive tree. "That tree is older than our village. My friends and I used to climb it. One day when you are a bit bigger, you'll be able to climb it too." Alexandros made no response, but his big brown eyes followed his father's finger. As they reached the outskirts of Vrouchas, the village came into view, a cluster of whitewashed houses with red-tiled roofs, surrounded by green fields and rugged hills. The sound of cicadas filled the air, a familiar symphony that Nikos had missed during his time in the city. They were greeted warmly by the villagers, who gathered around to meet Alexandros and to welcome Nikos home. Old friends and neighbours offered hugs and congratulations, their eyes filled with warmth and affection. One of the villagers, an elderly woman named Despina, stepped forward with a broad smile.

"Nikos, it's good to see you back. And this little one must be Alexandros. He's a handsome boy, just like his father."

Nikos blushed slightly, thanking her. "Yes, this is Alexandros. We're happy to be home." Despina nodded, her eyes twinkling.

"Come, I've made some fresh bread and cheese. You both must be hungry after your journey." Nikos followed her to a nearby house, grateful for the hospitality. Inside, the smell of baking bread and herbs enveloped them, making Nikos's stomach growl in anticipation. Despina set a table with bread, cheese, olives, and honey and Nikos settled Alexandros in a chair at the table.

As they ate, Despina told stories of the village and its people, filling Nikos in on all he had missed. Alexandros listened intently, his eyes darting around the room, taking in every detail. Nikos felt a deep sense of contentment. This was the life he wanted for his family: a life filled with love, community, and the rich heritage of their ancestors.

***

Vrouchas was a stark contrast to the city's hustle and bustle and the home Alexandros was used to. The village's pace of life was dictated by nature and tradition. For many days and nights, Alexandros was barely eating or sleeping, and Nikos was beginning to think that he had been wrong and that maybe he should have left his son with his parents. He still had to run the taverna and even though Despina was coming in to help with Alexandros, it was not working out quite as he had hoped.

The little boy, only three years old, seemed lost in the vast new world around him. His quietness was not just the silence of unfamiliarity but bore the weight of a child's unease, his teary eyes reflecting the enormity of the changes enveloping him. His initial days in Vrouchas were marked by a timidity that clung to him like a shadow. He was a quiet observer in a world that moved with an unfamiliar cadence, his interactions tentative, his laughter rare. Nikos watched, aching to bridge the gap that time and absence had carved between them, to reassure Alexandros that this place was a place of safety and love.

It was Nina, the Cretan hound Nikos had adopted who became the unexpected breakthrough. Nina seemed to sense the boy's need for companionship, her presence a gentle assertion that he was not alone in this new world. At first, Alexandros was wary of Nina, his initial encounters filled with hesitation. But Nina, with patience and understanding persisted. She would sit by his side, her head resting gently against his leg, or follow him, her tail wagging in silent camaraderie. Slowly the barriers Alexandros had built around himself began to crumble. The sight of Nina waiting for him each morning became a source of comfort, her eager greeting a highlight of his day. The sound of her bark, once startling, now elicited giggles from him. Their friendship blossomed in the sun-dappled afternoons. She became his guardian, his playmate with a bond that spoke volumes, a silent understanding that transcended species.

The quiet teary boy who had arrived in Vrouchas began to show signs of emerging from his shell, his moments of laughter and play more frequent. Nikos watched, his heart swelling with gratitude, as his son formed an inseparable bond with the dog. In Nina's steadfast presence, Alexandros found more than just a friend.

***

Alexandros' laughter echoed through the courtyard as he chased after Nina. The sun shone brightly, casting a warm glow over the landscape of their home. Nikos watched from a distance, a smile playing on his lips as he observed the pure joy radiating from his son. Nina was lively and affectionate and an unspoken bond had formed between the two. Wherever Alexandros went, Nina followed her protective instincts always on high alert.

"Papa, look!" Alexandros called out, waving a stick in the air triumphantly. "Nina found a stick!"

Nikos chuckled and walked over to his son. "Good job Alexandros. Nina is very clever, isn't she?"

Alexandros nodded enthusiastically, his eyes sparkling with delight. He tossed the stick a short distance away, and Nina bounded after it, her tail wagging furiously. She retrieved the stick and brought it back to Alexandros, dropping it at his feet. The little boy clapped his hands and hugged Nina around her neck.

"Good girl Nina! You're the best" Nina licked Alexandros's face, making him giggle even more. As the day went on, Nikos couldn't help but marvel at the bond between his son and the dog. Alexandros talked to Nina as if she were his closest confidante, sharing his little secrets and dreams with her. He would tell her about the adventures he wanted to go on, the stories he'd heard and his hopes of growing up to be just like his papa.

One evening, as the sun began to set, Nikos found Alexandros and Nina sitting under the olive tree in the garden. Alexandros was leaning against Nina, his small hand gently stroking her fur. Nikos approached quietly, not wanting to disturb the peaceful scene.

"What are you and Nina talking about?" Nikos asked softly.

"I was telling Nina about Mama."

Nikos' heart ached at the mention of his late wife. "What did you tell her?"

"I told her that Mama is watching over us from heaven," Alexandros said with a

solemn nod. "And that she would be happy we have Nina to take care of us, and the new lady that is coming soon."
Nikos felt a lump in his throat as he listened to his son's words. He reached out and pulled Alexandros into a gentle hug.

"Your mama would be incredibly happy Alexandros. She loved you very much and she would be proud of the brave and kind boy you're becoming." Alexandros hugged his father tightly, and Nina sensing the emotional moment, rested her head on Nikos' knee, offering silent comfort.

"Can you remember the new lady's name, Alexandros?" Nikos asked him.

"Yes, Mia-Mia" he said proudly. Nikos chuckled and hugged him tighter.

"Mia-Mia, it is."

As night fell and the stars began to twinkle in the sky, Nikos carried Alexandros inside, with Nina trotting closely behind. He tucked his son into bed, Nina curling up at the foot of the bed as she did every night. Alexandros reached out to pet her one last time, before drifting off to sleep. He had finally found a sense of belonging and the three of them, Nikos, Alexandros, and Nina began to spend many days together exploring the village and enjoying the simple life of the taverna, and each other.

Nikos knew that his decision to bring his son here was the first step towards building the future he envisioned, one that included Amelia and their child.

Chapter Twenty-Four

Florence
Milburn Manor
1906

In the dim light of her modest room at Milburn Manor, Florence sat with her diary open before her, the blank page a silent invitation to confide the thoughts and observations that weighed heavily on her mind. Her hand hovered over the page as she contemplated where to begin, the quiet of the room punctuated only by the soft ticking of a small clock on the mantle.

Florence had been born and raised in a small village where her parents although loving, were bound by the relentless pursuit of survival, their lives a struggle against the unforgiving embrace of poverty. It was in this village that Florence had learned the value of arduous work and the bitter taste of want. Her parents, determined to see her rise above the confines of their circumstances, instilled in Florence a love of learning. She would pore over books borrowed or gifted, each page a portal to a world beyond her own. Her quest for knowledge was not without its challenges for in a time when education was a privilege reserved for the few, her thirst for learning was often met with disdain.

Her move to Milburn Manor was not just a means to provide for herself and her family it was an escape from the predetermined path of poverty and obscurity that seemed her only inheritance. As she began to write, Florence's thought turned to Lady Isabella as always. Isabella possessed a spirit too wild for the confines of society's expectations and Florence could see that Isabella was experiencing the struggle of every woman who dares to dream of more than the life fate has allotted her.

Recently Florence had noticed subtle changes in Isabella. Moments of unexplained illness, a certain restlessness, and an air of secrecy that clung to her like a shadow. She had become closer to Isabella through the sharing of the secret meetings with James and Florence's part in enabling this to happen. As her maid, Florence was privy to the most intimate aspects of Isabella's life, managing her personal effects, her clothing, and even her laundry. It was in these mundane tasks that Florence found the first clues of Isabella's condition, the telltale signs that hinted at a secret too perilous to speak aloud.

Her heart was heavy with concern. She now feared that Isabella carried more than just the burden of an unwanted betrothal. If her suspicions were correct and Isabella was with child, the consequences could be devastating. She couldn't help but fear that such a revelation would not only ruin her reputation but could well endanger her life. The thought of Isabella facing such a dire predicament alone filled Florence with a profound sense of protectiveness and resolve. I must be vigilant she thought for Isabella's sake and the sake of the life she may be carrying. Florence knew she would stand by Lady Isabella and offer her support and if necessary, shield her from the storm that loomed on the horizon. Florence felt the weight of the secret they now shared; a bond of silence that drew them closer even as it threatened to upend the world they knew.

***

Downstairs, Pierre, the master chef of Milburn Manor, commanded the kitchen with the authority and precision of a general leading his troops into battle. Born in the south of France to a family of modest means, Pierre's journey to the prestigious kitchens of the English nobility was marked by ambition, determination, and an unwavering belief in his culinary talents. As a young boy, Pierre was enchanted by the flavours and aromas of his mother's cooking, spending countless hours by her side, learning the secrets of traditional French cuisine. However, it was the discovery of a tattered cookbook in his grandmother's attic, a collection of recipes from the finest Parisian chefs that ignited Pierre's dream of becoming a chef renowned for his culinary artistry. Determined to escape the constraints of his provincial life, Pierre left home at the age of sixteen, armed with little more than his passion for cooking and a fierce desire to succeed. He travelled across France, working in the kitchens of bistros and inns, each position a stepping stone toward his goal.

Pierre's talent and hard work did not go unnoticed; he quickly gained a reputation for his innovative dishes and his ability to transform the simplest ingredients into culinary masterpieces. His ambition eventually led him to Paris, where he apprenticed under some of the city's most celebrated chefs. It was here in the bustling heart of French cuisine that Pierre honed his skills, developing a style that blended traditional techniques with his own creative flair.

The call from Milburn Manor came at a time when Pierre was poised to make his mark on the Parisian culinary scene. The offer to become the head chef at one of England's most prestigious estates was both an honour and a challenge, an opportunity to bring his culinary vision to a new audience and to secure a position of influence and respect within the aristocratic world.

At Milburn Manor, Pierre quickly established himself as an indispensable part of the household. His menus were a highlight of the social season, drawing guests from near and far eager to experience his culinary creations. Pierre's kitchen was a place of relentless activity, where every dish was prepared with precision and artistry. He demanded excellence from his staff, his sharp eye missing nothing, his standards were uncompromising.

Despite his success, Pierre's ambitions extended beyond the accolades for his cooking. He understood the power of knowledge within the walls of Milburn Manor, and he was adept at navigating the complex web of relationships and secrets that characterised life in the estate. Pierre's keen observation skills and his strategic mind made him an expert in manipulation, using information to secure his position and to influence the household dynamics to his advantage.

It was during one of the manor's lavish dinners, an affair orchestrated to highlight Pierre's culinary brilliance that he first crossed paths with Percival, Lady Isabella's wealthy and influential betrothed. Percival, much like Pierre, understood the currency of knowledge and the subtle art of manipulation. Recognising a kindred spirit in the master chef, Percival saw an opportunity to extend his influence within the manor, particularly in matters concerning his betrothal to Isabella. Although his impending marriage to Isabella was more financial than romantic, he harboured doubts about her affection or rather the glaring absence of it. Whilst his romantic inclinations lay elsewhere, he wanted a wife who was obedient and to the aristocratic society to which he belonged was happy to marry him and outwardly adore him. He had the distinct feeling that Isabella's heart belonged elsewhere, though he had yet to pinpoint where or to whom.

Percival approached Pierre with the veneer of camaraderie, masking his intentions with a flattering commendation of the dinner.

"Your reputation does you little justice, Pierre. The meal was exquisite, a testament to your talent." Percival began, his words carefully chosen to appeal to Pierre's pride. "I understand, we both appreciate the subtler nuances of life at Milburn Manor. Perhaps there is a way we could be of mutual benefit to one another." The proposition was veiled but the implication was clear. Percival much like Pierre sought to wield information as a tool for his own ends. In Pierre, he saw not just a chef but a potential ally, someone whose access to the private quarters of the manor could prove invaluable.

Pierre understood that in a house as grand as Milburn Manor, gossip was as much a staple as the bread that graced the table. It was this understanding that he leveraged in his dealings with Percival. By positioning himself as a key informant on the happenings within both the upper and lower echelons of the manor, particularly regarding the delicate situation surrounding Isabella, Pierre saw an opportunity to bargain. In return for his insights, carefully curated titbits that would keep Percival apprised of Isabella's movements, then he hoped Percival would introduce his talents to the discerning palates of his acquaintances. Pierre had no intention at that time to inform Percival of the secret meetings between James and Isabella that Lily had seen.

"You have my assurance sir," Pierre looked at Percival, his mind already calculating how this request could serve his aspirations. "The staff confide in me, and they see all. Should anything out of the ordinary occur, I shall discreetly bring it to your attention."

Percival, satisfied with this arrangement saw no need to divulge his deeper suspicions, for now, he sought only vigilance, an insurance against the embarrassment of a public refusal or scandal.

"Your discretion in this matter will not go unrewarded Pierre. I trust you understand the delicacy of this situation."

"I do sir. You can rely on my utmost discretion and loyalty." Pierre assured him. The promise of furthering his standing and securing a patron in Percival motivated him, yes, but so too did the thrill of the intrigue, of being a player in the game, rather than merely a spectator.

For Pierre, this arrangement represented the culmination of years of ambition and hard work. The prospect of his culinary creations becoming the talk of

Lancashire's aristocracy was a tantalizing one, and he was willing to navigate the murky waters of intrigue and manipulation to achieve it. Yet, even as he basked in the potential glory of his future success, Pierre remained vigilant, aware that in the game of power and influence, fortunes could change as swiftly as the courses of a well-planned meal.

Chapter Twenty-Five
Amelia
Lancashire

Within the venerable walls of Milburn Manor's library, where knowledge and history whispered from every corner, Amelia was continuing her archiving of the records although her mind was on the latest pages of the diary she was reading. Each page unravelled further the complex tapestry of love, defiance, and the tragedy that had once pervaded the manor. The weight of their story, so intertwined with the fabric of the place she had come to care deeply about, felt both haunting and intimate.

As dusk crept across the sky, casting long shadows through the library's tall windows, Amelia felt a palpable shift in the atmosphere. The air around her grew colder, the kind of cold that seemed to seep into her bones, a herald of the supernatural that she had come to recognise. She looked up, her breath catching in her throat, as the figure of Isabella materialized before her. The apparition of Isabella stood at the edge of the dimly lit room, her presence no longer threatening. She looked almost serene but also sorrowful. She seemed to Amelia as if she were tethered to the world of the living by threads of regret and unfulfilled desires. Amelia held her breath as Isabella moved closer and gently touched Amelia's stomach, just briefly, their eyes meeting in a silent understanding. Isabella began to move, her steps soundless as she glided across the room toward a neglected corner of the library. Isabella stopped and then slowly began to fade until the library was once again empty, apart from Amelia. She moved towards the corner of the library where Isabella had been, a part of the library that she rarely explored. The books here were older, their leather bindings cracked, and their titles faded. As she reached for one, her fingers brushed against something unusual. The back panel of the bookshelf felt loose. Curiosity piqued, Amelia carefully pried the panel open, revealing a narrow, hidden compartment. Her heart quickened as she saw a bundle of yellowed letters tied with a faded ribbon. The top letter bore the elegant flowing script of Florence, the lady's maid who had written the diary. The letters had been hidden away, perhaps intentionally to protect their contents from prying eyes. Over the years, they had been forgotten, buried under layers of history.

Amelia picked up the letters and took them back to the table where she had been working. They appeared to be correspondence between Isabella and Florence, which meant that they must have been separated for some reason. With the letters clutched in her hands Amelia realised that her journey was far from over. Guided by the bond she felt with Isabella and armed with the truth that she hoped the letters contained, she vowed to uncover the fate of Isabella, to bring peace to a soul that had known too much suffering. In the silence that enveloped the library, Amelia felt an unbreakable bond forged between her and the woman who had lived, loved, and lost within these very walls. She would not rest until Isabella's story was told in full until every whisper of the past found its echo in the heart of the present.

***

Amelia had arranged to meet her father for lunch the following day and decided to take the box of letters with her. She hadn't mentioned the find to Rafe, yet. She was going to discuss this with her father and see if he could help as she was busy with finishing the archiving and reading the diary. The drive from Slaidburn to the village of Newton in Bowland was a lovely one, and Amelia enjoyed taking in the scenery from the fells, the old dry-stone walls, and the long winding road. She pulled into the car park of The Parkers Arms just as her father also arrived.

The Parkers Arms was a charming country inn located just outside Clitheroe in the village of Newton in Bowland. It was a traditional whitewashed building adorned with colourful baskets of flowers and shaded outdoor tables. Inside the rustic contemporary décor was casual, elegant warm, and inviting. They took their seats at a table near the fireplace and ordered a gin and tonic each. The gin was a local one which was infused with Yorkshire Rhubarb.

Amidst the whirlwind of revelations and emotional discoveries that had become her life at Milburn Manor, Amelia found herself grappling with a sense of urgency that propelled her forward. The letters she had unearthed, a tangible connection to Isabella and her story, weighed heavily on her mind. With her departure to Greece looming, a journey to reunite with Nikos and embrace the future they were building together, Amelia knew she could not leave these threads of the past untangled. It was with this in mind that she sought out her father, a man of quiet strength and understanding, who had always supported her endeavours no matter how unconventional.

As they settled over their meal, a 60-day aged red wine braised beef pie made with the pub's famous beef fat pastry, Amelia explained about the bunch of letters she had discovered.

"Dad," she began, her voice laced with the weight of her request, "these letters, they tell more of Isabella's story. I need you to read these while I focus on the diary and prepare for Greece. I can't shake the feeling that there's more to uncover. Isabella led me to these letters; her story deserves to be told in its entirety."

Her father, taking the letters, nodded solemnly, understanding the mantle of responsibility his daughter had placed upon him. "I'll read them, and together we'll ensure Isabella's voice is finally heard. You focus on your work and your journey to Greece and this… this I can do for you, for Isabella."

In the days that followed, Amelia's father became immersed in the world Isabella had left behind, his heart moved by the love, loss, and resilience that echoed through the words exchanged between Isabella and her lady's maid Florence. He began to piece together a narrative that, though marked by tragedy, also confirmed the enduring strength of the human spirit.

Meanwhile, Amelia's preparation for Greece continued her mind and heart a tapestry of anticipation for the future and reverence for the past. The diary and the letters, bridges across time, had intertwined the fates of those who dwelled within Milburn Manor, both living and long departed. With the letters in her father's care and the diary's secrets slowly yielding under Amelia's persistent gaze, the path forward was clear. They would honour the past by bringing its shadows into the light ensuring the voices of Milburn Manor, silenced by time, would finally be heard.

***

Amelia, sat at the window of the small restaurant, her fingers fidgeting with the handle of her teacup. Meeting up with Chloe always brought a sense of calm, but today her mind was preoccupied with her impending journey to Greece. As Chloe came through the door, her radiant smile eased some of Amelia's tension. "Amelia, it's so good to see you, and I'm so glad you picked this place, it's so appropriate" Chloe exclaimed, her arms outstretched for a hug.

"It is, isn't it." Amelia agreed, returning the embrace gratefully.

They had decided to meet at Brizola Bar & Grill, which was owned by a friend of theirs, Rachel, who although a local girl, specialised in Greek cuisine and the restaurant was renowned for its great food and atmosphere. It was in a picturesque courtyard just off the main high street in Clitheroe. Amelia chose the Pepper Pork Sandwich which she always had. It was delicious gyros pork on a flatbread with salad and the most amazing pepper sauce, whilst Chloe decided to have the Halloumi & Bean Stifado. After they settled with their meals, they chatted about Greece and the upcoming trip when Amelia looked at Chloe.

"So, what's new with you?" Chloe's sighed, her expression turning serious, and she hesitated for a moment before speaking.

"I saw Jack the other day."

Amelia's heart skipped a beat. "You did? What did he say?" Chloe took a deep breath, her gaze distant as she recounted the encounter.

"He seemed different, almost remorseful. He said he regrets everything, Amelia. All the pain he caused."

Amelia's mind whirled with conflicting emotions.

"I... I don't know what to make of that, he was so angry last time I saw him and then all the trouble he tried to cause." She admitted, her voice quiet and strained.

"I understand," Chloe replied softly, reaching out to grasp Amelia's hand. "Just remember, Amelia, you deserve someone who treats you with kindness and respect, no matter what Jack says now. You have Nikos, you have the baby, you're going to Greece. Forget Jack and look forward to the next chapter." Amelia smiled, grateful for Chloe's unwavering support.

"Thank you, Chloe. What will I do without you" she laughed.

"I'll be coming to Greece, as soon as you are settled, don't you worry," Chloe laughed too, and they hugged again.

As they continued to chat over their meals, Amelia felt a sense of comfort settle over her. With Chloe by her side, she knew she could face whatever challenges lay ahead in Greece.

Chapter Twenty-Six
Isabella
Lancashire 1906

In the quiet seclusion of Isabella's chamber, where the light of day filtered softly through the heavy drapery, a scene of intimate revelation unfolded. Isabella stood by the window, her silhouette etched against the light, as she turned to face Florence. The air between them was charged with anticipation and the weight of unspoken truths.

"Florence," Isabella began, her voice a mere whisper, betraying the turmoil that existed beneath her composed exterior. "I find myself in a …predicament. One that, I fear, will not only alter the course of my life but may also endanger yours, should you choose to stand by me." Florence, steadfast and unwavering, stepped closer, her loyalty to Isabella as certain as the dawn.

"My lady, there is nothing you could say that would sway my devotion. Speak your heart, and know it is safe with me."

With a deep breath, Isabella confessed, "I am with child Florence, James's child." The admission hung in the room, a declaration of both profound love and impending peril. "And I cannot, will not, marry Percival, knowing the truth that grows within me." Although Florence had suspected as much, the gravity of Isabella's situation settled over her like a shroud. To be with child out of wedlock was not merely scandalous, it was a transgression that society punished without mercy. Yet in the face of such daunting prospects, Florence's resolve did not waver.

"Then we must act, and swiftly," Florence responded, her mind already racing through the possibilities, each fraught with risk but illuminated by the glimmer of hope that defiance often carries. "Does James know?" she queried.

"James knows," Isabella was moved by Florence's unwavering support. "He is prepared to do whatever it takes. We've spoken of leaving, eloping to Ireland where his family has land. There we could be free, live as husband and wife without the shadow of scandal darkening our day, and I want you to come with me Florence, please." The plan was audacious but Florence understanding the magnitude of the decision, nodded her head.

"Certainly, my lady, I would be honoured to accompany you. We shall prepare for our departure, your future with James and your child, and now mine too is worth every peril we may face."

In the days that followed, Florence became the architect of their escape, leveraging her knowledge of the manor and its workings to plan their flight. She procured clothing suitable for travel, gathered what meagre funds she had and crafted a story to cover their absence, each step taken with a careful blend of haste and caution.

In the sanctuary of Isabella's chamber, the plans were laid, and the risks weighed. Together Isabella and Florence faced the dawning of a new chapter, one marked by uncertainty of the future but guided by the immutable light of hope and love.

***

Beneath the cloak of night under the whispering boughs of the ancient oak that stood sentinel at the edge of Milburn Manor, by the chapel, Isabella and James met, their hearts alight with a desperate hope. The moon, a sliver of silver in the velvet sky, cast a glow over their clandestine meeting, illuminating the path of their forthcoming journey.

"Isabella," James began, "tomorrow night, we shall leave this place. We must be swift, silent, and make for the coast where a ship awaits to carry us to Ireland." Isabella nodded and clasped his hand.

"We'll be ready. Florence has secured some provisions and a change of garments suitable for travel." James, his face a mask of resolve and fierce love, took Isabella's face in his hands.

Giving her a kiss he said "I have arranged for a carriage to be waiting beyond the north gate. From there we shall make haste to the coast. My cousin, who captains a ship, will see us safely across the sea. Isabella, my heart, every step we take from this moment forth is a step towards our future, one we shall build together away from the prying eyes and harsh judgments of this world. A future for our child."

Unbeknownst to them, hidden in the shadow of the underbrush, Lily listened, her heart pounding with the gravity of the words she overheard. Torn between her loyalty to Pierre and the undeniable wrongness of betraying a love as true as Isabella's and James's, Lily hesitated. But the memory of Pierre's instructions, his reminder of her place in the intricate hierarchy of the manor, and the consequences of disobedience, weighed heavily on her. With a heavy heart, Lily made her way back to the manor, her steps as silent as the secrets she now carried. In the kitchen, where the remnants of the day's meals were being cleared away, she found Pierre, his presence commanding even in the quiet of the late hour.

"Pierre," she whispered, drawing him aside with a glance that spoke of the urgency of her news. "I have something you must know." The words once spoken could not be reclaimed, and as she relayed the details of Isabella's and James's planned elopement, Lily felt the last vestiges of her innocence slip away.

Pierre listened, his expression unreadable, as Lily recounted what she had overheard. The implications of this information, the potential for manipulation, and the control it afforded sparked a dark satisfaction within him.

"You have done well, Lily," he said his voice smooth, betraying none of the turmoil that churned beneath the surface. "Your loyalty to the manor does you credit." As Lily retreated, the weight of betrayal settling like a stone in her heart, Pierre contemplated his next move. This knowledge was not just power, it was a currency with which he could further his ambitions, secure his position, and bind Percival to him in a web of indebtedness.

The elopement of Isabella and James, a defiance against the established order of things, had become a pawn in the greater game of secrets and lies that pervaded Milburn Manor. In the quiet aftermath of Lily's revelation, the manor stood on the precipice of a storm, one that promised to alter the lives of all within its walls. And at the heart of this impending tempest stood Pierre, ready to leverage the footsteps of fate to his own ends.

Chapter Twenty-Seven
Isabella
Lancashire 1906

In the kitchen garden at the back of the manor house, Percival had met Pierre, where his recent revelation had cast a pall over their clandestine meeting. The news of Isabella's intended elopement with James, a mere mill owner, was a blow to Percival's pride and his carefully laid plans. Percival his mind racing with the implications of Pierre's disclosure, saw in that moment not just a personal affront but a potential catastrophe that threatened the delicate balance of alliances and reputations he had worked diligently to cultivate.

"This cannot be allowed to proceed," he stated, his voice cold with determination. "Isabella's actions, should they come to light would be a scandal of considerable magnitude, not just for her but for all associated with Milburn Manor." Pierre sensing the shift in Percival's demeanour, from shock to strategic calculation, nodded in agreement.

"Indeed Sir, as you asked it was my duty to bring this matter to your attention. The consequences of inaction could be … most unfavourable."

With a decision made, Percival wasted no time. He sought an audience with Lord Rafe de Lacy to divulge the information that had come into his possession, a task fraught with the risk of exposing not just Isabella's indiscretions, but his own vulnerabilities. Lord de Lacy received Percival in the main drawing room, a space adorned with the portraits of ancestors whose gaze seemed to scrutinize the very fabric of their descendant's integrity.

"Lord de Lacy, "Percival began, his tone carefully modulated to convey both urgency and respect. "I come before you with news most distressing, regarding your daughter and my fiancée Lady Isabella. It has come to my attention that she plans to forsake our engagement, our family's agreement, in favour of a clandestine elopement with James Wycliffe !!" The revelation struck Lord de Lacy like a physical blow, the colour draining from his face as he processed the gravity of such a scandal.

"Are you certain of this?" he demanded, his voice a low rumble of contained fury. The de Lacy name, steeped in history and honour could ill afford the stain of such a scandal.

"With all due respect, my lord, I have every reason to believe the information is accurate," Percival replied, inwardly bracing himself against the storm he had unleashed. "I felt it my duty to inform you, that we might take appropriate measures to avert this crisis."

"Absolutely, but how did you come by this information?" Lord de Lacy was truly angry.

"Your chef, Pierre came across the information told to him by a young housemaid." Percival had started to sweat. The summoning of Pierre was immediate, a directive that brooked no delay. As the master chef was escorted to Lord Rafe's drawing room, the corridors of the manor seemed to pulse with anticipation, the staff whispering among themselves about the unfolding drama. Pierre aware of the gravity of the situation, entered the room with a measured calm, which belied the turmoil churning within him.

"Sit," Lord de Lacy commanded. Pierre complied, his posture erect, his hands folded neatly in his lap.

"Tell me everything "Lord de Lacy continued, his gaze piercing Pierre with an intensity that demanded nothing less than the complete truth. "Percival has informed me of Isabella's plan to forsake her betrothal and flee with James Wycliffe. I want to hear what you know of this matter." Pierre, choosing his words with care, recounted what he had learned from Lily. He spoke of overhearing the plans for the elopement and the preparations that had been made for their departure. Throughout his account, Pierre maintained a veneer of loyalty to the manor and its interests, emphasizing his role in bringing the matter to light out of concern for the de Lacy's family honour.

Lord de Lacy listened intently; his expression unreadable as Pierre spoke. The implications of Pierre's testimony were clear; Isabella's actions, if left unchecked, would not only scandalize the family but also undermine the carefully maintained social order that governed their lives. When Pierre had finished, Lord de Lacy sat back in his chair, his mind racing with the options before him. He didn't doubt the truth of what Pierre was saying but he doubted his reasons for gleaning this information were anything to do with loyalty to the family and probably more likely to further his career. This betrayal by Isabella, his daughter was a blow that struck at the very heart of his identity as both a father and a lord. He rose from his seat, the lines of his face etched deeper by the weight of the situation.

"This matter must be dealt with swiftly and discreetly. I will not allow the folly of youth and the rashness of emotion to undermine the standing of this family, nor the agreements we have entered. We will intercept this elopement and deal with James accordingly. Pierre, your diligence in this matter is noted and you Sir Percival are quite understandably upset. Tell no one of this matter, we will hide in the shadows, the three of us, and stop this ridiculous nonsense, together."

As Pierre left the drawing room, he felt that he had secured his position within the intricate web of the manor's secrets and power plays. His alliance with Percival and the lord himself, cemented by shared knowledge and mutual benefit, positioned him as a key player in the unfolding drama, a role he embraced with the cunning and foresight that had become his hallmark.

Chapter Twenty-Eight

Isabella
Lancashire

As the appointed hour of Isabella and James's elopement approached, Milburn Manor lay in a deceptive calm, its inhabitants asleep, unaware of the drama that was about to unfold beneath the cover of night. In the shadows, however, a different scene was set as Lord Rafe de Lacy, alongside Percival and Pierre, prepared to intercept the lovers, thwart their plan, and preserve the manor's honour.

They positioned themselves strategically near the north gate, the rumoured point of departure for Isabella and James. The moon hung low in the sky, casting an eerie glow over the grounds, its light a silent witness to the confrontation that loomed.

Percival, his heart a cauldron of betrayal and wounded pride, paced restlessly, his every step revealing the storm of emotions that raged within. Pierre, ever the opportunist stood by his presence a dark reminder of the role he played in setting this trap, and Lord de Lacy, stoic and imposing bore the weight of his lineage, determined to act as the arbiter of justice.

As whispers of movement broke the silence of the night, the tension among the three men reached its zenith. From the shadows emerged Isabella and James, their hands clasped, their resolve etched in the lines of their faces. Florence followed silently behind clutching two large bags. But before they could take more than a few steps towards freedom, they were confronted by the trio.

"Isabella, how could you shame me so?" Lord de Lacy's voice boomed, a mix of disappointment and anger. "Return to the house. This folly ends now." James, protective and defiant positioned himself between Isabella and the men.

"We seek only the happiness denied to us here. Stand aside and let us pass." Percival driven by jealousy and scorn stepped forward.

"You'll not take her anywhere, James. She is mine by promise and right." At this point, Isabella stepped forward and addressed her father.

"Father, I am sorry, I am in love, and I am going to marry James, we are going away tonight, and you can't stop us." She faltered slightly as she spoke, "I am having James's baby father …" James put his arm around her.

"I love Isabella Lord de Lacy and will make an honest woman of her and give her a good life."

"You will do no such thing, "Lord de Lacy exploded "You are not worthy of my daughter and if she is with child then you have brought shame and disgrace on my daughter." He turned to Isabella, "Get back into the manor and stay there, I will deal with you later. And you," he pointed to Florence, "You take her now, you will also be dealt with later." As he spoke Percival moved towards Isabella, and James desperate to protect her and their future lunged at Percival and pushed him aside. As the pair began to wrestle on the ground, Pierre intercepted and withdrew a knife from the folds of his coat, pushing Percival aside. The scuffle that ensued was chaotic, a maelstrom of desperation and fury under the cold gaze of the moon. Isabella was screaming and Florence ran to the manor to get help. Lord de Lacy attempted to intervene to bring some order to the madness that was unfolding before him.

Pierre was the first to strike, lunging at James with the knife gleaming ominously in the moonlight. The two men grappled fiercely, a desperate dance of survival under the watchful eyes of the ancient oaks that bordered the estate. In a twist of fate, James's hand found the knife, wrenching it free from Pierre's grasp with a force born of desperation. The struggle reached its crescendo as James, in a move to protect himself and Isabella, pushed Pierre with all his might. The momentum carried Pierre backward, his footing lost to the uneven ground until he fell with a sickening thud against a rock, the silence that followed as final as the grave.

Isabella's gasp of horror was swallowed by the night as Percival advanced on James. The grief and shock of Pierre's fall had barely registered before James found himself facing a new, equally deadly threat. The fight between James and Percival was brutal and brief. Percival fought with a reckless abandon. James despite his determination and love for Isabella was no match for Percival's cold fury.

In the ensuing melee, Percival had found the knife and plunged it into James with a precision that belied the chaos of their struggle. James's cry of pain echoed through the night, a sound that would haunt Isabella for the rest of her days. As James collapsed, the light fading from his eyes, Isabella rushed to his side, her world crumbling around her. Percival stood back panting, the reality of his actions dawning on him with chilling clarity. All was silent except for the sobbing of Isabella as she knelt beside the lifeless body of her true love. With trembling hands, Isabella brushed a lock of hair from James's lifeless face, her fingers lingering on his cold skin as if trying to imprint his image forever in her memory. In that moment, the world stood still, and all she could hear was the echo of her heart breaking.

***

In the grey light of dawn, the grounds of Milburn Manor felt like a world suspended in time, a silent witness to the night's tragic events. Lord de Lacy alongside a somber and resolute Percival, oversaw the grim task of burying James and Pierre in the shadow of the manor's chapel, a final resting place for a night that had spiralled into chaos.

With the deed done, a heavy silence hung between the two men, each lost in their thoughts of what had transpired and the irreparable changes it wrought upon their lives and the fabric of Milburn Manor. The grave, unmarked and hastily dug, indicated not just the end of lives, but the depth of secrets that the manor kept hidden within its walls.

***

The sun had risen higher in the sky by the time Lord de Lacy summoned Isabella to his study. The summons had come suddenly, a terse message that left no room for doubt: Lord de Lacy demanded her presence. With each step, Isabella's mind raced with the tumult of emotions threatening to overwhelm her, her memories of the night's tragedy fresh in her mind. She paused before the heavy oak door of the study, her hand trembling as she raised it to knock. As she entered, she could see her father seated behind his imposing desk, his countenance as stormy as the skies that brooded over the manor.

"Isabella," he began, his voice a controlled calm that belied the storm raging in his eyes. "Sit." She complied, taking the seat opposite him, her posture rigid, bracing herself for the onslaught of her father's wrath. Her father wasted no time on pleasantries. "The events of last night have brought disgrace upon our family," he stated each word a hammer blow to Isabella's already fragile state. "Your actions, your liaison with James Wycliffe, have tarnished the de Lacy name and brought about the unfortunate events that occurred last night." Isabella's heart clenched, the pain of James's loss a raw wound that seemed to tear further with her father's every word.

"Father, I loved James, I am having his child. He loved me and we honestly believed we could have a future where love outweighed duty."

Lord de Lacy's expression hardened. "Love? You speak of love when you have jeopardised everything this family stands for? No Isabella you have forced my hand." The pause that followed was heavy with dread, the air thick with the unspoken decree that loomed over them.

"You will be sent away," he declared, the sentence falling between them like a guillotine's blade. "To a convent far from here. There you will remain, far from the scandal you've wrought, far from the society that you have shamed." Isabella's breath caught in her throat, the reality of her father's words a cold voice around her heart, "A convent?" she whispered, disbelief and despair mingling in her voice.

Yes, a convent where you can reflect on your morals and your disgraceful behaviour." Lord de Lacy continued, his voice devoid of warmth. "I am not concerned with regards to the child, only that you never return here with it. Isabella, you are no longer the daughter I thought you were." The room spun, the walls closing in as Isabella grappled with the magnitude of her father's decree. To be torn from her home and all she knew, to be sent away to a life of penance for a sin she did not believe in was her punishment.

"Father please," she implored, tears spilling over, "do not do this, I have lost James, please do not send me away too."

"It is done, Isabella," Lord de Lacy was unmoved, his decision irrevocable. "You will leave at once." Isabella rose, her body trembling, her spirit shattered by the ruthlessness of her fate. She cast one last look at her father and without a word, she turned and exited the study. The corridors of Milburn Manor, once familiar, now felt alien, each step taking her further from the life she knew, from the love she had cherished, toward a future as cold and unforgiving as the stone walls that imprisoned her heart.

Chapter Twenty-Nine
Amelia
Lancashire

As Amelia delved deeper into the tangled web of Isabella's elopement and the tragic aftermath that unfolded in the pages of the old diary, her father embarked on a journey through the letters that Amelia had entrusted to him. Each letter, a reminder of a bond that refused to be severed by distance or circumstance, revealed the depth of the connection between Isabella, confined to a convent in Europe, and Florence, who faced her own trials back at Milburn Manor.

Through the letters, Isabella's father discovered that Florence, once Isabella's lady's maid, held in high regard, found herself demoted to the scullery, her status within the household irrevocably altered by the scandal that had enveloped Isabella. The manor's response to the events had been swift and unforgiving, leaving Florence to navigate a world far removed from the one she had known, a world of relentless toil and scarce recognition. Yet amid the hardships, Florence's resolve remained unshaken, her commitment to Isabella undimmed. The letters were her lifeline, a way to keep the promise she had made to stand by Isabella, no matter what the cost. Amelia's father as he read the letters, was struck by the poignancy of their contents. Isabella's letter spoke not only of her life within the confines of the convent, grappling with the reality of the loss of her beloved James but of her loneliness and struggles with the language.

"I find myself in a world far removed from the one we knew dear Florence," Isabella wrote in one letter. "Each day is a battle; one I fear I will not win. You were more than a lady's maid to me, you were a friend, a confidante in my darkest hours. I cling to the hope that my words find you, that in some way they bring us together again across the distance that divides us."

Florence's response, though few, reflected the hardship of her new life in the manor's scullery and her deep sadness for the loss of James and now Isabella. As Amelia's father came to the end of the letters, he had tears in his eyes as he read what appeared to be the final correspondence between the two women.

My Dearest Florence,

I hope this letter finds you well. I am writing to you in a moment of both great anticipation and deep uncertainty. As I approach the time to bring my child into the world, my heart is a tumult of emotions. The prospect of becoming a mother fills me with a profound joy that I can scarcely describe. I yearn to hold my child in my arms and see a little bit of James looking back at me. Yet alongside this joy, there is a shadow of fear and sadness. The circumstances that brought me to this place have not been kind, and the distance from home weighs heavily upon me.

I think often of Milburn Manor, of the life I left behind, and especially of my dear mother. In my heart, I hold onto the hope that the birth of my child will soften my father's heart and that he might find it within himself to forgive me. I long for the day when we can return home when the past can be forgotten, and I can once again be surrounded by those I love.

Florence, you have been more than my maid, you have been a steadfast friend, and your support has been a source of comfort to me. I know that if it were within your power, you would be here by my side. Your letters have been my lifeline, reminding me I am not alone, even when the nights are darkest.

Please convey my deepest apologies to my parents if you have the chance. Let them know that I carry their love with me, and that my thoughts are ever with them. I believe that once my child is born, we will find a way to reunite, to heal the wounds that have been inflicted by fate and circumstance.

Until then, I remain here, hopeful, and resolute. I trust in the mercy of God and the compassion of my family, that they will find it within their hearts to welcome us home.

*With all my love and gratitude
Isabella*

Chapter Thirty
Amelia
Lancashire

As the final preparations for her departure to Greece were underway, Amelia found herself in the quiet company of her father, surrounded by the familiar walls of her childhood home, Highcliffe House. The air between them was thick with anticipation, laden with the weight of discoveries past and those that lay just beyond the horizon. Her father presented her with a carefully curated compilation of the letters each one a fragment of the puzzle of Isabella's life. Among them, a singular letter, the last one received stood out as it was written in Greek.

"This was among the last of the letters," her father explained handing her the letter penned in Greek, the elegant script a whisper from the past that neither of them could decipher. "It's from a sister Agnes from the convent of Agia Marina in Heraklion and it's dated 1908." The letter, an enigma wrapped in the mystery of its language carried with it a sense of urgency, a palpable connection to Isabella's story that Amelia could not ignore. The name of the convent and Sister Agnes were the only clues legible to them, beacons that would guide Amelia's journey in Greece.

"I'll take it with me, Nikos should be able to translate it. This could offer some answers "Amelia said. As they discussed the rest of the letters and their contents and her father explained about the correspondence between Isabella and Florence, Amelia couldn't help but cry when she heard of her love for her child and her hopes for the future. She automatically put her hands on her stomach and vowed that nothing and no one would ever harm her child. After an emotional farewell with her father, she promised to call and email regularly and he would be coming out to Elounda soon to see her and Nikos and was especially looking forward to meeting Alexandros and the now infamous dog, Nina.

As they concluded their meeting, her father shared one last piece of news that closed the chapter on a lingering question from Amelia's past.

"Jack has left the area. I believe he has moved to Manchester. He too has decided to seek a fresh start. I have spoken to the solicitors and the proceeds of the house when it finally sells will all come to you, Amelia." The mention of Jack served as a reminder of how far she had come, of the growth and healing she had experienced within the manor's walls. It was a bittersweet acknowledgment; a letting go that was both liberating and laden with the melancholy of what might have been.

***

With the letters secured in her suitcase, Amelia prepared to leave Milburn Manor. The estate, with its sprawling gardens and echoing halls had become part of her, part of the journey she had undertaken. Yet as she stood at the threshold, her gaze cast toward the horizon, it was the future that called to her. A future where the story of Isabella, and her own story would continue to unfold.

As the car pulled away from the manor, Amelia thought she saw the ethereal figure of Lady Isabella staring out of a top-floor window, but when she looked again there was nothing. Greece awaited, with its ancient ruins and azure seas and Nikos, her new family.

Part one of Amelia's journey might have come to an end, but the adventure, the search for truth and connection, was just beginning.

PART TWO

Chapter Thirty-One

Isabella
Greece

The dawn had barely broken over Milburn Manor when Isabella, her belongings packed into a single, modest suitcase, made her silent departure. Beside her, William, her brother, carried himself with an air of detached obligation. There was no affectionate farewell from her parents, no comforting embrace, and from William only the solemn duty that cast a shadow over both their spirits.

Their journey commenced with a train ride to the coast, the English countryside blurring past the windows in a melancholic haze. Isabella sat quietly, her gaze fixed on the fleeting landscape, her mind full of fear and sorrow. William, for his part, seemed absorbed in his thoughts, an impenetrable barrier of reserve separating him from his sister's distress. The train's steady rhythm provided no comfort to Isabella, each clack of the wheels on the tracks a reminder of the distance growing between her and the life she once knew. She attempted conversation, a bid for some semblance of connection or comfort from William, but his responses were curt, his attention soon returning to the papers and documents he deemed more pressing than his sister's plight.

Upon reaching the coast, they boarded a steamship bound for Naples, Italy, a vessel that promised new beginnings for some but only the deepening of despair for Isabella. Her cabin, though private, felt more like a cell, the narrow bed and porthole window offering little solace.

The rolling sea matched the turmoil within her, and she found herself unable to venture out, staying confined to her cabin, her meals brought by a steward whose attempts at cheerfulness could not penetrate her gloom.

William, meanwhile, seemed to take to the journey with a sense of duty-bound stoicism. He visited Isabella occasionally, ensuring her basic needs were met, but his presence was more a reminder of her isolation than a source of brotherly support. His conversation revolved around practicalities, never touching the emotional depths of Isabella's heartache or the future that awaited her. The truth was that William was devastated by this turn of events but had no ideas how to help Isabella or even talk to her about it and so he remained detached and aloof, even though inside his heart was breaking too.

***

Isabella sat by the small window of her private cabin, watching the waves as the boat cut through the dark churning waters. The rhythmic sound of the waves against the hull was a constant reminder of the distance growing between her and everything she had known. She had been on the ship for several days now, bound for Italy and then onward to Athens.

The cabin was modest but comfortable furnished with a narrow bed, a wooden wardrobe, and a small writing desk. A single oil lamp hung from the ceiling, casting a warm flickering glow. Isabella rarely left her cabin, preferring the solitude and the comfort of her own thoughts. The memories of Milburn Manor and the life she once had haunted her, but the confinement of her cabin was a small mercy, allowing her to grieve in private.

The death of James weighed heavily on her heart. She couldn't shake the image of his lifeless body, the moment of their discovery forever etched in her mind. The love they shared, the plans they had made, all shattered in an instant. The pain of his loss was a constant ache, a wound that refused to heal.

Occasionally, she would venture out onto the deck, drawn by the promise of fresh air and the sight of the open sea. On one such evening, she wrapped herself in a heavy shawl and made her way up the narrow staircase to the deck. The sky was a blanket of stars, and the cool breeze carried the salty scent of the ocean. She leaned against the railing, letting the wind whip through her auburn hair, and closed her eyes, trying to find solace in the vastness around her. Despite her best efforts, she couldn't shake the feeling of dread that hung over her. The faces of her family, the laughter of friends and the warmth of the manor all seemed like distant memories, slipping further away with each passing wave. The realisation that she might never see them again was tearing her apart.

During the day, the ship was bustling with activity. The crew moved with practiced efficiency, tending to the needs of the passengers, and maintaining the vessel. Isabella watched them from the safety of her cabin, feeling a pang of envy at their camaraderie and sense of purpose. She felt like an outsider, adrift in a world that no longer made sense.

***

The port of Athens was bustling with activity, the sounds of seagulls mingling with the clamour of sailors and the constant rush of the waves against the harbour. It was here that Sister Agnes found them and greeted them in her heavily accented English. Isabella stood on the cobblestones, her eyes darting between the ship that had brought her and William to Greece and Sister Agnes waiting to take her away. The salty breeze whipped her auburn hair across he tear-streaked face as she clung to her brother's arm, her grip fierce with fear.

"William, you can't leave me here," she pleaded, her voice trembling as she glanced at the unfamiliar surroundings. "Please, don't let her take me. Take me home, I don't belong here." Her words were laced with desperation, each one a dagger of pain and panic. She tightened her hold, as though her sheer will would keep him at her side.

William's face was a mixture of sorrow and resignation. He looked at his sister, so fragile yet fierce, her eyes filled with a terror he felt powerless to soothe.

"Isabella, I wish I could," he said, his voice strained, heavy with the weight of their father's orders. "But this is where you need to be now. It's for your own good."

Isabella shook her head, stepping back and nearly stumbling as her knees buckled beneath her. "How can this be for my good?" she cried, her voice cracking with anguish. "I'm not sick William. I'm not crazy. You can't just leave me here like some…. prisoner!" He reached out to steady her, but she pulled away, her eyes wild with fear. She glanced over to where Sister Agnes stood, her calm watchful eyes waiting patiently. Everything about this place felt wrong. The foreign language, the strange faces, the sense of being utterly alone. It was as if she was being exiled to another world, and there was no way back.

"Please, William," Isabella begged, her voice lowering to a broken whisper. "I can't do this. I can't be alone in a place I don't understand." She reached out, clutching at his jacket, her tears flowing freely. "Take me back. Don't leave me here." William's heart twisted painfully. He wanted nothing more than to take her home, to undo everything that had brought them to this wretched moment. But their father's words echoed in his mind, cold and final. He placed his hands on Isabella's shoulders, trying to steady both her and him.

"I'm sorry Isabella. I truly am." He whispered. "But this is what must be done." Sister Agnes stepped forward, sensing the tension rising. Her presence was calm, but firm, a quiet force in the chaos of the moment.

"Miss de Lacy," she said gently, her voice soft but unyielding. "We need to leave now. Your brother has travelled a long way to bring you here, and he must return home. We are expected at the hotel." Isabella turned to the nun, her expression one of raw, uncomprehending pain.

"You can't take me," she whispered. "I don't belong with you. I'm not like them." Sister Agnes placed a gentle hand on Isabella's arm, her touch both soothing and resolute.

"I understand you're frightened, but you are not alone, Isabella. You will be safe with us." Her eyes flickered with empathy, but there was also a finality in her words. William stepped back, his eyes glistening with unshed tears as he looked at his sister for what felt like the last time.

"I'll write to you," he said, though the promise felt hollow. "And I'll do everything I can from home. But you must trust Sister Agnes." Isabella's tears fell harder and as William turned to leave, her legs gave out. She collapsed onto the cobblestones, her cries a wrenching mix of heartbreak and anger.

"William!" she screamed, reaching out as he walked away, his figure blurring into the crowd. He didn't look back, he couldn't. Each step felt like a betrayal but he forced himself onward, knowing that if he stopped, he would never leave.

Sister Agnes knelt beside Isabella, wrapping her arms around the trembling young woman.

"Hush now," she murmured, pulling Isabella close. "It's time to go." Isabella sobbed into the nun's shoulder, her voice muffled and choked with despair.

"I want to go home. Please, let me go home." A carriage was waiting to take them to the hotel and as she stepped inside, the door closed with a heavy thud. As the horses began to pull away, Isabella pressed her face to the small window, her eyes straining to catch one last glimpse of her brother. But he was gone, swallowed by the crowd, leaving her to the unknown fate that awaited. As the port faded from view, Isabella felt the full weight of her isolation. She was alone in a foreign land, with nothing but the haunting memory of the world she had left behind. The walls of her new world were closing in, and all she could do was weep.

***

The evening air in Athens was balmy, carrying the scents of the Mediterranean and the distant murmur of a city alive with the echoes of ancient civilization and the bustling progress of the modern era. For Isabella, stepping into this world under the guidance of Sister Agnes, the city was a tapestry of wonder and apprehension. The sights, the sounds, the smells were like nothing she had ever envisaged. The language was incomprehensible to her. How was she ever going to settle in this alien country?

In 1906, Athens was a city at the crossroads of history and modernity, its ancient ruins standing as silent sentinels over streets teeming with life. Electric lights were beginning to dot the cityscape, casting their glow alongside gas lamps, illuminating the faces of passersby and the facades of neoclassical buildings that spoke of Greece's rich heritage and its aspirations towards progress.

Sister Agnes, sensing Isabella's overwhelmed state, offered quiet reassurances as they made their way through the streets to a modest hotel where they were to stay for the night.

"Athens is a city of contrasts," she explained, "where the past and present walk hand in hand. It is much like life in the convent, rooted in tradition, yet always moving forward."

As they settled into the hotel that evening, they sat in a small courtyard and enjoyed a simple Greek salad which was made with ripe tomatoes, cucumber, and onion with a thick slice of feta cheese on top, accompanied by Dolmades, grape leaves stuffed with rice, pine nuts, and herbs, together with delicious fresh bread and olive oil. The food was amazing, and the flavours were something Isabella had never experienced.

Sister Agnes spoke of what awaited Isabella at the convent.

"Our days are structured around prayer, work, and the community," she began, her voice gentle. "You will share a room with Sister Thea, a kind soul with a nurturing spirit. She will be a guide for you, as you find your place among us." Isabella listened, a mix of fear and curiosity churning within her. The thought of sharing her life with strangers, in a land so far from home, was daunting. Yet, there was comfort in the knowledge that she would not be entirely alone.

"The work we do is varied," Sister Agnes continued. "We tend to the gardens, tutor the local children, and provide for those in need. Each sister contributes according to her abilities and talents. You will find your own way to serve in time." Then with a gentle tact, which belied the gravity of her words, Sister Agnes broached the subject of Isabella's pregnancy.

"Your child will be born into a community that values life in all its forms. We will ensure you have the care you need when the time comes. As for your baby..." her voice trailed off, searching for the right works. "The convent is not a place for a child to grow, Isabella so we will have to try and help you find somewhere suitable, see what work we can get you or you could look at adoption. However, this is not a discussion for today."

The night passed with little rest for Isabella, her mind grappling with Sister Agnes's words, the sounds of Athens a distant backdrop to her tumultuous thoughts. The reality of giving up her child, borne of love and now a symbol of her exile, was a pain sharper than any she had known, but she knew that whatever happened she would never give the child up for adoption, it was hers and a part of James. If she couldn't return home, then she would learn to survive in this alien country and support her child.

Morning found Athens awash in the golden light of dawn, the Acropolis casting its long shadow over the city as if in protection. For Isabella, the sight was a poignant reminder of the transient nature of all things, of civilizations that rise and fall, and of personal journeys that navigate the spaces in between.

As they departed Athens for the convent on the island of Crete, Isabella carried with her the weight of her conversation with Sister Agnes, the knowledge of the life she would soon lead, and the decisions that lay ahead regarding her child. As the vessel cleaved through the azure embrace of the Mediterranean, Isabella found herself drawn to the deck, compelled by a need to witness the approach to Crete, the island that heralded the final leg of her journey. The early morning sun, a radiant orb ascending from its nightly slumber, cast a golden hue over the sea, transforming the water into a shimmering tapestry of light and shadow. The horizon, once a mere line separating the sea from the sky, gradually revealed the silhouette of Crete, an ancient land emerging from the depths of history and myth. The island's rugged mountains rose majestically, their peaks crowned with the first light of dawn, while the shores, a blend of jagged cliffs and gentle sands, whispered tales of civilizations that had flourished upon their embrace.

Isabella, her gaze fixed upon the approaching island, felt a stirring within her, a mix of awe and apprehension. The air was crisp, carrying the scent of salt and the faint whisper of winds that had traversed continents and ages. Seabirds, companions of the ship since departure soared above, their cries a wild melody that spoke of freedom and the boundless skies.

As Isabella's boat approached the shores of Crete, she was greeted by a sight that spoke volumes of the island's rich history and vibrant culture. The rugged coastline loomed ahead its cliffs adorned with ancient ruins that whispered tales of bygone eras. The warm Mediterranean sunbathed the landscape in a golden glow, casting long shadows over the bustling port below. From afar, Isabella could see the colourful buildings of the port town, their terracotta roofs gleaming in the sunlight. Fishing boats bobbed gently in the harbour, their sails fluttering in the breeze. The sound of seagulls filled the air, mingling with the shouts of fishermen and the clinking of rigging.

As the boat drew nearer, Isabella could make out the town's architecture. Whitewashed houses with blue shutters lined the narrow streets, their facades adorned with vibrant bougainvillea and fragrant jasmine. The scent of salt and spices hung in the air, mingling with the tantalising aroma of freshly baked bread and grilled fish.

As she stepped onto the bustling quay, Isabella was struck by the lively atmosphere of the port. Vendors hawked their wares from colourful stalls, selling everything from ripe olives and juicy figs to handmade pottery and intricate lacework. Locals bustled about their daily tasks, their voices rising and falling in a melodic cadence as they went about their business.

In the distance, Isabella could see the imposing silhouette of a Venetian fortress, its weathered walls standing as a testament to the Island's tumultuous past. Beyond the port town, the rugged landscape stretched out into the horizon, dotted with olive groves, vineyards, and ancient ruins.

As Isabella and Sister Agnes made their way through the bustling streets, Isabella couldn't help but feel a sense of wonder and awe at the beauty and history that surrounded her. Crete was a land of contrasts, where ancient tradition mingled with the emerging modern life, and every corner held a story waiting to be told. With each step she took, Isabella felt herself drawn deeper into the island's embrace, eager to uncover its secrets and make her mark on its storied shores.

Little did she know that her journey would take her on a path she could never have imagined, leading her to a destiny that would forever change the course of her life.

Chapter Thirty-Two

Milburn Manor
Lancashire 1906

The atmosphere at Milburn Manor had grown tense and somber since Isabella's departure. The de Lacy household was fraught with secrets, lies, and an air of impending doom. As the days turned into weeks, Rafe knew he had to address the growing suspicions and rumours surrounding the disappearance of James Wycliffe, the mill owner.

Rafe had taken measures to ensure that Isabella's departure was shrouded in secrecy. The official story was that she had been sent abroad to recover from an illness. However, the suddenness of her departure and the whispers of scandal refused to die down. The local community, always quick to gossip, had started speculating about James's mysterious disappearance. James Wycliffe's absence was becoming increasingly difficult to ignore. His mill was a vital part of the local economy, and its continued operation depended heavily on his leadership. Workers were growing restless, and the town's merchants were starting to worry about the future of their livelihoods. The once thriving mill had begun to falter, with no clear direction or management in sight. Rafe understood that he needed to address the issue head-on, both to quell the rumours and to maintain his family's standing in the community. He could not afford to let the mill's decline draw unwanted attention to his own role in the events that had transpired.

Rafe arranged for a town meeting at the local inn, inviting the mill workers and prominent members of the community. He knew that presenting a strong front was crucial to regaining control of the situation. Standing before the gathered crowd, Rafe exuded a confidence he did not truly feel. His voice was steady as he addressed the anxious faces before him.

"Ladies and gentlemen, I understand your concerns regarding the recent changes and the absence of Mr Wycliffe. I assure you that the mill will continue to operate smoothly, and its future is secure. I have appointed a new manager. Mr Albert Shaw, a trusted and experienced individual, who will take over the day-to-day operations. I am confident that under his leadership, the mill will thrive." Albert Shaw, a seasoned overseer known for his competence and loyalty to the de Lacy family, stepped forward. His presence was meant to instil confidence and provide a sense of continuity. The workers, recognising Albert's reputation, began to calm.

Rafe continued, "I have also ensured that all wages will be paid on time, and any concerns you have will be addressed promptly. The de Lacy family is committed to the well-being of this community."

As the meeting progressed, one of the bolder workers stood up and voiced what many had been whispering. "What about Mr Wycliffe? It's not like him to just disappear. We've heard rumours …..."

Rafe's expression hardened, though he maintained his composure.

"Mr Wycliffe's sudden departure is indeed unusual. He left for personal reasons, which I am not at liberty to disclose. I ask for your understanding and respect for his privacy. Rest assured, the mill and your livelihoods are secure." The crowd though not entirely satisfied seemed placated by Rafe's reassurances and the appointment of Albert Shaw.

***

The air in the kitchen of Milburn Manor was thick with the scent of freshly baked bread and roasting meat. The clatter of pots and pans mixed with the chatter of the staff, who were busy preparing the evening meal. Rafe de Lacy entered the kitchen, his presence instantly commanding attention. The room fell silent as the staff turned to face him. Rafe cleared his throat, his expression grave.

"I have some news to share," he began. "Pierre Lafontaine, your chef, has been called back to France on a family matter and will not be returning to Milburn Manor. I am sure Mrs Hargreaves will continue to maintain the exacting standards for which we are known." Murmurs of surprise and concern rippled through the staff. Pierre's sudden departure was unexpected, and many of the staff exchanged worried glances. Pierre had been a talented chef, and his absence would surely be felt.

As Rafe turned to leave, his eyes briefly met those of Lily, the housemaid. She quickly looked away, her heart pounding in her chest. Lily knew the truth behind Pierre's disappearance. She had been in the gardens that night, hiding in the shadows, and had witnessed the terrible events that had unfolded.

Now standing in the kitchen, Lily could feel the weight of that night pressing down on her. She knew she held a dangerous secret, one that could destroy the de Lacy family if revealed. She had seen what Lord de Lacy and Sir Percival had done, and she would not forget. The events of that night were a dark secret that bound them together, a secret that gave her a dangerous edge.

Chapter Thirty-Three
Amelia
Greece

Under the clear, blue sky of Crete, Amelia stepped into the bustling atmosphere of Heraklion Airport, a mix of excitement and nerves fluttering in her heart. This was more than a journey; it was a homecoming of sorts, to a place that had captured a piece of her soul, to a man who had changed the course of her life, and to a future that awaited her with open arms and unknown promises.

Nikos, standing amidst the ebb and flow of arrivals, made Amelia's heart jump. His presence, strong and reassuring, immediately calmed the sea of uncertainty that had accompanied her on the flight over. As their eyes met, a myriad of emotions passed between them, joy, relief, and the unspoken trepidation of stepping into a new life together.

"Amelia," Nikos greeted, his voice carrying the rich timbre of the Aegean, a smile lighting up his face, reflecting the depth of his feelings for her.

Amelia moved towards him, and in that moment, their embrace spoke volumes, a silent acknowledgment of the journey they had embarked upon together and the one that lay ahead. She was here, in Crete, pregnant with their child, ready to start a life with Nikos and to meet Alexandros, the son who would soon be a big brother. With a gentleness that belied his strength, Nikos took Amelia's luggage, leading her to the car. As they drove from Heraklion towards Elounda and on to Vrouchas, the landscape unfolded like a living tapestry, each curve of the road revealing more of Crete's rugged beauty. Olive groves passed by the silver-green leaves shimmering in the breeze, vineyards stretched towards the horizon, and the distant mountains stood as silent guardians of the land. Amelia gazed out of the window, occasionally looking at Nikos, and smiled. The life growing inside her, a tangible symbol of her bond with Nikos, filled her with a profound sense of belonging and purpose.

As they travelled to the village of Vrouchas, the Mediterranean came into view, its vast expanse a brilliant blue that merged with the sky at the horizon. As they made their way along the road from Elounda toward Plaka, Amelia immediately felt as if she had come home. She asked Nikos if they could stop in Plaka, for some reason she felt she needed to soak up the atmosphere and look out at the Island of the Forgotten, Spinalonga. They stopped at the Taverna Spinalonga which had the most incredible views of the island. It looked so forlorn, and again Amelia was struck by the thoughts of the poor people with leprosy who had been imprisoned there, so close to the mainland yet so far. They chatted and laughed and held hands and enjoyed a lovely lunch of Saganaki cheese, and seafood linguine with a chilled glass of the local wine and discussed the letter that Amelia had brought with her which Nikos said he would look at later that day.

When they arrived in Vrouchas, the village seemed to embrace them, the stone houses, and winding streets showing a way of life that had endured through the ages. Nikos's home, nestled in the heart of the village, awaited them, a place where Amelia's new life would begin, where she would become a mother, a partner, and a member of a community that had its roots deep in the soil of Crete. Vrouchas was home to one of the largest windmill clusters comprising nine mills which gave it a unique charm.

    Nikos owned an old village house in the lower area of Vrouchas. It was an old dilapidated and deserted cluster of buildings that had once served as the village bakery. He had renovated it into a lovely, comfortable, and spacious home. It had three bedrooms with room for a fourth and a storage room which could be converted into a guestroom with an independent entrance. It had three bathrooms and a large living area. Upon entering the main arched doorway, Amelia found herself in a beautiful, pebbled courtyard that Nikos had lovingly made when he renovated the property. There was a staircase that led up to a large terrace with lovely sea, mountainside, and village views. After entering the front door, she was met by a fully equipped kitchen. To the left of this was the living room and to the right another room that appeared to be a dining area. From here there was access to a bathroom with a toilet and a shower. The corridor ahead of the kitchen led to all the bedrooms. All the bedrooms had large skylights which made them bright and cheerful. Nikos had kept all the traditional elements of the old village house, such as the arch in the kitchen and all the doors and windows had been kept and repaired. It had solar heated water and three air conditioners and ceiling fans in the bedrooms. There was even a wood burning stove and an electric storage heater for warmth in the winter. Amelia fell in love with it on sight and she was looking forward to meeting Alexandros who Nikos was collecting from the local nursery school later that day.

***

Alexandros came up the pebbled path onto the terrace, a shy smile on his young face as he clutched a toy boat in one hand. He looked up with curious eyes, taking in Amelia's presence with a mixture of interest and reserved caution. Nikos knelt beside his son, speaking softly in Greek, words that Amelia had begun to understand, though she couldn't catch every nuance.

"Alexandros, this is Mia-Mia," Nikos introduced, his hand resting gently on his son's shoulder. He looked at Amelia and mouthed "I'll explain later." Turning back to Alexandros he said, "She's going to live here with us now." Alexandrous's eyes widened slightly as he processed his father's words, then setting down his toy boat, he took a small step forward.

"Hello" he said in English, the word spoken with a soft accent that melted Amelia's heart. It was clear he had been practicing for this moment.

"Hello Alexandros," Amelia replied, kneeling to be at eye level with him. "I've heard so much about you, I've been very excited to meet you."

At that moment, Nina, bounded over to Amelia, her tail wagging furiously. She nuzzled Amelia's hand eagerly as if endorsing her acceptance into the family. "This is Nina," Nikos laughed, as the dog placed her paws gently onto Amelia's shoulder, licking her face warmly.

"As you can see, she's very welcoming." Amelia laughed, a sound of genuine delight as she petted Nina, enjoying the affectionate welcome.

"I can see that, she's beautiful," Amelia responded, giving Nina a scratch behind the ears.

Nikos watched his son and Amelia interact, a feeling of profound relief and happiness washing over him. Alexandrous, typically shy around new people, seemed taken with Amelia, his initial hesitation dissolving into a smile as they began to talk about his toy boat and the adventures he imagined with it. Amelia's Greek was extremely limited and so was Alexandros's English but somehow, they seemed to be communicating with the help of Nina who was trying to get involved too.

That evening as they sat down for a meal together, the table laden with dishes of Greek cuisine that Nikos had prepared, Amelia felt a sense of belonging she hadn't anticipated. The laughter, the shared looks between her and Nikos, Alexandros's animated stories and Nina patiently waiting for any scraps that might fall her way, all of it felt right. Later that evening, once Alexandros was in bed and Amelia and Nikos were sat on the terrace with coffee, listening to the cicadas and looking at the wonderful views, Amelia gave the letter from the Greek convent to Nikos, and he began to read it. When he had finished, he looked at Amelia with tears in his eyes.

"Amelia, I don't know how to tell you this ……." His face ashen, as he placed his hand in hers.

Chapter Thirty-Four
Isabella
Greece 1906

Isabella's first weeks at the convent were a blend of solace and solitude, marked by the slow passage of time and the rhythms of convent life which were both a comfort and a constraint. As she navigated the hallways and gardens of her new home, the presence of Sister Thea became increasingly significant. Sister Thea, a woman of gentle demeanour and insightful eyes, seemed to understand the unspoken depths of Isabella's heartache without the need for words.

Sister Thea was assigned to help Isabella acclimatise to the daily routines of the convent. Their room was sparse, furnished with simple beds and a small window that looked out over the gardens of the convent. Despite the room's austerity, there was peace to be found in the view of the gardens, where orderly rows of plants and the distant hum of the Aegean provided a backdrop to Isabella's new life. In the morning, they would wake to the soft tolling of the bell calling them to prayer. Isabella still clad in the vestiges of her former life with her elegant yet somber attire, would follow Sister Thea to the chapel where the air was cool and filled with the scent of incense and old stone. The prayers were chanted in a rhythmic flow that Isabella did not understand at first but felt deeply.

Sister Thea took it upon herself to introduce Isabella to the convent's garden, a lush parcel of land that was tended by the nuns as part of their daily duties.

"The garden teaches us patience and care," Sister Thea explained, handing Isabella a pair of gardening shears. "It reminds us that all things grow and flourish in time, and with love." Isabella found unexpected strength in her toil within the earth. Planting, weeding, and harvesting became mediative acts, roots connecting her to the moment, to the Earth, and somehow, to the child growing within her. The garden was where she felt closest to James, to the life she had left behind and to the child she would soon welcome.

***

Theodora Lykoudis, later known as Sister Thea, was born into a world of strife and upheaval in the small village of Kritsa, Crete. Her family, once prosperous landowners, found themselves embroiled in the political turmoil that swept through Greece at that time. Her father was a staunch supporter of Cretan independence and found himself at odds with the occupying forces. This dangerous alliance brought both respect and peril to the Lykoudis family. One fateful night when Theodora was just sixteen, their home was raided by a faction loyal to the Ottoman Empire. Her father was taken away and their family's property was confiscated. Theodora's mother struggled to keep the family together in the face of such adversity and the once loving home turned sombre, filled with whispers of fear and uncertainty. Amidst the chaos, Theodora found love in the arms of Cosmo, a young revolutionary who shared her father's ideals. Their love blossomed in secret, each meeting charged with the tension of their dangerous world. Cosmo was passionate and fearless, qualities that drew Theodora to him even more. They dreamed of a future where Crete was free, and they could live without fear.

However, their love was not to be. One evening while sneaking back from a clandestine meeting, Theodora was caught by Ottoman soldiers. To protect Cosmo and her family, she lied about her activities, claiming she was alone. Despite her efforts Cosmo was discovered and executed. Theodora's heart shattered, and she was left with the crushing guilt of his death. Haunted by grief and guilt,

Theodora decided to leave Kritsa. Her family's fall from grace and the loss of her beloved Cosmos had left deep scars. She sought refuge in the one place she believed could offer her redemption: the convent in Heraklion. At seventeen she entered the convent, taking the name Sister Thea, a symbol of her new life dedicated to God.

The convent, with its high stone walls and serene gardens, was a world apart from the turmoil Theodora had known. She immersed herself in prayer, work, and study. She found peace in the simplicity and predictability of convent life, yet the memories of her past never fully left her. She quickly became known for her dedication and compassion. Her experiences had given her a deep understanding of suffering, which she used to comfort others. Sister Thea was particularly drawn to the sick and the marginalized, seeing in them reflections of her own pain and loss. She became involved in the convent's outreach programs, visiting the poor and the sick in the nearby villages.

The arrival of Lady Isabella de Lacy at the convent brought a new chapter into Thea's life. Isabella, with her own heavy burdens found a kindred spirit in Thea. She saw the same lost look in Isabella's eyes that she had once seen in her own reflection. She reached out to Isabella, offering the comfort and understanding that had once been given to her. The two women formed a close bond, sharing their stories and finding strength in each other's presence. Thea's wisdom and compassion helped Isabella navigate the complexities of her new life, while Isabella's resilience inspired Thea to continue her own journey of healing and redemption.

***

As the sun began to rise over the tranquil hills of the Cretan countryside, Isabella found herself awakening to the soft chants of the morning prayers echoing through the convent walls. With a gentle sigh, she rose from her simple cot and began her morning routine, preparing herself for the day ahead. After the morning devotions and a frugal breakfast shared with the other sisters, Isabella made her way to the courtyard with Sister Thea. Together the embarked on their weekly visit to a nearby village, a journey that offered a brief respite from the solitude of convent life.

As they walked along the dusty path that led to the village, Isabella couldn't help but marvel at the natural beauty that surrounded them. The rugged landscape was alive with the vibrant colours of wildflowers, and the air was filled with the sweet scent of blooming jasmine. Such a contrast to the green fields and hills of her home in England.

Upon reaching the village, Isabella and Sister Thea were greeted warmly by the local villagers, who welcomed them with open arms. They made their way through the crowded streets, stopping to admire the colourful displays of fresh produce and handcrafted goods. They exchanged pleasantries with the villagers, offering words of encouragement and blessings to those they encountered. As they made their way back to the convent, their baskets filled with provisions for the week ahead, Isabella felt a sense of gratitude wash over her. Despite the challenges she faced, she found solace in the simple joys of community and companionship, and she felt hopeful that when her child was born, she would find a way to raise it away from the convent.

As the days turned into weeks, the relationship between Isabella and Sister Thea deepened. They would spend evenings together. Sister Thea was teaching her the Greek language and more about the history and cuisine of Greece. Isabella shared stories of her home, her voice soft but steady, weaving tales of the English countryside, of days filled with laughter and nights filled with love and dreams. In return, Thea spoke of her own journey, of the peace she had found within the convent walls, and of her belief that every soul was guided by a hand unseen.

One afternoon, as they sat beneath the shade of an old olive tree, Thea finally broached the subject of Isabella's pregnancy.

"You are carrying a new life, a precious gift," she said gently, her hand resting briefly over Isabella's own. "The child will need a home, a family to provide what we cannot here." Isabella's eyes filled with tears, her fears for her unborn child surfacing despite her newfound composure.

"I know," she whispered, "and it breaks my heart to leave here and you. But I have no choice, I must be with my child and provide for them somehow." Thea nodded, her expression one of compassionate resolve.

"I understand, my dear Isabella. But while it is a difficult path, it is also one of great love. To choose what is best for a child is the first act of motherhood."

Isabella looked at Sister Thea. "I will never give my child away, Thea, there has to be another answer, which I'm sure I will find, somehow."

In the weeks that followed Sister Thea became Isabella's confidante, a source of strength as the day of the birth drew near. Their friendship, forged in the shared simplicity of convent life and deepened through mutual respect and understanding became a pillar upon which Isabella could lean. As Isabella's time at the convent progressed, her belly swelling with the promise of a new life, she found herself grappling with the impending decision of her life and her child. Through it all her friend, Thea stood by her, a beacon of support, reminding her of the strength she possessed, and of the hope that lay in the possibility of a future where love, in all its forms, could find a way.

As Isabella settled into life within the convent walls, she found solace in the simple rhythms of daily life. Amidst the routine of prayers and chores, she discovered a hidden talent that lay dormant within her: her voice. It was during one quiet evening, as the sisters gathered for vespers in the chapel, that Isabella's voice first emerged. As the hymns rose and fell in gentle cadence, she found herself drawn to the music, her heart swelling with a longing she couldn't quite articulate. Isabella tentatively joined her voice with the others, her voice rising above the chorus like a delicate lark in flight. At first, her voice faltered, uncertain and untested, but with each passing note, she gained confidence, her melodies weaving effortlessly into the tapestry of sound that enveloped the chapel. The other sisters turned to look at her, their faces alight with surprise and wonder and from that day forward she allowed her voice to become a beacon of hope and light in a world fraught with darkness.

The months at the convent had passed with the relentless pace of the changing seasons. Each day was a test of Isabella's resilience and the inevitable approach of her due date. Thea had helped prepare her for childbirth, sharing whispered words of wisdom and comfort as the day drew near.

***

The labour began on a stormy night, with the winds of the Aegean howling like ancient spirits across the Cretan landscape. The convent, usually a beacon of tranquillity, echoed with the tempest's fury, as if nature itself were voicing the pain and turmoil that wracked Isabella's body. In the small, austere room that had become her sanctuary, Isabella clung to Thea's hand, her grip tight and desperate. The midwife who was from the village, a kindly woman of gentle hands and soothing words, guided her through the contractions, her voice a steady presence in the chaotic symphony of the storm. As the hours slipped by, marked by the rhythm of the rain against the windows, Isabella's labour intensified. Each contraction was a wave, overwhelming and all-consuming, crashing over her with inexorable force. Through it all, Isabella felt a profound loneliness, as though she were both connected to the life emerging from within her and irrevocably isolated by the act of its coming.

Finally, with a cry that mingled despair with relief, Isabella brought her son into the world. He was small, his cries feeble yet fierce, a sound that was the sweetest melody and the most wonderful sound she had ever heard. Sister Agnes who had come to assist, took the newborn in her arms, wrapping him in a clean white swaddle.

"A beautiful boy, "she announced, her eyes meeting Isabella's, were filled with an unknown sorrow.

Isabella reached out, her hands trembling, her heart splintering within her chest.

"Please, let me hold him," she begged her voice a whisper torn from the depths of her soul. Gently Sister Agnes placed the infant in Isabella's arms, and for a moment, the storm outside ceased to exist. There was only Isabella and her son, their breaths mingling, their warmth shared. She traced her finger along his delicate cheek, memorised his face, and whispered promises of love and hope that seemed as fragile as it was fierce.

"I love you, my darling. You are my heart, my soul. I shall call you Dimitri," she spoke to him, each word a vow, each breath a wish. "Remember Dimitri, that even if I am not by your side, my love will always find you."

The midwives, experienced and compassionate attended to her needs with gentle hands and reassuring words. But as they worked to clean the newborn and tend to Isabella's discomfort, their trained eyes noticed something amiss. In the soft glow of candlelight, the midwives observed faint lesions on Isabella's skin, small marks that seemed out of place amid such a momentous occasion. Concerned for both mother and child, they exchanged worried glances before quietly finishing their duties.

In the soft glow of the morning light filtering through the small window of her chamber, Isabella cradled her newborn son in her arms, his tiny form nestled against her chest as she marvelled at the miracle of his existence. With each gentle breath he took, she felt her heart swell with a love so pure and profound it transcended the bounds of human understanding. As she traced the delicate contours of his tiny features with trembling fingers, a sense of wonder washed over her, filling her soul with a radiant warmth that banished the shadows of doubt and fear. In that moment there was only the two of them, mother, and child, bound together by an unbreakable bond forged in the crucible of love. She felt James with her and for the first time since the tragedy that had befallen her, she felt peace.

Days slipped by unnoticed as Isabella revelled in the simple joy of motherhood, her heart overflowing with a sense of gratitude and awe. She whispered words of love and tenderness to her son, her voice a soothing melody that calmed his restless cries. She sang lullabies to him and dreamt of a future with him.

***

Isabella woke with a start, her heart pounding in her chest. She blinked against the morning light filtering through the thin curtains, momentarily disorientated. The room felt empty, too quiet. Her eyes darted to the small cradle beside her bed, expecting to see the familiar sight of her sleeping baby. But the cradle was empty. A wave of panic surged through her. She threw off the covers and stumbled out of bed, her legs weak and unsteady.

"Dimitri?" she called out, her voice cracking. She searched the room frantically, opening the wardrobe, and checking under the bed as if he could be hiding somewhere. But deep down she knew the truth.

The door creaked open, and Sister Agnes stepped into the room, her face etched with sorrow. She had a folded letter in her hands, her eyes avoiding Isabella's desperate gaze.

"Where is he?" Isabella demanded, her voice rising in hysteria. "Where is my son?"

Sister Agnes approached her slowly, extending the letter.

"Isabella, please read this," she said gently, her voice trembling. Isabella snatched the letter from her hands, her fingers shaking as she unfolded the paper. She recognised her father's handwriting immediately, the familiar script that once brought comfort now filling her with dread. She began to read, each word cutting deeper than the last.

Milburn Manor
Lancashire England

My Dearest Isabella,

It is with a heavy heart that I write to you today, knowing the profound joy you must be experiencing at the birth of your son. However, it is my duty as your father to inform you of the decision that has been made, one that weighs heavily upon my conscience.

As you are aware, the circumstances surrounding your child's birth are far from the standards our family upholds. To ensure the preservation of our name and reputation, your son has been placed with an adoptive family. He will be cared for and loved, but he will never know the heritage of Milburn Manor, nor will he have any claim upon it. This decision, though painful is necessary for the protection of our lineage.

Although I am still angry with you, your mother is distraught, and you are still our beloved daughter. Should you wish to return to Milburn Manor, you will be welcomed back under the condition that you live in seclusion. This arrangement is imperative to maintain the dignity of our family. The world must never know the truth of your situation or the terrible events of that fateful night. However, if you choose to remain in Greece, understand that you will be entirely alone, as either way the child you have brought into this world will grow up without you.

This decision was not made lightly and brings me no joy. My love for you remains steadfast, even as I uphold the duties that come with our family name. I implore you to consider your options carefully and to act by what is best for your future, and the future of our family.

Sir Rafe de Lacy.

Isabella's vision blurred with tears. She crumpled the letter in her fist and sank to her knees, a guttural sob tearing from her throat.

"No!" she screamed, her voice echoing through the small room. "No, he can't be gone! My baby, my Dimitri!" Sister Agnes knelt beside her, wrapping her arms around Isabella's shaking shoulders.

"I'm so sorry, Isabella," she whispered, tears streaming down her cheeks. "I'm so, so sorry."

Isabella pushed her away, rising to her feet with a surge of raw, furious energy. "You knew," she accused, her voice a venomous hiss. "You knew and you did nothing!"

Sister Agnes shook her head, her grief evident. "I wanted to tell you, but it was not my place. I am bound by my vows, by my duty to your father."

"To my father?" Isabella spat, her voice dripping with contempt. "He has taken everything from me. My home, my dignity, my true love and now my child. How could he do this?" She stumbled towards the door, driven by a primal need to find her son, to hold him in her arms once more.

"I have to find him," she muttered to herself, half-mad with grief. "I have to bring him back." Sister Agnes reached out, her voice pleading.

"Isabella, please, there's nothing you can do. The family has taken him away. You won't be able to find him."

Isabella turned to face her, her eyes wild and desperate. "Then what is left for me?" she cried. "What is left of my life without my child?"

The weight of her father's betrayal settled on her shoulders, crushing her spirit. She sank to the floor once more, her body wracked with sobs. Sister Agnes knelt beside her again, this time just holding her, letting her grieve. Hours passed, or maybe minutes. Time had lost all meaning. Isabella's cries eventually quieted, replaced by a hollow emptiness. She stared at the crumpled letter, the words a cruel reminder of her loss. Her heart shattered, and Isabella knew she had a choice to make. Return to England and live a life of seclusion, or stay in Greece, alone but free. She thought of Dimitri, of the life he would have without her, and the tears flowed anew.

"I will stay," she whispered to herself. "I will stay here, and I will find a way to live, for him."

She surrendered to the darkness that threatened to consume her, her spirit broken and her soul adrift on an ocean of sorrow. For in that moment, she knew that she had lost not only her son but a piece of her own heart as well.

Left in the quiet of her room surrounded by memories of her baby, Isabella wept. She wept for her son, for James, for herself, for the life they would not share. In the pain, in the solitude, Isabella's love for Dimitri remained unbroken, unwavering, it was a beacon that would endure the passing of seasons, the silence of the halls, and the ache of her empty arms. But she made a vow that she would never leave Greece if she knew Dimitri was here and she would never return to England without him.

Chapter Thirty-Five

**Milburn Manor
Lancashire 1906**

Milburn Manor was shrouded in a heavy silence, a stark contrast to the vibrant life it once knew. The events that had transpired left a profound impact on Isabella's parents Lord Rafe de Lacy and Lady Eleanor de Lacy. Rafe had always been a man of stern demeanour, but the murder of James Wycliffe and the subsequent scandal surrounding his daughter broke something deep within him. The guilt of his actions, coupled with the fear of exposure, gnawed at his conscience daily. The decision to send Isabella away and ensure her child was adopted was a means to protect the family's reputation, but it came at a great personal cost.

Lady Eleanor, once the epitome of grace and composure, found herself engulfed in a deep melancholy. The departure of Isabella, her daughter, left an irreplaceable void. The whispers among the servants, the dark rumours, and the heavy burden of their secrets took a toll on her health. One frosty winter evening, Eleanor sat by the fireplace in the drawing room, staring into the flickering flames. The weight of her sorrow was almost tangible, and tears streamed down her face as she clutched a faded photograph of Isabella. Rafe, her husband entered the room, his face etched with lines of worry and regret.

"Eleanor," he began softly, his voice betraying the torment he felt, "I did what I thought was best for the family."

"But was it best for Isabella?" Eleanor whispered. "We sent her away when she needed us the most. We took her child from her." Rafe sighed deeply, sinking into a chair opposite his wife.

"I know, but what choice did we have? The scandal…it would have ruined us." Eleanor's eyes flashed with a rare fire. "We sacrificed our daughter for our pride, Rafe. Our family is torn apart."

In the months that followed, the tension between Rafe and Eleanor grew. The once close-knit couple found themselves estranged, each lost in their grief and guilt. Rafe threw himself into his work and his estate, trying to distract himself from the relentless whispers of his conscience. Eleanor's health continued to decline, and she spent more and more time confined to her room, her spirit broken. One morning she was staring at the stack of letters that had just been brought to her. Among the letters, one caught her eye, a letter from Greece, however it was addressed to Miss Florence Wilson. Curiosity piqued, Eleanor summoned Rogers, the Butler.

"Who is Florence Wilson?"

Rogers shifted uncomfortably. "She's the scullery maid, Lady Eleanor. She used to be Lady Isabella's maid but after……the incident, Sir Rafe demoted her to the kitchen." Eleanor's heart tightened. She had spent so much time alone since Isabella had left that she hadn't known the full extent of what had transpired.

"Bring Florence to me," Eleanor instructed firmly.

A few moments later, Florence entered the bedroom, her hands wringing the apron she wore. She looked worn and tired, but there was a spark of surprise and curiosity in her eyes.

> "You wanted to see me, Lady Eleanor?" Florence asked, her voice hesitant. "Yes, I understand you were once Isabella's maid. I had no idea you were demoted, and now working in the kitchen." Eleanor looked at her

with sympathy.

Florence nodded, "Yes Lady Eleanor. After Lady Isabella left and everything that had happened, Sir Rafe sent me to the kitchen."

"I see, "Eleanor nodded, holding up a letter. "This arrived for you today. It's from Greece." Florence's eyes widened and she took the letter with trembling hands. Tears welled up in Florence's eyes as she saw the familiar handwriting and knew it was another letter from Isabella. Eleanor looked at Florence.

"So, you two have been corresponding?" she asked. Florence nodded. "Yes, my Lady, her letters mean so much to me and I hope that mine do to her too. She likes to hear about home and you, of course." Florence whispered with tears streaming down her face.

Eleanor reached out and took Florence's hand. "I'm so sorry Florence, I hadn't realised you were so close. This must have been incredibly difficult for you. I had no idea. However, I want to make things right. I would like you to become my personal lady's maid. Having you close will make me feel connected to Isabella and make your life more comfortable, which is what you deserve."

Florence looked stunned. "Me, Lady Eleanor? But I'm just a scullery maid now..." Eleanor shook her head.

"You are much more than that Florence. You are Isabella's confidante and friend. I trust you and I need someone like you by my side." Later that day, after Florence had moved her belongings into new quarters upstairs, near Lady Eleanor, she read Isabella's latest letter which from the date had taken a couple of months to reach Milburn Manor and Florence. Isabella spoke of her plans to return to Milburn Manor with her baby, hoping for her father's forgiveness and the warmth of home. Florence's heart ached for Isabella, but she couldn't ignore the nagging worry about what would happen if Isabella's hopes were dashed. She knew she had to speak with Lady Eleanor.

Florence stood quietly in Lady Eleanor's dressing room, and as she styled her hair she began, her voice shaky.

"My lady, I have read the latest letter from Isabella, and I need to tell you about it." Eleanor's face softened with concern.

"What is it, Florence?" Florence took a deep breath

"She hopes to return with the baby. She believes that if she comes back, she may be forgiven."

Eleanor's eyes filled with tears as she listened. If only they had received this letter earlier. Would Rafe have forgiven her darling daughter? She knew the painful truth about her grandchild, a truth that Florence was unaware of. Gathering her composure, Eleanor took Florence's hands in hers.

"Florence," Eleanor began, her voice trembling. "There is something you must know. Isabella's baby…. Lord de Lacy arranged for the child to be adopted. The baby was a boy, and he will never be allowed to return to Milburn Manor." Florence gasped, her eyes wide with shock.

"But why? How could he do such a thing? Eleanor's tears began to flow freely.

"He told Isabella that she could return, but only without her child. He wanted to ensure that the baby would never have a claim to the estate and that no one would know of the scandal of a baby born out of wedlock."

Florence was silent, the weight of the revelation pressing down on her. Eleanor wiped her tears, trying to compose herself.

"We must hope Isabella will come home," she said her voice trembling. "She needs to know she isn't alone." Florence nodded, her heart heavy with the latest revelations as she knew how heartbroken Isabella would be. She could see Eleanor's pain and she decided to focus on supporting her lady in any way she could.

Florence left the room, her mind racing. She prayed that Isabella would find the strength to endure this pain and hoped that one day, they would all be reunited. She was determined to help Isabella find her way back to Milburn Manor.

Back in the dressing room, Eleanor sat alone, staring into the distance. Her heart ached with the weight of their betrayal and the pain it must have caused Isabella. She vowed to herself that she would do everything in her power to make amends, to bring Isabella home, and to support her in any way possible, and as the days turned to weeks, Eleanor and Florence clung to the hope that Isabella would return.

Chapter Thirty-Six

Isabella
Greece 1907

The days following the removal of her son were marked not by the joy of new motherhood, but by an all-consuming void that Isabella felt within her heart. The convent, with its stoic serenity and the rhythmic prayers that echoed through its stone corridors, seemed to amplify the silence left in the wake of her child's absence. Isabella, once vibrant and full of purpose, now felt herself adrift, caught in the tides of insurmountable grief. Sister Thea had managed to find out that Dimitri had been adopted by a family in Elounda who were desperate for a baby and had been delighted with the turn of events, but even though Isabella was heartened by the news, nothing could take away the pain of the separation.

As the weeks slipped by, her physical health began to mirror the desolation that plagued her spirit. She was listless, often found gazing out of her small window overlooking the convent's gardens, her eyes vacant and her thoughts miles away. The other sisters, including Sister Thea, watched over her with worried whispers, their concern growing with each passing day.

Sister Agnes, ever the pragmatic soul, decided it was time to intervene when Isabella missed morning prayers for the third consecutive day. She had also missed several mealtimes and was spending most of her days alone in her room.

"Isabella," Sister Agnes began softly after finding her in her room one morning, "I have called for the doctor to visit. You have not been yourself, and we must ensure your well-being." Isabella's response was a faint nod, the gesture listless and devoid of the strength that once defined her.

When the doctor arrived, a middle-aged man with a kind face and a gentle manner, Isabella submitted to his examination with a detached compliance. As he inspected her, his brow furrowed in concern at the patches of skin that showed unusual pigmentation and texture changes, symptoms that had gone unnoticed under the long sleeves and high collars Isabella wore. After what seemed an eternity the doctor came out of Isabella's room where Sister Agnes had been patiently waiting, her face pale and her eyes fixed on the floor as if in prayer.

"I need a word Sister. Somewhere private." He said, his tone grave. Sister Agnes nodded and showed the doctor the way to her office. Behind the closed door, the doctor spoke in hushed tones, his expression filled with the heavy burden of his findings. Sister Agnes listened, her face gradually draining of colour as the truth unfolded before her eyes. She clutched her rosary beads tightly, her fingers trembling, her eyes filled with a mix of fear and sorrow. After the doctor left, Sister Agnes stood there for a moment, trying to steady herself, but the weight of what she had just heard seemed almost too much to bear.

***

Sister Agnes sat across from Isabella in the small room, her gentle eyes filled with compassion and understanding. She clasped Isabella's trembling hands in her own, offering a reassuring smile before beginning to speak.

"Isabella," she began softly, her voice gentle yet firm. "We need to talk." Isabella looked up, her eyes filled with a mixture of despair and defiance.

"What more is there to say?" she asked bitterly. "My child has been taken from me, my one true love dead, and my family has cast me aside. What else can you possibly tell me." Sister Agnes took a deep breath, steeling herself for the difficult conversation ahead. She sat down beside Isabella.

"There is something else, Isabella. Something especially important. I have been waiting for the right moment to tell you, but I fear there is no right moment for such news."

Isabella's eyes narrowed, a sense of foreboding creeping into her heart. "What is it?" she demanded, her voice trembling. "What more can you take from me?" Sister Agnes reached out and placed her hand near Isabella's hand, her presence warm and reassuring.

"It's about your health, Isabella," she said gently. "The doctor has expressed some…concerns."

"Concerns?" Isabella repeated, her mind racing. "What do you mean?" Sister Agnes sighed, her eyes filled with compassion.

"You have been showing symptoms, Isabella. Symptoms that we have come to recognise in others who suffer from a serious illness." Isabella's heart began to pound, fear clawing at her chest.

"What illness?" she whispered.

"Leprosy" Sister Agnes said softly, the word hanging heavily in the air. "The doctor has confirmed that you have leprosy, Isabella." The room seemed to spin around her, the walls closing in. Isabella felt a wave of nausea wash over her, her mind struggling to process the information.

"Leprosy?" she repeated her voice shaking. "But how? How could this happen?" Sister Agnes, near to tears, looked at Isabella.

"Leprosy is a disease that can affect anyone, Isabella. It is not a punishment or a curse. It is simply an illness, one that we do not yet fully understand."

Isabella's eyes filled with tears, her mind reeling. "What will happen to me?" she asked, her voice breaking. "Does my baby have this illness? Have I passed it to him?" Her voice was barely audible.

"Leprosy is contagious, yes," Sister Agnes replied. "However, your son has been examined and is showing no signs of the disease, please be rest assured." Isabella looked Sister Agnes in the eyes.

"What will become of me?" Sister Agnes took a deep breath, her expression grim.

"There is a place, Isabella. An island called Spinalonga, where those with leprosy are sent to live. It is a place of isolation, but it is also a place of community. There, you will be cared for and protected. You will not be alone." Isabella's heart sank, the reality of her situation crashing down on her.

"An island?" she whispered, her voice filled with dread. "I will be sent away, to live among the sick and dying?" Sister Agnes nodded slowly, her eyes filled with sorrow.

"It will not be an easy life, but it is a life. And there is always hope. On Spinalonga you will find others who understand what you are going through. You will find a new community, a new family."

Isabella's tears flowed freely, her body trembling with fear and grief. "I don't want to go." She cried, her voice filled with desperation. "I don't want to be sent away." Sister Agnes wrapped her arms around Isabella, holding her close. "I know dear child," she whispered. "I know. But we must face this together. We must find the strength to carry on, no matter how difficult the journey." Isabella clung to Sister Agnes, her sobs wracking her body. She felt the weight of her father's betrayal, the loss of her child, the loss of James, and now the terror of her illness.

As the two women sat together in the dimly lit room, Isabella's tears began to subside, replaced by a quiet determination. She would face this new challenge with courage and grace. She would find a way to endure, survive, and perhaps even thrive on the island of Spinalonga. For herself and her son.

***

The dawn was breaking, its first light washing over Crete with a tender glow that belied the heavy hearts of those at the convent. The air was thick with a mournful silence as Sister Thea accompanied Isabella on the carriage ride to Elounda. Each turn of the wheels over the rugged path felt like a slow rending of the ties that bound Isabella to her past life. Isabella sat cloaked in her heavy shawl, her hands clasped tightly in her lap, staring into the distance with a vacant gaze. The landscape rolled by, a blur of olive groves and vineyards, ancient and indifferent. Sister Thea watched her closely, the lines of worry etched deeply into her face.

"Isabella," Sister Thea finally said, her voice barely above a whisper, as if afraid to break the fragile peace, "Spinalonga has its own kind of mercy. The isolation is daunting, yes, but there, you will not suffer the scorn of the ignorant. You will live among those who understand, who fight the same battles." Isabella's eyes met Sister Thea's, a flash of raw, silent fear passing between them.

"Will I ever feel the sun as warmly, Thea? Will it reach me there, through the walls of my exile?" her voice cracked, laden with despair too heavy to bear. "I hope so, Isabella, I truly do," Thea replied with tears in her eyes. Isabella turned to Thea,

"Please, do one thing for me. Please take this letter I have written. It's for my son, for Dimitri. It explains everything. I may never return from this island and never see my son, so please make sure he gets it." Sister Thea took Isabella's hand, holding it between her own.

"I will make sure your son gets this letter; I promise." She vowed.

The little port of Elounda was bustling with the morning's activities as fishermen prepared their boats and merchants opened their stalls. The salt air carried the sounds of the sea, the cries of the gulls mingling with the shouts of men. Isabella felt every gaze upon her as she alighted from the carriage, the weight of each look adding to the burden she already bore. A young couple caught her eye. They stood a little apart from the crowd, their attention focused on the baby in the pram before them. The woman, with her soft features and kind eyes, cooed gently to the infant, while the man looked on with a mixture of pride and tenderness. Isabella felt waves of sorrow and envy. That should have been her moment of joy, her chance to cherish and nurture her child. Instead, her baby had been taken from her, and now she was being sent away, banished to an island of suffering and isolation.

The couple glanced at her, their eyes filled with pity as they realised, she was about to board the boat to Spinalonga. Their faces radiated happiness as they gazed adoringly at the new baby they had recently adopted. They were strangers to each other, their paths crossing in a fleeting moment of shared existence, each unaware of the other's profound significance.

Isabella and Thea made their way to the dock where a small boat bobbed gently in the water, its destination clear: Spinalonga. Sister Thea stood beside Isabella, her eyes brimming with unshed tears. The bond they had formed was strong, one forged in shared prayers, whispered confidences, and mutual support.

"I can't believe this is happening," Isabella whispered, her voice trembling. "I feel like I'm walking into a nightmare." Thea placed a comforting hand on Isabella's shoulder.

"I know. This is a difficult journey, but you are stronger than you realise. Spinalonga may be a place of isolation, but hopefully, it is also a place where you can find peace and purpose." Isabella turned to face Thea, her eyes searching her friend's face for reassurance.

"What if I never see you again?" she asked. Thea's grip on Isabella's shoulder tightened. "We will see each other again, Isabella. In this life or the next, our spirits are bound by a connection that distance and time cannot sever." Isabella nodded, drawing strength from Thea's words.

"I don't know how to thank you for everything you have done for me. You've been my anchor, my guide." Tears finally spilled over Thea's cheeks.

"And you have been my light, Isabella. Your courage, and your resilience, have inspired me every day.

"Remember, even on Spinalonga, you are never truly alone. You carry our prayers and love with you."

Isabella started to weep. "I don't want to go, please Thea please.." The sight of Isabella's despair tore at Sister Thea's soul, but there was no other choice. She hugged Isabella tightly, tears streaming down her face.

"I would do anything to spare you this Isabella. I would take your place if I could. But this is not a punishment-it's a chance to survive. To find hope in the darkest of places."

The boatman, a grizzled old man with sympathetic eyes, helped Isabella aboard. As the boat pulled away from the shore, Isabella stood at the stern, watching Elounda and Sister Thea recede into the distance, the figure of her friend growing smaller and smaller, the distance between them expanding with each passing second.

Isabella turned her gaze forward. The island loomed in the distance, its imposing walls cutting a stark silhouette against the brightening sky. It was no longer just a name or fate she had to accept. It was real, it was near, and it was waiting.

Chapter Thirty-Seven
Amelia
Greece

Dear Florence,

It is with a sorrowful heart and a reluctant hand that I write this letter, informing you of the grievous circumstances that have befallen our dear sister Isabella. She has recently been diagnosed with leprosy which has necessitated her removal from our community to the island of Spinalonga, as per the regulations of health and isolation mandated for such afflictions.

Isabella's condition has deteriorated quite swiftly, a testament to the cruel nature of her illness, which allowed us little time to prepare for the immediate and necessary actions that followed. Given the stigma and the requisite seclusion associated with leprosy, Isabella was taken to Spinalonga, an isle that now serves as her place of exile, where hopefully she can receive the care and treatment this disease demands. In her final hours at the convent, Isabella was enveloped in a palpable shroud of solitude, yet she bore her fate with grace and fortitude that we have all come to admire. She requested that I write to you, hoping to offer you solace in the knowledge that she thinks of you fondly and with affection, a connection undimmed by distance or circumstance.

Furthermore, she implored that a similar letter be sent to her son's adoptive family, to explain her absence and to reassure them of her enduring love and prayers for his wellbeing and happiness. Her deepest regret, as you are aware, was the involuntary severance of this maternal bond, forced upon her by her father and now this unexpected and cruel disease.

Please know, Florence, that Isabella's thoughts often lingered on the memories of brighter days, and on the hope that her son would grow to know of her love for him. She spoke of her desires for his future with a mother's love that knows no bounds, her spirit indomitable even as her body faltered.

Though Isabella is now beyond the reach of our care and correspondence, her legacy of courage and love endures. She departed from us in body but never in spirit and we feel her absence profoundly within the walls of our convent.

With deepest sympathies and heartfelt prayers.

Sister Agnes

Amelia held the letter from Sister Agnes with trembling hands. Nikos, sitting beside her, had translated the solemn words, the harsh realities faced by Isabella in those dark days. The letter, dated and faded, seemed to weigh heavily in her hands. The words echoed in her mind, each sentence unveiling the grim truth of Isabella's fate: her diagnosis with leprosy, her subsequent isolation, and her relocation to Spinalonga. It was a story of heartbreak and resilience, of a woman caught in the merciless grip of her era's social and medical stigmas. Amelia felt a sharp pang in her chest as she absorbed the reality of Isabella's suffering. Her eyes blurred with tears, not just for the pain and loneliness Isabella must have endured, but also for the stark reminder of how cruelly the diseased were ostracized, even by those they loved.

"Isabella was sent away, alone to die. That's why her spirit at Milburn Manor was so disfigured and in pain. Now I can understand her sorrow and the desperation she must have felt. No wonder she is not at rest." Amelia's words were caught in her throat.

Nikos reached out, placing a comforting hand over hers.

"She was loved Amelia," he said gently. "This letter is full of pain but also deep care and respect. Sister Agnes wrote it with such affection." Amelia nodded, wiping her tears with the back of her hand.

"It's just so unfair," she managed to say. "To be ripped away from your child and then sent to an island because of an illness… it's barbaric."

They sat in silence for a few moments. "She said she held onto hope, for her son, for a better future, Amelia continued. "She wanted her son to know of her love, despite everything. It's beautiful and tragic. We need to find her son's family and visit the convent. We must do something to make sure she can finally rest in peace."

They decided that Nikos would visit the convent in Heraklion to see if he could confirm any details of Isabella's stay there and her subsequent banishment to Spinalonga, but as it was such a long time ago, neither knew whether the records would go back that far but Nikos felt it was worth trying. Amelia was going to research online using her skills and knowledge and had also decided to go to the bookshop she had first seen in Elounda.

She knew the wi-fi was good in there and she also thought that there might be books on Spinalonga that could help with their research, and together they would search the public and church records for birth and adoption records around the time that Isabella's son was born, if the convent wasn't able to divulge that information.

Feeling emotionally drained, Nikos suggested that, as the taverna was closed that day, why didn't they all go down to Elounda and spend the day on the beach and then have dinner before heading home? Alexandros was more than happy with that idea and with Nina in the back of the car too, they all set off down the long mountain road into the bustling village of Elounda.

***

The soft hum of the Mediterranean evening filled the air as Nikos, Amelia, Alexandros, and Nina, the ever-faithful dog by his side, made their way into the heart of Elounda. The small seaside village with its quaint charm and bustling energy was the perfect setting for an evening out. Elounda's main square around the harbour was alive with the sounds of laughter, conversation, and the clinking of glasses. Tavernas lined the square, their tables spilling out onto the street, lit by strings of lights that twinkled like the stars above. The aroma of grilled seafood and fresh herbs wafted through the air, a tantalizing invitation to indulge in the local cuisine. Nikos led them to his favourite spot, a family-run taverna, The Moonspinners, which was a lovely restaurant that was right on the sea. The lights under the water meant that they could eat their meals whilst watching the fish swim in the water, something that Alexandros and Nina found mesmerising.

They started with a selection of meze: tzatziki, taramasalata, freshly baked bread, olives, and saganaki, that sizzled delightfully on a hot plate. As they waited for their main dishes, grilled octopus for Nikos, calamari for Alexandros, and moussaka for Amelia, Amelia took in the scene around her. Families and friends gathered, enjoying the food and the ambiance, a stark contrast to the solitary sadness of Spinalonga which she could see from the restaurant.

The waiter had just set down their main courses when Nikos steered the conversation towards the future, specifically the new addition to their family. "So, Amelia," Nikos began, a smile playing at the corners of his lips as he took a sip of his chilled white wine, "Have you thought about names yet? For the baby, I mean." Amelia who had been sharing a tender morsel of calamari with Alexandros, paused, and looked up, her face glowing.

"I have been thinking about it yes," she replied her hand subconsciously resting on her belly. "If it's a girl, obviously Isabella? And if it's a boy, I haven't thought yet I'll need your help," she laughed.

Nikos nodded approvingly, "Isabella is a beautiful name and choice. It's a way to honour her memory too." Alexandros who had been quietly listening, chimed in, "Can I help pick a nickname for the baby?" his eyes were earnest, eager to be involved in the life of his soon-to-be sibling. He was picking up a few words in English and Nikos was constantly translating and trying to teach Amelia Greek at the same time.

"Of course," Amelia laughed, ruffling his hair affectionately. "What do you think about Bella if it's a girl for a nickname?

"Bella," Alexandros repeated, testing the name. "I like it. Bella and I can play soccer together when she's older. I'll teach her." As they all laughed the conversation shifted towards preparations for the baby, from decorating the nursery to choosing the right hospital for the delivery. Nikos mentioned how the community in their small village was eagerly anticipating the birth, offering clothes, cribs, and countless words of advice.

"It's amazing, "Amelia mused, "how much love and support we've received. Back home in England, communities aren't always so involved. Here it feels like the entire village is excited."

"It's the Cretan way, "Nikos explained. "Children are considered a blessing, a new life that renews our own. Everyone will want to play a part in his or her upbringing. As they talked Nina lay quietly at their feet, occasionally lifting her head to nudge Amelia's hand for attention.

As the meal came to an end, they lingered at the table savouring the last bits of their dessert, honey drizzled baklava, and the last moments of the evening together. Alexandros was getting sleepy, and Nikos carried him as they got up to leave. Walking back through the square, Amelia felt a profound connection to the place and its people. Amelia was beginning to feel more at home in this beautiful, rugged land that was now her own.

***

The convent was nestled on the outskirts of the bustling city of Heraklion, its stone walls, weathered by time exuded a sense of timelessness and tranquillity. It was surrounded by lush gardens, meticulously maintained by the nuns, where vibrant flowers and aromatic herbs created a fragrant, peaceful atmosphere. As Nikos approached the entrance, he was greeted by a tall wrought-iron gate, intricately designed with floral patterns and religious symbols. The gate creaked open to reveal a cobblestone path leading to the main building. The path was lined with olive trees and bougainvillea, their branches providing a canopy of shade and colour. The main building of the convent was a large three-story structure with a red-tiled roof and whitewashed walls. Tall arched windows allowed sunlight to stream into the interior, creating a warm and inviting ambience. The entrance was adorned with a simple yet elegant wooden door, above which hung a small, weathered icon of the Virgin Mary.

Inside, the convent was a haven of calm. The air was filled with the faint scent of incense and beeswax candles. The floors were made of polished stone, worn smooth by centuries of footsteps. Nikos was led to the convent's archives, located in a quiet wing of the building. He had already explained his mission, that he was hoping to uncover any records of Isabella de Lacy, a former resident who had tragically been sent to Spinalonga due to her leprosy diagnosis. Sister Anastasia led him to a small dimly lit room filled with rows of ancient ledgers and dusty documents.

Together they pored over the records, and soon, Nikos's fingers traced the lines of an entry dated back to 1907 confirming Isabella's presence at the convent, her diagnosis, and her subsequent transfer to Spinalonga. It noted her giving birth, but the details about her son were scant, only that he was adopted by a family in Elounda, shortly after his birth.

"Is there nothing more about her son?" Nikos asked a hint of desperation in his voice.

"I'm afraid not," Sister Anastasia replied softly. "Records then were sparse, and many personal details were lost or never recorded property, especially for those sent to Spinalonga."

Thanking Sister Anastasia for her help, Nikos took copies of the records, his mind heavy with the thought of Isabella's lonely and stigmatized journey, and her son's uncertain beginning in Elounda.

Just as he was making his way back towards Vrouchas, his mobile phone started ringing. He pulled over and looked at the screen. It was a Heraklion number. He answered and Sister Anastasia said breathlessly,

"I continued having a good search after you had left, and I found the birth certificate for Isabella's baby. He was named Dimitri, and his mother and father are listed as Isabella de Lacy and James Wycliffe. Attached was a note to say that the baby was adopted by the Kostas family in Elounda in 1907 who kept the name Dimitri. I do hope that this is of some more help to you." She finished.

Nikos could not thank her enough and she promised to post a copy of the certificate and note that same day. With a much lighter heart, Nikos continued the long winding road home, grateful that he had some encouraging news for Amelia.

Chapter Thirty-Eight
Isabella
Spinalonga Greece

The boat's keel grated against the pebbles of Spinalonga's shore with a harsh, scraping sound that seemed to echo off the high, encircling walls of the island. Isabella stood at the bow, her frame silhouetted against the searing Mediterranean sun which was beginning to dip towards the horizon casting long shadows and turning the sea a burnt orange.

The fisherman who had brought her here handed Isabella a small satchel, her only possessions now.

"God be with you," he muttered, his voice a low rasp as he avoided her gaze, pushing the boat back into the water with a haste that spoke of fear, or perhaps pity.

Isabella turned away from the receding boat and faced the island. Before her lay a narrow rocky path that disappeared into a dark, gaping tunnel that looked as if it had been carved straight out of the cliff face. With a deep steadying breath, she stepped forward, her shoes crunching on the gravel, the sound unnaturally loud in the oppressive silence of the island. As she entered the tunnel, the light dimmed, and the temperature dropped sharply. The air was damp and heavy with the smell of the sea and something else, something decaying. Isabella's heart pounded in her chest, her steps quick and uncertain as her eyes struggled to adjust to the darkness. The walls of the tunnel seemed to close in around her the darkness cold and menacing.

Halfway through, a sudden movement to her right made her stop dead. A figure detached itself from the shadows, its features obscured, its form bent and twisted. A low moan filled the air, and then a rasping voice:

"Food… do you have food?"

Isabella recoiled, clutching her satchel to her chest. More figures appeared, stumbling towards her, their limbs grotesque with deformities from the ravages of leprosy. Their eyes were desperate, haunted with hunger and pain. She backed away her breath coming in sharp gasps, her back hitting the cold damp wall of the tunnel. Just as a hand reached out to grab her sleeve, a strong authoritative voice cut through the darkness.

"Enough, stand back!" A tall figure emerged from the deeper shadows of the tunnel, a priest, his robe a darker blot against the gloom, a large cross swinging from his neck. He moved forward with a lantern in one hand, its light flickering and casting eerie shadows on the walls.

"This lady has come from the convent and is now under my protection, she brings nothing with her, as you all well know from when you first arrived, leave her be." He announced firmly, stepping between Isabella and the reaching hands of the afflicted. He offered Isabella a brief, kind smile.

"Come, my child, I will take you to the village, you are safe now."

Grateful, Isabella nodded, her relief palpable as she followed the priest out of the tunnel, the displaced residents falling back, their moans still echoing in the musty air. The village was spread out before her as she stepped out of the tunnel's mouth. It was a collection of stone houses, some in disrepair, others with signs of life like laundry on lines or pots of herbs on windowsills. The streets were narrow and winding, laid out like a labyrinth, and as she walked, faces peered out at her, some curious, some indifferent. The priest led her to a small house, explaining that it would be her home.

"I hope you will find peace here, Isabella," he said as he left her at the door with her satchel. "Tomorrow, we will talk about how things are done on the island, but for tonight, rest."

The door creaked loudly as she pushed it open, revealing a single room with a straw mattress in one corner and a small table with a chipped basin on top. The walls were bare, and the floor was cold stone. Isabella's eyes filled with tears as she took in her surroundings. She thought of her room at Milburn Manor, with its plush carpets, warm fireplace, and the soft bed that had always brought her comfort. This place was a far cry from the life of privilege she had once known. She felt a profound sense of loss and isolation. The stark reality of her situation hit her with full force. She had been cast out from her family, her home, the convent, and everything she had ever known. Now she was just another leper, condemned to live out her days in this forsaken place.

As night fell, the island grew eerily quiet. Isabella lay on the hard mattress, staring at the ceiling. The sounds of the ocean waves crashing against the shore filled the silence, a constant reminder of her isolation. Sleep was elusive, her mind racing with thoughts of her past and fears for her future. Her heart ached with a grief so profound she thought it might consume her.

***

The pale streaks of dawn cast a soft glow over Spinalonga as Isabella awoke to her first full day on the island. The initial light of morning brought little warmth to her stark small house within the village, where the stone walls did little to fend off the sea's chill or the dampness that seemed to seep into her bones. Isabella rose from the thin, worn mattress that was laid on a crude wooden bed frame. Her body ached a deep, relentless ache that had become her constant companion. Her hands, already showing the telltale signs of leprosy's cruel touch, trembled as she attempted to button her dress. Each fumbled attempt was a stark reminder of the capabilities she was losing to the disease.

Stepping outside, Isabella was greeted not by the quaint charm of a Cretan Village but by the harsh, barren landscape of Spinalonga. The ground was rocky and uneven, the narrow paths were dusty, and the few patches of vegetation were hardy and sparse. The sea, visible from every point on the island, crashed against the rocky shores with a relentless ferocity that mirrored the turmoil she felt inside. The priest had called that morning to explain where the communal area was where residents gathered for meals. As Isabella made her way towards it, she felt the weight of isolation pressing down on her. Conversations bubbled around her, the rapid interchange of Greek syllables sounding musical yet incomprehensible. Her knowledge of Greek was rudimentary at best, having learned only a few phrases and words during her time at the convent. Now, those phrases seemed woefully inadequate.

Attempting to communicate her need for food, she repeated one of the few sentences she had memorized, only to be met with blank stares or nods that led to no action. The frustration of not being understood, of being so fundamentally alone even in a crowd, was overwhelming. Tears pricked her eyes, but she fought them back, stiffening her spine as she finally managed to procure a small piece of bread and a cup of water. The meal was meagre, reflecting the scarcity of resources that the colony's isolation imposed. The bread was stale, and the water had a slight brininess that made her stomach churn. As she ate, the despair that had been simmering within her began to boil over. The reality of her situation, the permanence of it, settled in with crushing clarity.

After the meal, Isabella wandered towards the edge of the island, where the ruins of the Venetian fortifications stood as a reminder of the island's history as a fortress before it became a leper colony. Sitting on a crumbling wall, she looked out over the water, the barrier that separated her from the rest of the world. The salty wind whipped her hair around her face, and the sound of the seagulls mocked her with their freedom. Tears finally escaped her eyes, tracing clean lines down her dirt-streaked face. She allowed herself to weep for everything she had lost. Her health, her home, her lover, her sense of belonging, and most painfully, her son. The baby boy she would never get to raise, whose face she knew she would never see again.

Father Yannis found her there. He approached quietly, respectful of her grief, and sat beside her on the ancient wall. They sat in silence for a long time, watching the horizon.

"You are not alone here, Isabella," he finally said, his voice gentle. "It may feel like it now, but this place, these people, they can become your family if you let them. We are all bound by our fate, but we are also bound by our resilience. You are stronger than you know." His words, kindly meant and softly spoken, were a small comfort. Isabella knew the road ahead would be fraught with more pain and loneliness, but in that moment, the priest's presence, and the solidarity he offered gave her the faintest glimmer of hope.

As night fell and the first stars appeared in the darkening sky, Isabella stood and made her way back to her new home, her heart heavy but her resolve slowly strengthening. Tomorrow would be another day, and she would face it head-on, with whatever strength she could muster.

Chapter Thirty-Nine
Amelia
Greece

The Mediterranean breeze was gentle the following day when Amelia had gone to Elounda, mainly to go to the market, but also to visit the little bookshop she had seen when she was first in Elounda. The bookshop was on a back road above the harbour going out of Elounda towards Agios Nikolas. The shop with its faded blue shutters and the soft chime of the wind bell, seemed to call out to her, promising whispers of forgotten tales and secrets within its dusty shelves. There was a sign over the door that read "Nostos Books."

Amelia pushed open the door, the old bell ringing a quaint welcome. Inside the shop was a cavern of books; rows upon rows of old leather spines and newer bindings filled the air with the musky scent of paper and time. She moved slowly among the shelves, her eyes scanning titles and authors, searching for anything related to Spinalonga.

"Looking for something in particular?" The voice came from a woman about Amelia's age, standing behind a wooden counter.

"Yes, actually," Amelia replied, approaching the counter. "I'm trying to find any records or books about Spinalonga, not fiction though, facts. My research." she hesitated, wondering how much to share, "is rather complicated."

"I'm Sophia," the woman said with a smile. "And you've come to the right place. My own fascination with Spinalonga started many years ago. I try to collect as much as I can about it. What exactly are you looking for?" Relieved by the warmth in Sophia's voice and her excellent English, Amelia pulled out a copy of the birth certificate and the letters she had obtained from the convent.

"I'm following the story of a woman who was sent to Spinalonga in 1907 from a convent in Heraklion and the son she had there who was adopted by a family here in Elounda."

Sophia's eyes lit up with interest as she took the papers Amelia offered. "Let's see what we have," she murmured spreading them on the counter. "You know, Spinalonga's history is as deep as it is somber. Many lives were shattered by the disease." As they pored over the documents, Sophia suggested looking at several old ledgers and photo albums that were believed to have belonged to a doctor who once worked on the island. They flipped through the pages, each photograph and entry a poignant reminder of the lives touched by the island's grim legacy.

"This could be useful," Sophia pointed to a faded photograph of a group of island residents. Amelia took the photograph carefully, her heart pounding as she stared at the small grainy image. In the foreground, a group of women stood near the crumbling walls of a building, their faces worn and weary. One woman in particular, caught her eye. She was tall and slender, dressed in dark clothing, her expression unreadable, yet hauntingly familiar. Amelia's breath hitched. The woman's auburn hair was pulled back, just as she'd seen it before, and there was something about her posture, the way she held herself, that sent a chill down Amelia's spine. Could it be…. Isabella? Amelia's grip tightened on the photograph, her pulse quickening. She could barely focus on Sophia who was still talking, all she could see was the face of the woman in the picture, a face that had visited her in her dreams, weeping and lost wandering the halls of Milburn Manor.

Amelia's mind raced, a mix of disbelief and recognition. It was Isabella. It had to be. But she

She couldn't tell Sophia that she knew this woman, not from stories or photographs, but from ghostly encounters in the dead of night.

"We could check the local archives for more on her. And as for the son, the church records might have something on the adoption." Sophia continued looking at Amelia."

"Thank you, Sophia. That would be great" but inside, her thoughts were in chaos.

***

The afternoon waned as they examined books and discussed possibilities. Amelia felt a growing connection with Sophia, bound by their mutual interest in the island's history.

"Why don't you come back tomorrow, around lunchtime and we could go together to the church? Eleni, the owner is coming in tomorrow. She's in her eighties but still comes in a few days and I'm sure she won't mind if I pop out for an hour or so. Her father was also a doctor and I know he had a lot to do with the treatment of Leprosy, so I'm sure she would be interested too." Sophia said. Amelia nodded, grateful for the offer.

"I'd like that very much. Thank you, Sophia."

As Amelia walked away from the quaint bookshop, she glanced back one last time. There in the large front window, hung a faded sign that seemed out of place amid the old-world charm of the shop. The sign, bold and jarring against the backdrop of ancient tomes, was in Greek, but underneath in English, it read For Sale. Eleni Manolakis, with a phone number.

Amelia was intrigued and looked forward to seeing Sophia and the owner, Eleni, tomorrow.

***

Amelia's footsteps echoed softly on the street as she approached the quaint bookshop once again. Pushing open the door, she was greeted by the familiar musty smell of books old and new, a perfume of history and mystery mingled together.

Inside, Sophia was arranging some books at the counter but looked up and smiled warmly as Amelia entered.

"Good morning, Amelia! I've told Eleni about your research. She's eager to meet you. Let me fetch her," she said disappearing through a door behind the counter. Moments later, Sophia returned with an elderly woman whose graceful demeanour belied her age. "Amelia this is Eleni Manolakis, the owner of the shop," Sophia introduced.

"Pleased to meet you," Amelia said, extending her hand respectfully. Eleni's handshake was firm, her eyes sharp with intelligence and curiosity. "Sophia tells me you're looking into a woman's story related to Spinalonga. It's a subject close to my heart." Eleni remarked. Amelia carefully pulled out the letter she had safeguarded, the letter from Sister Agnes at the convent and the copy of the birth certificate, Nikos had given her. Amelia explained about her work in England and how she had come across the diary of Florence and the story of Isabella de Lacy. She didn't mention the sightings of Isabella at that stage as she wasn't sure if she should or even if these two women would understand. Eleni could speak some English, but Sophia was also doing a lot of interpreting too. "This letter was written by sister Agnes at the convent where Isabella was sent by her father. She gave birth to a baby boy who was adopted by a family here in Elounda, according to this note their name was Kostas." Amelia explained, handing it over to Eleni.

Eleni read the letter intently, her expression turning contemplative. After a long pause, she reached into her bag and retrieved a worn, yellowing envelope. "I wondered when Sophia mentioned you and your research whether it could be true, and it is. She said with tears in her eyes, "This was my father's most treasured possession. It's from his biological mother. My family name was Kostas before I married. My father's name was Dimitri, and this letter was given to his adoptive parents by a sister Thea when they first took him home," she said, her voice a soft echo of past pain. There was silence, Amelia was stunned, as was Sophia. They watched as Eleni unfolded the letter with reverent hands:

My Darling Dimitri

As I write this letter, my heart aches with the sorrow of our separation. You were taken from me when you were only a few days old, and it was not my choice to let you go. My love for you remains strong and I want you to know that this decision was made against my will. Though you are too young to understand, I hope that one day you will read this letter and know that I loved you more than words can express. You were born into a world where circumstances beyond my control forced us apart, and it is my deepest regret that I could not keep you with me.

I hope and pray that your adoptive parents will provide you with the love and care that I wish I could have given you. Hopefully, they will offer you a life of opportunities and happiness. As you grow, I pray that you will understand and forgive the choices made by others that led to our separation. I hope that you will always feel the love that I have for you, even from afar. You are in my thoughts and my heart every single day.

May your life be filled with joy, kindness, and love. I will cherish the brief days I had with you and hold onto the hope that one day we will meet again, and you will understand the depths of my love for you.
With all my love
Now and always
Your mother, Isabella

Eleni clasped her hands together, her eyes reflecting the pride and poignancy of her words.

"Let me tell you about my father, Dimitri Kostas," she began, her voice steady and clear. "He was not only a doctor, but he was also a healer in every sense of the word. Dimitri was adopted by the Kostas family, who were well-respected doctors in Elounda, growing up he knew only that he had been born in a convent and that his birth mother was banished to the Leprosarium of Spinalonga.

It was this knowledge that kindled the fire in him to pursue medicine like his adoptive parents. He excelled in his studies, driven by a purpose stronger than most. After medical school, instead of pursuing a lucrative practice, he chose to work on Spinalonga. It was as if he needed to face the disease that took his mother head-on. He spent years on Spinalonga, working tirelessly to improve the conditions there. He was pivotal in introducing new treatment protocols and collaborated with researchers to trial new drugs. His compassion and dedication brought him respect and admiration from patients and peers alike. But it wasn't just his medical prowess that defined him," Eleni continued, her eyes distant as if visualizing the past.

"He believed deeply in the dignity of each patient, fighting not just the disease but the stigma associated with it. When the first effective treatments for leprosy were developed, Dimitri was among the first to administer them, witnessing miraculous recoveries that many thought impossible. His work helped change the perception of leprosy. He saw it not as a curse but a disease that needed understanding and compassion. Through his efforts, many lives were saved, and the shadows over Spinalonga began to lift."

Sophia brought in some coffee for them all, and Eleni continued.

"He kept his mother's letter all his life, as a reminder of the love he had lost but also of the love he chose to give to others every day. This bookshop," she gestured around, "is filled with stories, but none so powerful as my father's."

Amelia listened, deeply moved by the depth of Dimitri's character and achievements.

"Let me show you something else Amelia." Eleni said as she led Amelia to a secluded corner of the bookshop where the air was thick with the scent of aging paper. The walls were lined with ancient ledgers and manuscripts, each a bearer of untold stories. Eleni reached for a particularly worn ledger on the top shelf, its leather cover cracked, and pages yellowed with time.

"This is the record of all the patients admitted to Spinalonga from 1904 onwards." Eleni explained as she laid the heavy book on a reading table with care. "Let's see if we can find Isabella's entry."

They turned the pages slowly, scanning the faded handwriting for Isabella's name. Finally, Amelia pointed to a line in the ledger.

"Here she is, "she said, her finger trembling slightly over the text. Eleni leaned closer, her eyes tracing the words that detailed Isabella's entry:

Name: Isabella de Lacy
Date of Admission: March 1907
Date of Death: October 1912
Cause of Death: Heart Failure due to Leprosy

Chapter Forty
Isabella
Spinalonga, Greece

Isabella's first days on Spinalonga were a blur of confusion and fear. The stigmatized air of leprosy hung heavily about the island, filling its new residents with a silent dread for their future. However, as time passed, Isabella began to see the island differently, through the community of fellow sufferers who were, like her, exiled but clinging to remnants of hope and humanity. The disease was frightening, and some residents had lost facial features such as their eyes, or nose, whilst others had lost limbs. Many had open wounds that leaked pus which made their ragged garments stick to their skin and there was a constant awful stench. The medical treatments were minimal, with a doctor or nurse visiting once a week with minimal supplies and not much comfort. Each day began with the harsh reality of her condition.

Life on Spinalonga was a harsh existence, a daily struggle against the relentless grip of leprosy and the unforgiving elements of the island. Isabella found herself thrust into this world of isolation and despair, her every waking moment consumed by the grim reality of her surroundings. Each day began with the faint glimmer of dawn as the first rays of sunlight crept over the horizon, casting long shadows across the crumbling ruins of the abandoned village. For Isabella and other residents of Spinalonga, there was no respite from the relentless march of time, no escape from the prison of their bodies.

Their leader was the Priest, Father Yannis, a man of unwavering faith who guided them through the darkest days with his words of wisdom and compassion. It was he who provided a semblance of order in the chaos, who offered a glimmer of hope in the face of overwhelming despair. Each day was a battle against the ravages of disease, a constant struggle to maintain some sense of normality in a world turned upside down. Water was scarce and rationed out in small quantities to ensure that every drop was used sparingly. Food was brought in by boat from the nearby village of Plaka, a meagre supply of fish and vegetables that barely sustained them through the long, lean months.

There were no mirrors on Spinalonga, no reflections to remind them of the faces they once knew. Instead, they lived in the shadows, shrouded in darkness and uncertainty, their identities stripped away by the cruel hand of fate. Yet, despite the hardships they faced, their spirits were resilient, with a determination to survive against all odds.

***

The sound of the morning bell signalled the start of the day's activities. The residents would gather in the main square, where tasks were assigned by Father Yannis. Some would head to the communal kitchens to help prepare meals, while others tended to the gardens or took care of maintenance work. Food was a constant concern. Supplies were brought from Plaka by boat, but they were never enough. The islanders supplemented their diet with whatever they could grow or catch. Initially, Isabella kept to herself, struggling with her illness and the isolation. But slowly, she began to observe the daily routines of the islanders. The village had its own rhythm, a fragile order maintained by those who had been there the longest. The Priest, Father Yannis, was a steady presence, offering spiritual and practical support.

Father Yannis was born in 1865 in a small village nestled in the mountains of

Crete. His parents, Nikolaos, and Iris were devout Christians who instilled in him a keen sense of faith and compassion from an early age. Nikolaos was a humble farmer, and Iris managed their household with unwavering dedication. The family lived a simple but contented life, guided by the rhythms of the seasons and their unwavering belief in God.

As a boy, Yannis showed an unusual depth of understanding and empathy, often spending time with the elderly and sick in his village. He was drawn to the stories of the saints and the teachings of the bible, finding solace and inspiration in their words. His parents noticed his pious nature and encouraged his spiritual growth, hoping that he might one day serve the church.

At the age of eighteen, Yannis left his village to study theology in Heraklion. He spent several years immersed in his studies, learning not only about the doctrines of his faith but also about the human condition. His education broadened his perspective and he became passionate about helping those in need. His mentors recognised his potential and nurtured his development, impressed by his dedication and humility. After completing his studies, Yannis was ordained as a priest and assigned to a small parish in a coastal town. There he quickly gained a reputation for his kindness and tireless work. He visited the sick, provided for the poor, and offered counsel to those in distress. His parishioners loved him, seeing him not just as a spiritual leader but as a devoted friend.

In 1904, Yannis's life took an unexpected turn when he was asked to become the priest for the leper colony on Spinalonga. The position was a challenging one, as it required a level of compassion and resilience that few possessed. Despite the daunting task, Yannis accepted, believing it was his calling to bring hope and comfort to those suffering from leprosy. Father Yannis made the difficult decision to live on Spinalonga, choosing to serve and comfort the afflicted despite the heartache of leaving behind his family. His unwavering faith and compassion compelled him to embrace this path, seeking to bring hope and solace to those in need.

***

One morning, while sitting outside her small stone dwelling, Isabella was approached by a woman named Maria. Despite the language barrier, Maria's kind eyes and gentle manner put Isabella at ease. Through gestures and broken phrases, Maria invited Isabella to join her in the communal kitchen. She was hesitant at first but decided to follow Maria and see what happened.

The kitchen on Spinalonga was a stark contrast to the opulent kitchens Isabella had known at Milburn Manor. It was a small, dimly lit room with rough stone walls that absorbed the heat from the constantly burning stove. The floor was made of uneven, worn flagstones, and the air was thick with the scent of boiling stew and baking bread. In one corner, a large, iron pot hung over an open fire, where a thin, weary-looking woman stirred the contents with a wooden spoon. Near the crude wooden table at the centre of the kitchen, another woman chopped vegetables with hands that trembled from the disease. Her face was gaunt and her movements slow but she smiled and waved as Maria and Isabella entered the kitchen.

Cooking became a bridge between Isabella and the other women on the island. She learned the basics of Greek from Maria, picking up words and phrases as they prepared meals together. The kitchen was a place of warmth and camaraderie, a refuge from the harsh realities of their condition. They cooked simple dishes, lentil soup, vegetable stews, and bread, using ingredients brought over from the mainland.

Isabella's skills improved and she found joy in contributing to the community. Her involvement in the kitchen gave her a sense of purpose and belonging. Despite the worsening of the condition of her hands, Isabella remained determined to be useful. The lesions spread, and her fingers began to curl, making even simple tasks painful. But she persevered, driven by the bonds she had formed and the need to distract herself from her illness.

One morning, Isabella stood at the rocky shore, her eyes fixed on the horizon where the supply boat was slowly making its way towards the island. The sun was high in the sky, casting a golden glow over the azure waters of the Aegean Sea. This was one of the few moments of anticipation on Spinalonga, where the arrival of supplies brought a semblance of connection to the world beyond their existence.

As the boat drew nearer, Isabella noticed something unusual. Amidst the usual crates of food and medical supplies, there was a small figure standing at the front of the boat, clutching a worn satchel to his chest. As the boat docked and the gangplank was lowered, the figure hesitated for a moment before stepping onto the island. The boy couldn't have been more than ten years old. His face was pale, eyes wide with fear and confusion. He scanned the crowd nervously, his small frame trembling as he gripped his bag tightly. Isabella's heart ached at the sight of him; it was clear he was terrified and alone.

The boy's eyes met Isabella's for a brief moment before he looked away, tears welling in his eyes. She took a step forward, wanting to comfort him, but before she could reach him, he turned and bolted, disappearing into the narrow alleys of the settlement. Isabella hurried after him, her mind racing. How had this boy ended up here? Who had sent him, all alone? She wove through the labyrinthine streets, calling out softly,

"It's all right, little one. I won't hurt you. Please, come back." Her words were met with silence, and for a moment Isabella feared she would never find him. But then she heard a faint, muffled sob coming from behind one of the stone buildings. She approached cautiously, not wanting to startle him further. Kneeling, Isabella peered behind the building and saw the boy curled up in a ball, his face buried in his arms. She reached out a hand gently, her voice soft and soothing.

"Hey there, it's okay. My name is Isabella. What's your name?"

The boy lifted his head slightly, his tear-streaked face coming into view. "Loukas," he whispered.

"Loukas," she repeated with a smile. "That's a lovely name. How old are you, Loukas?"

"Nine and a half "he replied, sniffing, and wiping his nose on his sleeve. "I don't want to be here. I want my mama and I want to go home." Isabella's heart broke as he spoke. She knew all too well the feeling of being torn away from loved ones.

"I know, Loukas. It's scary being in a new place. But you're not alone. We are all here together, and we will look after you." Loukas looked up at her, his eyes filled with hope and despair in equal measure.

"Can I stay with you, until my mama comes to get me?" Choking back tears at his words, Isabella extended her hand to him.

"Of course, come on, let's get you settled and find you something to eat. You must be hungry after your journey."

He hesitated for a moment before taking her hand, allowing her to lead him away from his hiding place. They walked back towards the main square, where some of the other residents had gathered, curiosity etched on their faces. Isabella guided Loukas to a small bench and sat beside him, offering him a piece of bread from the supplies. He took it gratefully, nibbling at it while glancing around nervously. The other residents watched with a mix of sympathy and sadness. They knew what it meant for a new arrival, especially one so young. Isabella spoke to them softly, asking if anyone knew more about Loukas's arrival.

One of the older women stepped forward, a grim expression on her face. "His family sent him here," she said quietly. "They couldn't bear the thought of living with the shame of his condition. It's a terrible thing, but not uncommon." Isabella nodded, her heart heavy with sorrow for Loukas and his family. She turned back to the boy, who was now staring at the ground, tears silently falling onto his tattered shoes.

"You're not alone, Loukas. I will take care of you whilst you are here. I will ask Father Yannis if you can stay with me. Would that be ok with you?" He looked up at her, his eyes searching her face for any sign of deceit. Finding none, he nodded slowly and Isabella squeezed his hand gently offering him a reassuring smile. She led him to her small dwelling, a simple but cosy space she had tried to make her own. She gave him some water and let him rest. Over the following weeks, Loukas and Isabella began to form a bond. She became a surrogate mother to him, providing him with the love and care he so desperately needed. She told him stories, sang him lullabies, and taught him some English words. Loukas began to open up, sharing stories of his family and his life in Plaka.

Despite the bond they formed, Loukas never stopped believing that his parents would come for him. Every day, he would ask Isabella if a boat had arrived with news from his family. Each time she had to tell him no, his eyes would fill with hope and then quickly dim with disappointment. One evening as they sat outside watching the sun set over the sea, Loukas turned to Isabella. "Do you think my mama and papa will come for me soon?"

Isabella smiled gently, brushing a lock of hair from his forehead.

"I hope so, Loukas," she said softly. "But until then, you have me. And I promise I will always be here for you." Loukas leaned into her, seeking comfort. "Thank you, Isabella." His lips were wobbling as he tried not to cry, his eyes already back gazing at the horizon searching for the boat he was sure would come.

Chapter Forty-One
Isabella
Spinalonga, Greece

Death was a constant presence on Spinalonga. The leprosy ravaged the bodies of the inhabitants, and many succumbed to the disease. Every death was a reminder of the fragility of life on the island. One day, a young man named Andreas passed away. He had been one of the brighter spirits on the island, always quick with a smile and a joke despite his suffering. His death cast a pall over the community.

Isabella and her friend Maria attended his simple funeral, standing with the other residents as Father Yannis said a few words. Tears streamed down Isabella's face as she watched the coffin being lowered into the ground. She felt the weight of the island's sorrow pressing down on her. Maria squeezed her hand.

"We have to be strong, Isabella. For ourselves and each other." Maria's warmth and kindness were a balm to Isabella's weary soul. As they worked side by side in the kitchens every day, Maria would share stories about the island and its residents. Isabella learned that Maria had been sent to Spinalonga after contracting leprosy, leaving behind a husband and two young children. Despite the hardship, Maria never lost her hope or her sense of humour.

Together they shared stories of their past lives, clinging to the memories of better days. They celebrated small joys, a satisfying meal, a sunny day, or a visit from the priest who brought news from the outside world. In the evening, when the day's work was done, Isabella and her fellow companions would gather around the communal hearth, their faces illuminated by the flickering of the fire. They would share stories of the past, their hopes for the future, and the dreams that kept them going in the darkest of times. Yet, even amidst the camaraderie, there were moments of profound sadness and despair. Isabella would often find herself gazing out across the shimmering waters of the sea, longing for the life she had once known, and the loved ones she had been forced to leave behind. She gazed out at the horizon, at the lights from the village of Plaka, and her heart broke over and over as she knew her baby was out there somewhere.

***

As the morning sun cast its golden glow over the rugged landscape Isabella found herself drawn to the edge of the sea, the rhythmic waves offering a soothing melody that echoed the song in her heart. With each gentle swell, she felt a stirring within her, a longing to give voice to the emotions that lay buried beneath the surface. Taking a deep breath, Isabella closed her eyes and began to hum softly, the sound weaving its way through the salty air like a delicate thread. As she surrendered herself to the music, she felt a sense of peace wash over her, as if the notes carried away the weight of her worries and fears. A few of her fellow islanders had gathered nearby, drawn by the sound that filled the air. They watched in silent awe as Isabella's voice soared, as she sang an old Irish ballad, each note carrying with it a message of hope and resilience.

Father Yannis approached Isabella with a gentle smile.

"Your voice is a gift, Isabella," he said softly. "It brings light to even the darkest of days." Later that evening, after word had spread about Isabella's singing and her lovely voice, when she went down to the central square where all the residents ate and she was sat with Maria and Loukas, an older resident, appeared, his weathered hands cradling a Cretan Lyra. With a nod from Father Yannis, he began to play, the mournful strains of the lyra providing a haunting melody that filled the air, echoing off the stone walls of the ancient buildings. Isabella joined in and began to sing along. She wasn't sure the words quite fitted being English, but no one seemed to mind and gradually others joined in. Some even tried dancing, whilst others simply closed their eyes, lost in the bittersweet beauty of the music.

She sang a lullaby her mother had once sung to her, her voice soaring and echoing through the narrow streets, carried by the gentle evening breeze. She sang the lullabies she used to sing to Dimitri in the convent, her voice loud and clear.

Across the water, in the small village of Plaka, a young couple was having dinner at a local taverna. Katerina and Mattheo, the adoptive parents of baby Dimitri, were taking a rare moment to relax and enjoy a meal together. The child, now a few months old, was restless in his pram, fussing and crying despite their best efforts to soothe him. As Katerina cradled the child, attempting to calm him with gentle rocking and whispered words, Mattheo heard the faint strains of Isabella's song. He stood up and walked to the edge of the sea, and realised the singing was coming from the Island. He let the soft melody wash over him. Her voice was clear and beautiful, unlike anything he had heard in a long time. "Katerina, listen," Mattheo said, motioning her to come closer. She approached holding the crying child close to her chest. The baby's cries began to subside, his little face relaxing as the soothing melody wrapped around him like a warm embrace. Katerina rocked him gently, following the rhythm of the distant song. "It is calming him," she whispered, a smile of relief spreading across her face.

Neither Mattheo nor Katerina knew that the woman singing was Isabella and Isabella was unaware that her voice was reaching her son as she sang with a heart full of longing and love. Her voice was filled with the pain of separation and the hope that somehow, her love would find its way to him. Isabella's lullaby, carried by the wind, reached Dimitri's ears like a mother's caress. Though he was too young to understand, the connection was undeniable. His eyes fluttered closed, his tiny hands relaxing as he drifted into a peaceful sleep.

Back on Spinalonga, Isabella continued to sing, her eyes closed and her thoughts far away. Her spirit seemed to transcend the physical boundaries of the island, reaching out to the child she had been forced to abandon. She imagined holding him, rocking him gently, and singing him to sleep. As the night deepened, the poignant connection between mother and son remained unnoticed by the world around them. At that moment, the distance and the circumstances that separated them seemed to vanish, replaced by the timeless bond of love and music. Isabella's song was a lullaby of love, unknowingly soothing her son, and in turn bringing a moment of peace to her own troubled heart.

Mattheo and Katerina, still gazing towards Spinalonga, marvelled at their peaceful sleeping child.

"Whoever she is, she has a gift," Mattheo said softly. Katerina nodded, holding their sleeping baby close.

"Yes, she does. It's as if she knows exactly what he needs."

Chapter Forty-Two
Isabella
Spinalonga, Greece

One day, as Isabella left the kitchen, she heard a commotion near the entrance to one of the old, crumbling buildings that served as a makeshift home for some of the residents. Curious, Isabella approached and saw a group of people gathered around, their expressions a mix of frustration and fear. Standing in the centre, was a tall, gaunt man with piercing eyes and an air of defiance. He was in the middle of an argument with Father Yannis, who was trying to calm him down.

Isabella hesitated at the edge of the gathering, her hands throbbing from her work in the kitchen. She watched as the man's voice rose, his words sharp and filled with anger.

"I don't need your pity, Yannis," he spat, his eyes blazing. "And I certainly don't need your charity. I can fend for myself." Father Yannis remained calm, his voice gentle but firm.

"Sebastian, we are all in this together. The community needs your help, and you need theirs. It's the only way we will survive here." Sebastian scoffed, turning away from the priest. As he did, his eyes met Isabella's. For a brief moment, the anger in his gaze softened, replaced by a flicker of curiosity. But it was quickly gone, replaced once more by his hardened exterior.

"Who's this?" he demanded, pointing a finger at Isabella. "Another one come to tell me how to live my life?" Isabella stepped forward, her heart pounding.

"I'm Isabella," she said, her voice steady. "And I'm not here to tell you how to live. I'm here just trying to live, like everyone else." Sebastian's eyes narrowed. "We'll see about that," he muttered before pushing past her and disappearing down a narrow alley.

Over the following weeks, Isabella learned more about Sebastian from the other residents. He had been a merchant, prosperous and well-respected until leprosy had taken everything from him. His bitterness stemmed not just from his illness, but from the loss of his former life and the way society had cast him aside. Despite his abrasive nature, Sebastian was a valuable member of the community. His resourcefulness and old connections meant he could acquire goods that others couldn't. But his help always came with a price, and he often exploited the desperation of his fellow islanders, to maintain a sense of control.

Isabella found herself both repelled and intrigued by Sebastian. She could see the pain beneath his anger, and she wanted to help him, though she knew it wouldn't be easy. Their interactions since the first meeting were tense, often filled with sharp words and cold stares, but slowly, a grudging respect began to form between them.

One evening, as Isabella was tending to a sick child, Sebastian approached her, a rare softness in his eyes.

"Why do you care so much?" he asked, his voice low. Isabella looked up, meeting his gaze.

"Because we're all we have," she replied simply. "If we don't care for each other, then what do we have left?" Sebastian said nothing, but the next day, he left a small bundle of much-needed supplies at Isabella's door.

***

Maria's health had been declining for weeks. Despite her resilient spirit, the disease had taken its toll on her body. She continued to work in the kitchen as long as she could, refusing to let the illness define her. But eventually, she grew too weak to stand, and

Isabella took over her duties, preparing meals with a heavy heart. One morning as the sun rose over the island, Isabella sat by Maria's bedside. Maria's breathing was shallow, her once bright eyes dull with pain. She reached out a frail hand to Isabella, who clasped it tightly.

"Don't be sad, Isabella" Maria whispered. "I've lived a good life, and I've found family here. Take care of our kitchen, while you can, and take care of yourself." Tears streamed down Isabella's face.

"I will, Maria. I promise."

Maria passed away peacefully that night. The island mourned the loss of one of its most beloved residents. Isabella was inconsolable, feeling the weight of her friend's absence keenly, and in the days following Maria's death, Isabella struggled to cope with her grief. It was during this grim time that Sebastian stepped forward to offer his support. He had a reputation for being gruff and aloof, but Isabella saw a different side of him as he quietly helped her with the kitchen duties and a listening ear. With Sebastian's support, Isabella began to find her footing again. Sebastian became a trusted friend, always there to lend a hand or offer a kind word.

As the disease progressed, Isabella found it increasingly difficult to work in the kitchen. The simple tasks she once performed with ease became exhausting, and her strength waned. Sebastian noticed her struggle and stepped in to help, taking on many of her duties to ensure she could rest. The other islanders and Father Yannis were surprised at the change in Sebastian but secretly pleased that he had found some peace and Isabella had found a friend again after she lost Maria.

As Isabella's physical condition worsened, she found herself spending more time in her small modest house that she shared with Loukas. She could no longer work in the kitchen, her strength depleted by the disease. Yet, despite her physical limitations, her spirit remained unbroken.

As the years wore on the disease took a heavier toll on Isabella. She lost the fingers of her right hand, making the simplest tasks arduous and Sebastian became indispensable to her with his help and unwavering friendship and support. However, the hardest blow came when she began to lose her sight, the world fading into an indistinct haze, then finally darkness.

Blindness isolated her in ways leprosy had not, trapping her in a perpetual night. But her friends became her eyes, describing sunsets, guiding her steps, and ensuring she never felt alone in the darkness. Sebastian would narrate the changing hues of the sky, while Loukas would bring flowers, describing their colours and textures, keeping Isabella's world vibrant with words. Loukas rarely left her side to make sure she was safe. He felt as if she was the mother he had lost, and in turn, he became the son she never had. Even as Isabella's world dimmed to darkness, her voice remained a beacon of light. Weaving through the air like a thread of hope. With each note she sang, she brought comfort to the weary souls of Spinalonga, infusing the desolate island with a sense of warmth and joy.

Despite her blindness, Isabella's spirit soared, her songs resonating with a newfound depth and clarity. Her fellow residents marvelled at her resilience, dubbing her the "Songbird of Spinalonga" in honour of her unwavering spirit and the solace she brought to their troubled hearts. And so, with each melody that echoed through the stone streets of Spinalonga, Isabella's legacy grew, her voice becoming a symbol of strength and unity for all who called the island home.

Chapter Forty-Three
Amelia
Greece

Under the soft glow of the afternoon sun, Amelia and Nikos made their way to the charming bookshop in Elounda, where so much of Isabella's story had come to light. They were there to meet Eleni, the elderly owner who had helped them connect the historical dots of Isabella's life and her son Dimitri's legacy. As they entered, the familiar bell chimed above them, heralding their arrival. Eleni greeted them with a smile, though her eyes hinted at the weariness that often accompanied her age.

"Hello, Eleni," Amelia began, her voice warm with gratitude. "This is Nikos and we wanted to thank you for all the help you have given us. Your insights and obvious connections have been invaluable in piecing together Isabella's story." Eleni waved her hand modestly.

"It was my pleasure. I'm glad I could help and learn of Dimitri's mother and where she came from. It brings closure to such a poignant tale." Nikos, ever the direct one, got straight to the point.

"We were wondering if you would be interested in setting up an exhibition of some sort here in the shop. A way to tell Isabella's story to everyone that comes in."

Eleni sighed softly, a trace of regret crossing her features. "I would love nothing more, but I'm afraid I have other news. I'm selling the shop. I'm not as young as I used to be. My husband is unwell, and I need the money. Also, the shop needs more energy and presence than I can give."

Amelia and Nikos exchanged a quick look, a silent conversation passing between them. Amelia had the money from her house sale back in England and they had already been discussing looking for some sort of shop for her.

"What if we took over the shop, Eleni?" We would keep Sophia on as when Amelia gives birth she may have to take a step back for a short while, but we'll buy it from you. That way, you can rest knowing it's in hands that genuinely care about preserving its legacy, and we can set up the exhibit, maybe as a new opening for it?" Nikos suggested, his voice hopeful.

Eleni looked taken aback, her eyes widening in surprise before a soft smile spread across her face. "I can't think of a better outcome. I would love that, and yes, I would still like to help organise this exhibition. It would be a fitting tribute to my father and Isabella. A fitting goodbye to the shop but also a new chapter for it, how wonderful." She beamed.

With the decision made, they went to a local restaurant, Rusteak, and spent the next hour discussing ideas for the exhibition. Over a delicious meal of appetizers including tzatziki, spicy cream cheese, zucchini balls, and Greek salad they envisioned panels detailing the history of Spinalonga, personal items from Dimitri that Eleni had kept, copies of the letters and interactive sections where visitors could learn more about the treatment of leprosy through the ages. As the main course arrived, they all stopped to admire and take in the delicious smells of the pork dish that Eleni had ordered. It was Gourounopoula (pork in the oven) with the crispiest crackling Amelia had ever seen. Eleni and Sophia were enjoying a glass of the local white wine and Nikos had a pint of ice-cold Mythos. As they thanked their hosts and owners, Joanna, and George, talk turned once again to the exhibition.

"It's going to be educational and moving," Amelia said, excited about the project's potential and the thought of owning Eleni's beloved bookshop. "A place where history is respected and remembered."

"I think we should plan a visit to Spinalonga," Sophia added. "A sort of pilgrimage to honour Isabella and all the souls who lived their lives on that island." They all nodded in agreement and as they left the restaurant and headed home, Amelia felt a profound connection to everything that had transpired. They were not just preserving history; they were keeping alive the memories of those who had suffered and triumphed over incredible adversities.

***

In the weeks that followed, Amelia, Eleni, and Sophia worked tirelessly. The community's interest was piqued as word spread of the new owners and the upcoming exhibition. Support poured in, with locals donating time, resources, and even artifacts related to Spinalonga's history.

The journey to Spinalonga began on a bright, crisp morning. Amelia, Nikos, and Sophia boarded the boat at the picturesque harbour of Elounda. The harbour bustled with activity as fishermen prepared their nets and tourists snapped photos of the stunning scenery. The boat was modest, but sturdy, its wooden planks polished by years of use. The air was filled with the scent of salt and seaweed, and the cries of seagulls echoed overhead. Amelia seated at the front of the boat, felt a mix of anticipation and solemnity. She clutched a small bouquet of wildflowers she had picked that morning, their delicate petals trembling in the breeze.

As the boat glided across the water, the island of Spinalonga came into view. The fortress walls, imposing and ancient loomed against the backdrop of the clear blue sky. The island seemed both beautiful and haunting, a silent reminder of the history it held within its stone walls. The closer they approached the more details emerged. The remnants of the old leper colony were visible; crumbling buildings, narrow pathways, and the remains of what once were homes. Amelia's heart ached as she thought of Isabella, who had spent her final years on this desolate island. As they reached the shore, the boat slowed, and they disembarked onto weathered wooden planks. The sound of their footsteps echoed in the stillness, and for a moment, it felt as if they were stepping back in time. Together, they walked up the path leading to the graveyard. The air was heavy with history, and each step seemed to resonate with the memories of those who had once called Spinalonga home. Amelia held the bouquet tightly, feeling a profound connection to the woman who had endured so much. They left the flowers by the unmarked graves, a simple yet poignant gesture of remembrance and respect

***.

Amelia stood on the rocky shore of Spinalonga, gazing out at the shimmering waters of the Aegean Sea. The sun was beginning its descent, casting a golden hue over the island and its abandoned buildings. Beside her Nikos and Sophia were deep in conversation, reminiscing about the island's history and its tragic past. As the voices of her companions faded into the background, Amelia felt a strange pull, an almost magnetic force drawing her towards the heart of the island. She wandered away from the group, her footsteps echoing softly against the ancient stones. The air was thick with memories, and she could almost hear the whispers of the past swirling around her.

It was then, as she walked among the ruins, that she heard it: a soft ethereal singing. The voice was hauntingly beautiful, filled with a longing that resonated deep within her soul. Amelia paused, straining to hear more, her heart pounding in her chest. The melody was familiar, a song that bridged the gap between the past and the present. She turned to see Nikos and Sophia had found her and she looked at them, her voice trembling with excitement.

"Did you hear that?" she asked, her eyes wide with wonder.

Nikos looked at her, a puzzled expression on his face. "Hear what?"

"The singing," Amelia insisted. "It was so clear, so beautiful." Sophia shook her head gently.

"There's no one here, Amelia. It must have been the wind or a bird. This island has a way of playing tricks on people's minds."

But Amelia knew what she had heard. She felt a deep connection to the voice as if it were calling out to her across time. Ignoring their dismissals, she ventured further into the ruins, her heart guided by the strange melody. The song grew louder, more distinct, filling her with a sense of peace and sorrow all at once. She found herself standing before a crumbling stone building, its door hanging ajar. Hesitantly she stepped inside, the cool shadows wrapping around her. The singing enveloped her completely now, a lullaby of heartache and hope. She closed her eyes, allowing the music to wash over her, tears slipping down her cheeks. In her mind's eye, she was sure she could see Isabella, a figure in white, her eyes lifted towards the heavens as she sang her soul into the twilight.

Amelia felt a hand on her shoulder, bringing her back to the present. She turned to find Nikos standing beside her, his expression a mix of concern and tenderness.

"Are you all right?" he asked softly. She nodded, wiping away her tears. "Yes, I'm fine. It's just…. this place, it is so full of memories."

Sophia joined them her eyes scanning the empty room, "Sometimes the past speaks to us in ways we can't explain." Amelia smiled through her tears, feeling a profound sense of connection to the island and its history.

"Possibly, as you said before, it must have been a bird."

As they left the building and made their way back down to the shore, Amelia glanced back one last time, and for a fleeting moment, she thought she saw a figure standing in the shadows, a soft smile on her lips. The vision faded quickly, but the feeling of warmth remained.

As they set sail from Spinalonga and the island receded into the distance, the haunting melody of Isabella's song lingered in her heart, a timeless echo of love and loss, guiding her forward into the future.

Chapter Forty-Four
Isabella
Spinalonga, Greece
1912

Although Isabella's world was now an impenetrable blackness, she had learned to navigate her small house by touch, her fingers trailing along the rough walls and worn furniture, but the island had become an even more daunting place without her sight. Her health had deteriorated further. A persistent cough wracked her frail body, each fit leaving her gasping for breath, the fingers of her left hand were now twisted and painful. Her skin was thin and fragile, marred by deep cracks and sores that refused to heal. She spent most of her days lying on her straw mattress, listening to the distant sounds of the island. The once familiar noises had taken on a haunting quality, a constant reminder of her isolation and impending fate.

One morning, Isabella's breathing became laboured, her chest heaving with effort. She lay in her bed, her ravaged hands clutching the thin blanket that offered little warmth. The sun had risen, casting a dim light into the house, but Isabella's world remained shrouded in darkness. Sebastian who had become her closest friend, sat by her side. He held her hand gently, his rough fingers a comforting presence. He had seen many succumb to the disease, but watching Isabella suffer was a different kind of torment.

Isabella's breathing grew more ragged, her strength ebbing away with each passing moment. She squeezed Sebastian's hand weakly, trying to convey her gratitude for his companionship.

"Thank you," she whispered. Sebastian leaned closer, tears glistening in his eyes.

"You're not alone, Isabella. Loukas is here too." He said his voice choked with emotion.

"I can feel him," she murmured. "And I can feel you. Thank you for being my friend." Sebastian's heart ached as he watched her struggle. He wished he could take away her pain, to ease her suffering in some way. But all he could do was hold her hand and be there in her last moments.

Loukas, knelt beside her bed. His face was streaked with tears, his heart breaking at the sight of the woman who had shown him so much love and kindness. He held her other hand, his fingers intertwined with hers.

"Isabella," he whispered, his voice trembling. "Please don't leave me."

Isabella's heart broke for the boy she had come to love as her own. She wished she could stay, to continue guiding and protecting him. But she knew her time was short.

"Loukas," she said softly, "you must be strong. Remember what I've taught you. I love you and you have Sebastian now." Loukas just nodded, tears spilling down his cheeks.

As the day wore on, Isabella's breaths grew shallower, her grip on Sebastian and Loukas weakening. She could feel the end approaching, a mix of fear and relief washing over her. She thought of her family, of James, and of the life of which she had once dreamed. She prayed for Dimitri and hoped he was happy.

In her last moments, Isabella's mind drifted to a memory of Milburn Manor, of the gardens filled with laughter and music. She imagined herself dancing with James, surrounded by the people she cared about. The vision brought her a sense of calm, a reminder of the joy she had once known. With a final, shuddering breath, Isabella whispered, "James…I'm here." Her body relaxed, her spirit finally finding the peace it had sought for so long.

Sebastian and Loukas sat in stunned silence, the weight of their loss pressing down on them. The small house seemed to grow colder, the light dimmer. They wept openly, their tears for Isabella whom they had both loved deeply.

***

As the sun set, casting a golden glow over the island, the residents stood in silent tribute, their hearts heavy with grief. They had all lost friends and loved ones to the disease, but Isabella's death felt especially cruel. She had brought light and hope to their lives, even in the darkest of times. Sebastian and Loukas stood side by side, their faces streaked with tears. They knew they would carry Isabella's memory with them always, her spirit a guiding light in their hearts. As they mourned her loss, they took solace in the knowledge that she was finally free from pain, and reunited with her loved ones in a place where suffering could no longer touch her.

The diagnosis was heart failure due to Leprosy, but those who knew her best understood that it was as much from a broken heart as from the disease.

***

Isabella was buried in an unmarked grave on the island, like many before her.

There were no flowers, no epitaphs, just the barren earth and the sound of the sea. Isabella's legacy lived on through the stories and songs of Spinalonga, a symbol of grace and strength in the face of unimaginable hardship. And in the quiet moments, when the wind whispered through the ruins, it was said that you could still hear her voice, a haunting reminder of the footsteps of fate that had led her to this place.

Chapter Forty-Five

Dimitri
Greece

Dimitri Kostas had a charmed childhood, growing up in the warmth and affluence of his adoptive family in Elounda. The Kostas family, known for their wealth and generosity, ensured that Dimitri wanted for nothing. His parents Mattheo and Katerina were kind-hearted and deeply loving, instilling in Dimitri a sense of compassion and a strong moral compass from an early age.

When Dimitri turned fifteen, he discovered that he could sing and his voice, rich and melodious, captivated all who heard it. The Kostas family encouraged his passion for music, enrolling him in singing lessons. Dimitri's talent flourished and he became well known in the local community, often performing at town events and celebrations. Dimitri's childhood was filled with laughter, music, and the close-knit bond of a loving family. His days were spent exploring the beautiful landscapes of Crete, attending school, and practicing his singing. Surrounded by friends and family, Dimitri life was idyllic and his future was full of promise. Although he had always known that he was adopted, he had never asked about his birth parents and loved Mattheo and Katerina deeply.

However, on his eighteenth birthday, everything changed. Along with the traditional celebration and gifts, Katerina gave him the letter from the convent where he had been born. The letter, carefully preserved and kept by his adoptive parents, was from his biological mother Isabella. The letter was filled with love and sorrow, explaining the circumstances that had led to his adoption. Isabella wrote about her love for him, her dreams for his future, and her hope that he would understand why he had been taken from her and that she would never stop loving him.

As Dimitri read the heartfelt words, a wave of emotions washed over him. He felt a profound sense of loss for the mother he had never known, but also a newfound determination. His parents explained Isabella's tragic fate on Spinalonga, her struggles with leprosy, and her ultimate death. The revelation of his heritage and his mother's suffering ignited a fierce desire within him to honour her memory.

Encouraged by Mattheo who was also a doctor, Dimitri set aside his dreams of becoming a professional singer and enrolled in medical school. His adoptive parents supported his decision, proud of the man he was becoming. Dimitri pursued his career in medicine, focusing on infectious diseases. His journey was not easy, but his determination and compassion saw him through the rigorous years of study and training. He attended the University in Athens, working in various hospitals and clinics there and although it was hard being away from his family he enjoyed his training. Upon completing his medical education, he returned to Elounda, specifically to work on Spinalonga, where his mother had spent her final years. He felt an indescribable bond with the place and its residents as if he were walking in the footsteps of his mother. The island, once a place of isolation and despair, became his home and the centre of his life's work.

As a doctor, Dimitri brought hope and healing to the residents of Spinalonga. He treated their physical ailments with advanced medical knowledge and their emotional wounds with empathy and kindness. His dedication to finding better treatments and ultimately a cure for leprosy earned him the respect and admiration of his peers and patients alike.

Dimitri work extended beyond the confines of Spinalonga. He collaborated with researchers and medical professionals around the world, contributing to significant advancements in the treatment of leprosy. His efforts played a crucial role in the eventual closure of the leper colony in 1957, as effective treatments became widely available, allowing patients to reintegrate into society. Despite his professional achievements, Dimitri never lost sight of the personal mission that had driven him. He kept his mother's letter close, reading it often as a reminder of the love and sacrifice that had shaped his destiny.

In the footsteps of fate, Dimitri found his calling, transforming a legacy of sorrow into one of hope and healing. His life's work ensured that Isabella's sacrifice was not in vain, and their story became an inspiration for generations to come.

Chapter Forty-Six

Lily Bates
Lancashire

Lily stood in the vast, echoing kitchen of Milburn Manor, her hands busy scrubbing pots, but her mind far from her task. The events of that fateful night haunted her, the image of Sir Percival and Mr Wycliffe locked in a violent struggle replaying in her mind repeatedly. She had been hiding in the garden on Pierre's instructions when she witnessed the brutal murder of James Wycliffe and Pierre's fatal fall. The knowledge weighed heavily on her and she struggled to decide what to do with it. The kitchen was abuzz with activity, the other servants chattering and bustling about as they prepared the evening meal. Lily worked silently, her eyes darting around nervously. She needed to tell someone, but who would believe her?

As Lily wrestled with her thoughts, a sharp voice cut through the kitchen noise.

"Attention, everyone!" It was Mr Edmund Rogers the butler, standing at the entrance with a stern expression. The kitchen fell silent as all eyes turned to him.

"I have an announcement," Mr Rogers continued. "Due to recent changes in the household, Lord de Lacy has decided to reduce the staff. With fewer guests and social events, he feels it is no longer necessary to maintain a full complement of servants. Unfortunately, this means that some of you will be let go." A murmur of concern rippled through the staff, and Lily's heart pounded in her chest. This couldn't be happening.

Mr Rogers began reading off names, dismissing servants one by one. When he reached Lily, her heart sank.

"Lily, your services are no longer required. You must leave by tomorrow." Desperation clawed at her. She couldn't leave without telling someone what she had seen.

"Please, Mr Rogers, I have nowhere else to go." She pleaded. Mr Rogers's expression remained unyielding.

"I'm sorry Lily, but there is nothing more I can do for you. You must leave by tomorrow." Panic surged through her as she watched Mr Rogers turn and leave. She couldn't let this happen. Determined she sought him and the housekeeper Mrs Thornber out later that evening in their rooms.

"Mr Rogers, Mrs Thornber, I need to speak to you. It's important." She said, her voice urgent. They both looked up with a mixture of pity and annoyance.

"What is it, Lily" Mrs Thornber said, her expression stern.

"I saw something that night in the garden. I saw what happened to Mr Wycliffe and Pierre." She blurted out, her eyes wide with fear. Mr Rogers sighed, shaking his head.

"Lily, you've always had a vivid imagination. Pierre has returned to France and Mr Wycliffe has returned to his family. We were at the meeting held by Lord de Lacy himself. It's best not to spread tales that can't be substantiated."

"But it's true! I saw Sir Percival and …she began, but Mrs Thornber cut her off.

"Lily, enough. These wild accusations won't help you. You've been dismissed. It's time to move on. It is best if you leave now."

With her pleas ignored and her employment at Milburn Manor terminated, Lily had no choice but to leave. She packed her few belongings, tears streaming down her face, and set out for the only place that would take her: the workhouse where she had grown up.

The workhouse was a grim, oppressive place, a far cry from the relative comfort of

Milburn Manor. It was a place where the destitute and the desperate were forced to toil long hours for meagre rations. The air was thick with the smell of sweat and despair, and the walls seemed to close in on her as she entered. Lily tried to tell her story to anyone who would listen, but her words were met with disbelief and scorn.

"I saw them, I swear. Sir Percival and Lord de Lacy," she insisted. The other inmates shook their heads, some laughing cruelly, others looking at her with pity. "You're mad," one of them said. "Just like old Lizzy, over there" pointing to a frail old lady sitting rocking in the corner of the room. Labelled insane, Lily was confined to the workhouse's most dismal quarters. The overseers, uninterested in her tales, treated her like any other troubled soul, and her protests were quickly silenced.

Days turned into weeks, and weeks into months. Lily's life in the workhouse was a relentless cycle of hard labour, inadequate food, and isolation. She was given menial tasks, scrubbing floors, and washing clothes, her hands raw and blistered from the work. The overseers showed no mercy, driving inmates to exhaustion. At night she lay on a thin lumpy mattress, her mind racing with the memories of what she had witnessed and the injustice she had suffered. She clung to the hope that someone, someday would believe her story and bring justice to the wrongful deeds that had occurred at Milburn Manor.

But as the months wore on, that hope began to fade. The harsh reality took its toll, and Lily's spirit was crushed under the weight of her circumstances. She became a shadow of her former self, her dreams and aspirations buried beneath the relentless grind of survival. In the end, Lily's fate was sealed by the very system she had hoped to escape. Her claims of witnessing murder were dismissed as the ravings of a madwoman, and she was left to endure the harsh, unforgiving life of the workhouse. The truth she carried remained locked within her, and the bodies of Pierre and James remained undiscovered in the chapel grounds of Milburn Manor.

Lily's life, once filled with hope, ended in the cold, unforgiving walls of the workhouse, where she perished alone, a victim of cruel circumstances and the relentless footsteps of fate.

Chapter Forty-Seven

Percival Ashcroft
Lancashire

Sir Percival Ashcroft stood at the grand entrance of Ashcroft Lodge, in Bashall Eaves, his family seat. The estate was a symbol of his family's wealth and status, and Percival was determined to continue his life as if nothing had happened on the night of Isabella's elopement. However, without the structure and respectability that his engagement to Isabella had provided, Percival's darker tendencies began to surface more prominently. He was aware of the whispers about his true nature, and this together with the knowledge of his actions that fateful night, haunted him. He sought solace in gambling, initially seeing it as a harmless diversion. It began with small bets at private clubs, and games of cards and dice with other gentlemen. The thrill of the gamble provided a temporary escape from his troubled mind. But as his luck began to wane, his bets grew larger and more reckless. He started frequenting seedier establishments, where the stakes were higher and the risks greater.

Percival's gambling addiction quickly spiralled out of control. He lost vast sums of money, funds that were meant to maintain his lodge and its grounds. Desperate to recoup his losses, he borrowed from anyone who would lend it to him, promising to pay back double once his luck turned. But luck was a fickle mistress, and soon his debts mounted beyond his ability to repay.

The once proud and arrogant Sir Percival was now a familiar face in the dark corners of gambling dens. He avoided old acquaintances, unable to face their pity or disdain. His days were spent chasing after fortunes that slipped through his fingers like sand. To dull the pain of his failures and the shame of his addiction, Percival turned to drink. What started as a glass of brandy to steady his nerves became a nightly ritual of drunken oblivion. His charm and wit were eroded by the alcohol, leaving behind a bitter and resentful man. His staff noticed the change in him. His once immaculate appearance became dishevelled, his sharp mind dulled by drink. He lashed out at servants and the estate fell into disrcpair.

One evening, after losing a particularly hefty sum at the gambling tables, Percival returned to the lodge in a rage. He stumbled through the halls, shouting curses and knocking over priceless antiques. His descent had reached a point of no return, and he could no longer hide the man he had become. In a moment of drunken clarity, Percival realised the full extent of his ruin. He saw the broken remains of his life and knew that he had no way out. The weight of his guilt, his addiction, and his failures pressed down on him, suffocating any remaining will to fight.

On a chilly winter night, Percival made his way to his study. The room was dark, the only light coming from the moon filtering through the curtains. He sat at his desk, a bottle of brandy in one hand and a loaded pistol in the other. As he drank, he penned a final letter, his handwriting unsteady and blurred by tears.

To whom it may concern,

I have disgraced my family and myself. I am a coward, a gambler, a drunk. I have taken a life and destroyed my own. There is no redemption for me, I cannot face the consequences of my actions.
Forgive me, or do not. It matters little now.

Sir Percival Ashcroft.

With the letter finished, Percival placed the pistol to his temple. The shot echoed through the empty halls of Ashcroft Lodge, a final punctuation to his tragic descent.

Percival's death sent shockwaves through the community. Rumours of his gambling debts and secret vices spread, tarnishing the once revered Ashcroft name. Ashcroft Lodge, once a beacon of prestige, became a somber reminder of Percival's downfall. In the wake of his death, the Lodge was sold off to cover his debts. The new owners, unaware of its dark history, moved in but the shadow of Percival's death lingered. The estate had become a monument to the dangers of hidden vices and the excessive cost of maintaining appearances.

For Sir Percival Ashcroft, the footsteps of fate had led him down a dark path, and in the end, he found only despair.

Chapter Forty-Eight

**Florence Wilson
Lancashire**

Florence had always been prudent with her earnings, and the new opportunity of becoming a lady's maid again had allowed her to save even more diligently. She stashed away every extra penny, dreaming of a life where she could one day return to her village, free from the burdens that had plagued her at Milburn Manor. The months turned into years and Florence's presence became a comfort to Eleanor. Despite the pain that lingered over Isabella, a genuine bond formed between the two women. Florence's empathy and quiet strength helped Eleanor navigate her grief, and in return, Eleanor provided Florence with the means to secure her future. When they learned of Isabella's death, the weight of this finality hit them both hard, but it also brought with it a sense of closure for Florence.

With a heavy heart but clear resolve, Florence had approached Eleanor with her plans. She had saved enough to buy a small cottage and she was moving back to her village, Waddington. She had secured a job as a teacher at the local school. With Eleanor's blessing and a generous parting gift, Florence left Milburn Manor. She returned to Waddington, the village of her birth, and moved into her quaint cottage near the edge of the village. Her modest home was filled with sunlight and hope, a stark contrast to the dark corridors of the manor she had left behind.

Florence quickly integrated herself back into village life. She found immense joy in teaching the village children, imparting not just knowledge but also the values of kindness and perseverance she had learned through her hardships. It wasn't long before Florence's warmth and intelligence caught the eye of Thomas, a kind-hearted widower and local craftsman. He admired her dedication and the way she had turned her life around. Their courtship was gentle and respectful, and they married in a small, joyful ceremony surrounded by friends and villagers. Florence's life blossomed in ways she had never imagined. She and Thomas created a loving home, and Florence continued to teach, earning the respect and admiration of her community. In the quiet moments of her life, Florence would sometimes feel Isabella's presence, a gentle reminder of the bond they had shared.

As she walked through the village, hand in hand with Thomas, Florence felt a deep sense of contentment. She had overcome her past, forged a new path, and found her true calling. Her journey had been long and difficult, but the footsteps of fate had finally led her to a place of peace and fulfilment.

Chapter Forty-Nine
Lord & Lady de Lacy
Milburn Manor
Lancashire

As the years passed, the grandeur of Milburn Manor stood in stark contrast to the modest cottage where Rafe and Eleanor de Lacy now resided. The manor, under the stewardship of their son William, flourished becoming a beacon of prosperity and kindness that reflected William's gentle nature and just leadership. William deeply regretted his treatment of his sister Isabella and wished that he had done more to help her after that fateful night.

Lord Rafe de Lacy, once a man of unyielding power and cruelty, had been reduced to a shadow of his former self. The weight of his sins, particularly the murder he had covered up and the death of his daughter, had become a heavy burden he could no longer escape. His health deteriorated, and he often found himself wandering the grounds of Milburn Manor, lost in his morbid thoughts.

One crisp autumn afternoon, Rafe decided to take one of his last remaining pleasures: a solitary ride on his favourite horse. He set out from the cottage, hoping the familiar rhythm of the ride would provide some measure of peace. The day was quiet, the manor's grounds painted in the golden hues of the season.

As he returned, the manor looming in the distance, Rafe's path took him past the old chapel. The ruins, hidden away and forgotten by many, held dark secrets that only a few remembered. As he rode by, a sudden chill swept through the air, making the hairs on the back of his neck stand up.

Rafe's horse, sensing something unseen, began to prance nervously.

"Easy boy," Rafe murmured, patting the horse's neck. But the animal was not to be calmed. It reared back, eyes wide with terror. Rafe struggled to maintain control, but the horse bucked wildly, throwing him to the ground.

He landed with a sickening thud, the bones in his neck snapping instantly. As he lay there, the world fading to black, he caught a glimpse of the old chapel, the very spot where James and Pierre were buried. The wind howled, and for a moment he thought he heard the voice of his daughter, Isabella.

Eleanor, concerned by the delay, found Rafe's horse wandering riderless and panicked. She followed its path and discovered Rafe's lifeless body near the chapel. The sight was eerily poignant, the past and present colliding in a tragic twist of fate.

William and the servants arrived, their faces pale with shock. They gently carried Rafe's body back to the cottage, where Eleanor sat beside him, her heart heavy with a mixture of sorrow and relief. In his last moments, Rafe had found the peace he sought, and in his death justice had been served.

***

Eleanor had endured profound suffering since the tragic death of her beloved daughter. The pain of losing Isabella had etched deep lines of grief on her face, and for many years the weight of her sorrow was a constant companion. However, as time passed after Rafe's death, Eleanor went back to live at the manor with her son and his family. Surrounded by the innocence and exuberance of her grandchildren, she found her spirit gradually lifting. Their giggles and playful antics breathed new life into her weary heart, and she began to see the world through their eyes, a place filled with wonder and possibility.

Yet, even in these moments of joy, thoughts of Isabella were never far from

Eleanor's mind. She often found herself reflecting on the child Isabella had borne, the grandchild she had never known. The decision to have the baby adopted, orchestrated by Rafe, had been a source of immense heartache for Eleanor. She wondered about the boy, his life, his fate, and whether he knew of his true heritage.

As she watched her grandchildren grow, Eleanor couldn't help but imagining how different life might have been if Isabella had been able to keep her child. She pondered on the boy's journey, hoping that he had found happiness and purpose despite the cruel twist of fate that had separated him from his mother.

Eleanor often sat in the manor's gardens, finding a quiet spot where she could think about Isabella. In these peaceful moments, she found a measure of acceptance and that through her grandchildren, a part of Isabella lived on. The pain of the past would never fully disappear, and her life, marked by loss and secrets ultimately succumbed to the inexorable march of time.

***

In the gardens of Milburn Manor, where shadows of the past lingered, the footsteps of fate echoed softly, a haunting reminder of the paths Lord and Lady de Lacy had trodden and the destiny that awaited them all.

Epilogue

Amelia's life had blossomed in ways she had once only dared to hope. Greece had become her permanent home, rich with the love of her husband Nikos and their children Alexandros and the new baby girl Isabella Thea. Amelia's father had moved to Greece to be closer to his grandchildren, delighting in his new role as a grandfather, his days filled with laughter and joy.

In Elounda, the bookshop continued to thrive as a beacon of history and learning, even after Eleni Manolakis, the beloved previous owner and friend, had passed away. Her spirit, much like Isabella's, seemed to infuse the very walls of the shop with a warmth and wisdom that drew people from all walks of life. Amelia and Nikos had made sure that Eleni's legacy of knowledge and passion was carried forward. The shop had become not just a place to buy books but a place to connect with the past and the stories that needed to be told. As Amelia walked through the vibrant market of Elounda, she knew she had come home. Her thoughts drifted to Milburn Manor. She felt the pulse of Isabella's legacy beat in sync with her heartbeat, a rhythmic dance of past and future steps.

***

Isabella's spirit, once known as the Weeping Widow, had transformed into a vision of ethereal beauty and serenity. No longer shrouded in sorrow, she now appeared as an entity with an otherworldly glow that filled Milburn Manor with warmth and peace. Her once ragged and disfigured appearance had been replaced by an exquisite gown of flowing white silk, adorned with delicate lace and intricate embroidery that shimmered in the soft light. The gown seemed to be woven from the very essence of moonlight, casting a gentle luminescent aura around her. Her face, no longer marked by the anguish of her earthly struggles, now bore a serene and timeless beauty. As she moved through the manor, she brought a sense of calm and comfort to all who glimpsed her. Her touch was as light as a whisper, and her presence as soothing as a gentle breeze. She was often seen in the gardens or wandering the halls and there was always a soft glow that accompanied her.

She was renamed the White Lady, a benevolent spirit watching over the manor and its inhabitants. She was a reminder of the enduring power of love and the possibility of redemption. Her presence was a reminder that transformation can come from enduring life's greatest trials with grace and courage. In her radiant form, Isabella's spirit had finally found peace, illuminating Milburn Manor with the light of hope and the promise of a brighter tomorrow. The White Lady was a symbol of the beauty that can emerge from even the darkest of circumstances.

***

Life, Amelia realised, was much like the books she cherished: stories of beginnings and endings, of challenges and triumphs, and paths determined by fate. In Greece, with her family and the memory of Isabella's indomitable spirit surrounding her, Amelia had found her place. And, back at Milburn Manor, Isabella's spirit rested, her journey complete.

***

In the quiet moments of twilight, as the world around her whispered of continuing legacies and new beginnings, Amelia knew she was exactly where she was meant to be, guided by the footsteps of fate.

THE END

SPINALONGA

Spinalonga Island was once a formidable sea fortress, built by the Venetians in the late 16th century to defend the Gulf of Elounda and the northeast coast of Crete. Under Venetian rule, the area around the island and the entrance to the Gulf of Elounda was used to harvest salt from the sea. Spinalonga later served as a last refuge for the Ottoman Turks who fled there during the Cretan revolt of 1878.

In the 1900s Spinalonga took on an entirely new population: nearly 1,000 sufferers from the infectious disease known as leprosy. This disease was once considered incurable, and an automatic "death sentence." For over fifty years, Spinalonga served as Europe's last active leper colony. When the cure for leprosy was discovered in 1948 the residents of Spinalonga were gradually treated, returned to good health, and sent back to the mainland to rejoin the rest of society. The colony was permanently closed in 1957. Because of the absence of official records, the history of Spinalonga is preserved through the stories of its former residents.

In 1936 Epaminondas Remoundakis, a young law student from Athens discovered he had leprosy and went voluntarily to Spinalonga where his sister already was. He founded the "Brotherhood of the Sick of Spinalonga." The group worked to improve living conditions for inhabitants of the island and formed its own fully functioning society, including restaurants, a church, and a school. He later lost an arm and went blind due to the disease.

**"If you are walking along the path of Spinalonga, dwell for a moment and consider your breath.
From some of the ruined houses, you will hear the lamented song of a mother, a sister, or the pain-filled breath of a man. Let two tears escape from your eyes and you will see the shine of millions of tears that have watered this same way, on which you stride along today."
Epaminondas Remoundakis
1914-1978**

Acknowledgments

First, I would like to thank my husband, Eddie for his patience and help whilst I was writing this book. He has read, read, and re-read the book numerous times. He has also made some helpful (and some not-so-helpful!) suggestions, so a big thank you and all my love.

All the places in Lancashire and Elounda do exist, (except Milburn Manor) however, all the characters are completely fictional. I was brought up in Lancashire and my love of the countryside, specifically the Ribble Valley, has helped me to write this story. I have visited Elounda, so many times and I always fall in love with it all over again each time I visit. The Greek people are so lovely and of course, the food is amazing. For anyone going to Elounda, I would highly recommend a visit to the island of Spinalonga.

Finally, a big thank you to my readers, for taking the time to read this novel. If you could take the time to give me a review on Amazon it would be a great help for authors like myself who don't have a big marketing budget.

This is my second novel.
My first novel, which is set once again in Lancashire, is **The Book of Shadows**. A dual timeline story set in the present and 1612, the era of the Pendle Witch Trials. The story is unravelled through an old recipe book and is a tale of magic and mystery.

With Love

Juliet xx

Printed in Great Britain
by Amazon